Polished Glass

By the same author

Angel's War
Mirror on the Wall
Mirror Images
To Reason Why
Ties of Blood
All Manner of Things
The Foolish Virgin
A Lesser Peace
A Chained Satan
Season of Sins
The Decent Thing
Silk Stocking Spy
Looking Glass
Broken Glass

Polished Glass

C. W. Reed

ROBERT HALE · LONDON

Typeset in 11/13½pt Baskerville
by Derek Doyle & Associates, Shaw Heath
Printed and bound in Great Britain
by Biddles Limited, King's Lynn

As long as there is any sex dominance such a thing as world peace may be psychologically impossible. . . . Non-differentiation in clothing, in education, in general treatment, is an essential factor in equality . . . it is important that the exclusively male and female names should be discontinued . . . a revised idea of courtesy on a non-sexual basis is essential.

Paul Bousfield, *Sex and Civilisation*, 1925

PART I

KISS ME GOODNIGHT, SERGEANT-MAJOR

CHAPTER ONE

'She's done a splendid job at this end of the line,' Subaltern Edwards affirmed, a shade too heartily, as though she was on the defensive or expected some kind of opposition from her superior officer.

Junior Commander Jean Nossiter nodded her head in agreement, glanced down at the name on the file in front of her. *GLASS (Alice) A5196M. Sgt.* 'Couldn't agree more, Sheila. She's kept the whole of the motor pool ticking over, virtually. Absolutely first class. Highest commendation.' She glanced up again at the tall, solid figure perched awkwardly on the edge of the desk. 'She has a way of getting the best out of our gang of harpies that astonishes me. But come on! Officer material? Can you see it? That accent of hers! And dining in on mess nights. Can you see it? Honestly?'

'She could learn to sort out which knife to use.' But already the subaltern's tone was reluctantly accepting defeat.

'She'd stick out like a sore thumb. Besides, the girl wouldn't thank us for it. She'd be like a fish out of water. You know she would. I agree, she deserves recognition for the past few weeks.'

And a lively period it had been, with the sudden springing on them of the Cairo Conference, with Winny and Roosevelt and that Chinese fellow, Chiang Kai-shek meeting in the Egyptian capital on 22 November. It had meant a major headache for the Auxiliary Territorial Service Transport Section, operating from their base at Burg-el-Arab. The road between Alex and Cairo had been clogged all the way with a constant stream of vehicles, and constant demands for more. Yes, indeed, Sergeant Glass had earned her commendation, keeping the unit on its toes day and night until everyone had collapsed with exhausted relief when the bigwigs had cleared off to Teheran, for their meeting with Uncle Joe Stalin to plot old Adolf's downfall, and the sooner the better.

But Sheila Edwards was going a bit over the top with her desire to send Alice Glass off for an officers' training course, and her senior studied her with newly awakened interest. A fetching enough girl, Sheila, in a large-boned, jolly-hockey-sticks, healthy English way. Her fair complexion had never taken well to the hot and often fierce desert climate. Her face was usually flushed and wore a slightly flustered, uncomfortable look. In a bathing costume, at the beach or at the pool at the officers' club in Cairo or Alexandria, her skin did not react favourably to the hot sun, taking on a sore and angry redness if exposed for even the shortest spell. Coming off the tennis courts in her whites, she positively dripped, and glowed like a tomato.

Not like that other little thing, the kid that was rumoured to be such a special chum of the gallant Sergeant Glass. Lynne Manning. Brown as a berry that one, or more appropriately, as a wog, and looked like one, too, when she wandered about in that *thobe*, the striped gown the locals wore. 'Ahmed Two', some of the girls called her, after the dhobi and cha-wallah youth who looked after them. And saw far more of them than he should, their junior commander suspected, for one of such tender years. She continued to observe her subordinate with veiled, speculative attentiveness.

Bitching and scandalmongering were rife in the camp; par for the course, she accepted, when a group of young, healthy women were cooped up together under such stringent circumstances. And let's face it: some of those under her command were sluts – no other word for it. But the whispers she had heard (nothing more than salacious gossip recounted in confidence by her servant, the main source for her 'keeping a finger on the pulse', and not to be acted upon) were that rough diamond Glass and the boyish waif, Manning, were a combination that strayed beyond the bounds of comrades-in-arms – unless one were to view the term in a literal sense. For a split second, Junior Commander Nossiter entertained the intriguing and libidinous thought that Sheila might be smitten with Sapphic feelings for the sergeant herself, but then dismissed the outrageous idea. Sheila was far too proper, and far too sensible, to betray her rank and her class by such an unforgivable lapse. Nevertheless, her speculations brought to Jean a possible solution that might kill at least two birds with one stone: scotch any possible hint of public embarrassment or disgrace by nipping it in the bud, and present for Sheila's benefit the reward for Glass's excellence so sought after by her subaltern.

'Tell you what we'll do, Sheila.' Nossiter glanced meaningfully towards the closed door and leaned forward, dropping her voice to a confidential murmur. 'Keep this under your hat, but I have this on rock-solid authority from Colonel Fowles. Most of the unit's going to be disbanded soon into the New Year. Now that the war's moved on into Italy, they won't need us here. Some of us might get the chance to stay on. Staff HQ in Cairo.' She grinned and winked. 'Mum's the word, mind. But most of our girls should be transferred back home. Second front should be coming in the next few months. What I can do is ship Glass out pronto. Recommend her to go on a staff sergeant or quartermaster sergeant's course. That's where her strength lies, believe me. She's a first rate non-com. You know she'll be happier with that. Backbone of the army and all that, eh? And she'll be back in Blighty for Christmas, if she's lucky. She'll be delighted!'

It was appropriate, Alice thought, that her transfer back to Blighty should come so close to the Christmas season. She had arrived in Egypt the day before Christmas Eve, a year ago. They hadn't actually got off the troopship until Christmas Eve itself. Beth's letter had been waiting for her. It had been written weeks before, of course, and been sent to the camp at Nottingham, telling her that Beth was pregnant, by Arty Clark, and that they were going to get married, in haste, on 18 December. She'd already been married a week when Alice read the letter. She remembered vividly how she'd made her way to the upper deck, how she had managed to find herself alone among 2,000 others, had sat in the weirdly warm, exotic night, with all the stars overhead, and wept for her lost love. She'd been pissed when she'd scribbled off a short, stilted note of congratulations, '*to both of you*', on Christmas night, her head dizzy and her guts churning with the fizzy foreign beer and Syrian wine. It was six months before she heard from Beth again, this time to announce the birth of their daughter, Elaine Ruth, on 23 June. Al had got drunk again, but just a little. That had been the night she made her first move with the girl sitting opposite her now.

She watched Lynne Manning's dark, narrow tongue flicker out, and lap at the ice-cream cone. The sticky dribbles of white ran down the sides of the wafer, dripped on to the thin, dark fingers. Lynne saw her watching, and those shining black eyes danced, she pulled a monkey-faced grin, and giggled. The black thatch of hair glistened as though brilliantined. It was thick and unruly on top, but shaved close on her neck and at the sides, about her small ears, leaving them clear. 'Short back and sides', she always said with a grin when she came fresh from the barber and the girls teased her.

'You won't miss me at all, will you?' Alice said, keeping her tone light.

Lynne lifted the cone high, lapped carefully around its sides. 'I'll weep buckets when you've gone, Sarge. You know I will. I'll be wringing out my pillow every morning.'

'Lying little cow!' Alice reached across and took hold of the skinny wrist across the little round table of the café. Quickly she released it again. The last day of the year. They would see the New Year in together tonight. 1944. Would it bring the end of the war? A lot of people were getting their hopes up. Everybody was talking about a second front, an invasion across the Channel. They said Britain was packed with Yanks nowadays. They would run the whole show, they reckoned. She might well be in on it in some way. That was why she was being sent home. Two more days and she'd be on her way. She'd expected to be away two or three weeks ago, soon after Captain Nossiter had called her in to tell her. She shouldn't call her captain. Her rank was junior commander, just to remind them that they were ATS, not pukka army. But it was such a mouthful, and anyway it was equivalent to captain, down to the three pips on the shoulder. That reminded her. If she made it to staff sergeant, Alice would have some sewing to do – a crown to go above her three stripes. Damn good show! as Colonel Fowles would say – and probably try to cop a quick feel, if given half a chance.

But she'd been tickled pink, and no mistake. She certainly hadn't expected to progress beyond sergeant. That had been the dizzy heights, as far as she was concerned. The thought of going home again, after a year out here, made her guts squeeze with excitement; and that in turn brought a sense of guilt. She gazed fondly at the figure opposite her, who had now nibbled away the pointed bottom of the cone, and was messily sucking at the melting cream inside. 'God! You're a mucky little pup! Here. Clean yourself up!' She dug a khaki handkerchief from the pocket of her uniform skirt and passed it across the table. She would miss Lynne a hell of a lot. The acknowledgement was a sop to her conscience, for her secret shame at the pleasure she felt at her imminent return to England.

All right, that first time, way back in the boiling July heat, had been a reaction against her own terrible misery at Beth's news, and the pain it caused. Just for fun, for the physical pleasure – and the excitement. But she wasn't that calculating, or cold-blooded. She really did feel something tender towards the kid. That was another thing. Everyone treated Manning as though she was about fourteen or so. She was less than two years younger than Al, and Al had celebrated her twenty-second birthday only a couple of weeks ago. Sometimes Lynne seemed no more mature than Doreen, Alice's youngest sister, who was not yet fourteen. Not always, though.

Alice had been afraid they might not be able to have this last private time together, and, in spite of her eagerness to begin her long voyage home, she was glad that they had managed to fit in the weekend break, at the very last minute, booking into one of the armed forces' hostels in Cairo for two nights. They had done the trip to Giza, struggled up those massive stones at the base of Cheops' tomb, Lynne scrambling ahead like a goat, laughingly cursing at the hindrance of their regulation skirts, and hoisting hers so high on her thin, tanned thighs that the view, especially from where Alice struggled below her, was indecently arous-ing. They had perched precariously on a very smelly, flea-bitten camel, Al cradling her companion tightly in her lap, while the beast lurched and heaved and threatened to send them tumbling, before trotting off at a bouncingly uncomfortable speed, while its driver promised still more speed unless they paid more baksheesh. They had visited the museum. They planned to go to the open-air cinema show organized by the NAAFI, after which there would be a dance, scheduled to last until the arrival of the New Year.

'There'll be randy pongoes and matelots queuing six-deep to get at you, Sarge.' Lynne pulled a wry face of amused resignation.

'Don't talk daft! Couldn't think of anything worse. In fact . . .' she hesitated a little, her voice thickened with awkwardness. 'I'm only going for your sake. I'd rather we had our own party.'

They had a double room at the hostel, with its own narrow balcony. The rusting, curled patterns of the wrought-iron railing and the blistered surface of the painted strip of flooring looked unsafe, but they were able to open the long wooden shutters and stand at the window. The noise of the busy street below came up through the darkness. The spiky silhouettes of palm trees stood out against the gleam of the River Nile as Alice stared out towards El Duqqi, and the gardens. She felt a hand rest lightly on her shoulder.

'Close the netting or we'll get bitten to death.'

They had not put on the lamps in the room, and Alice noted the dark brilliance of Lynne's eyes as they held her gaze. She smelt the clean, scented smell of soap, and the fresh lightness of her perfume. Alice closed the metal-framed netting across the window opening and turned. Lynne moved closer, into her embracing arms, and lifted her face until her warm breath mingled with Alice's. 'You little hussy!' Alice breathed, as the thin arms came up to close around her neck. 'You didn't bring your pyjamas.'

'I want to give you something to remember me by. Not that you will. Soon as that boat leaves the quayside, you'll forget all about me. I know bloody well who you'll be thinking about then, all right.'

As though in immediate response to Lynne's softly reproachful words, Alice found herself staring at her partner's slight breasts, the dark and surprisingly large nipples, with scarcely any areolae, and picturing the whiteness of Beth's bosom, and the tiny pale buds, circled by their more generous, pink surrounds. 'Shut up!' she said harshly, and bore her backwards to the creaking iron bed.

A long time later, a few hours into the New Year, their limbs and bodies still entangled, they lay in sweating and sated tiredness, the sheet kicked down about their feet. 'Does she know you're going home?' Lynne's husky voice carried no trace of resentment, and Alice felt a fresh wave of tenderness sweep over her.

'No. I haven't heard from her since September.'

'Will you go and see her?'

The question hung there for a second, and Alice shifted, felt the slippery sheen of Lynne's flesh against hers. 'No, I reckon not. It would be too awkward. The baby. Her husband.'

'She might have changed – I mean from the way she felt when you split up.' Lynne paused, and cleared her throat. There was a suggestion of reluctance in her rusty murmur. 'I bet she has. Being married, having the sprog and all that. I bet she'd love to see you again.'

'Hark at you! The wise old Witch of the West! Tell me fortune, will you?' Lynne's thin frame squirmed against her in feigned annoyance, then her fingers twined in Alice's bronzed, damp curls, playing with them.

'What about that lad of yours? Davy. I bet he'll be over the moon to have you back again. You can't deny it. He'll be there at the dockside waiting to propose, if you give him half a chance!'

'Nay, lass. He's given me up as a bad job, an' all. There's nobody in the whole wide world cares about me now.'

'You poor old thing!' Lynne wriggled round, and flung a leg over Alice's hip, pressing herself even closer. 'You'd best stay true to me, then, eh, Sarge? Will you wait for me till we meet again?'

'Cheeky young bugger! And will you *please*, stop calling me "sarge", at least while we're in bed?'

CHAPTER TWO

The *Empire Indus* was vastly overpopulated in terms of her pre-war complement, which made for an uncomfortable voyage for the 2,000 personnel, including Sergeant Alice Glass, who boarded at Alexandria. But it was scheduled to be a much shorter journey than most had anticipated. There was a mixed reception to the news that they were not after all to head through the Canal and down the Red Sea for a cruise southward along the east coast of Africa and round the Cape of Good Hope into the South Atlantic. Quite a few of Alice's fellow passengers had been looking forward to a leisurely trip through tropical waters, to say nothing of the possibility of some exciting visits ashore in Mombasa, Durban, and Cape Town, soaking up the sun while the folks at home eagerly awaiting their loved ones shivered through a freezing January.

Joan Parish, a Q.A. nurse, who occupied the bunk above Alice in the crowded non-coms mess, leaned beside her at the rail soon after leaving harbour and expressed her dismay. 'The Atlantic wouldn't have bothered me at all. They seem to be cracking the U-boat packs these days. And this old thing can shift, even if it is crammed like the Black Hole of Calcutta.' She gave a theatrical little shiver of disapproval, and straightened her thin brown arms, bare to above the elbow, where her khaki-drill sleeves were neatly and identically folded.

'At least we'll get home a lot quicker. A couple of weeks at the most.'

Joan Parish glanced at her, the thick, dark eyebrows raised, her mouth curled in an expression of scepticism. 'Yes, but the Med! No room to run, is there? And Jerry's still on Crete, and all those other islands. Easy to get at us from the air.'

Alice nodded her head back, to indicate the land still close behind them. 'But we've got the whole of the North African coastline now. There's bags of air cover if we need it. Sicily's ours now, too, and we're well stuck into Italy. The Eyeties are with us. We'll be in Rome in a few weeks.'

Parish gave a scornful laugh. 'The Eyeties? Hah! Christ! I remember shipping out their POWs. There were more of them than our boys!'

Another of these old-timers! Alice thought, more in humour than in anger. The old get-your-knees-brown brigade! Sure enough, the senior nurse came out with the anticipated question.

'How long have you been out here, Sergeant?'

'Just over a year. A year and two weeks to be precise!' Alice mocked herself for her subterfuge. 'My name's Alice, by the way. Me mates call me Al.' She held out her hand. Parish was a few inches taller. She stared down at her as though slightly taken aback, then took hold of the proffered hand and gripped it tightly.

'Hello. I'm Joan.'

'How long have you been out, Joan?' Alice asked dutifully.

'Oh, I landed way back. In the days of Wavell. Before Monty. He forgot to take me back with him when he shoved off.' The thin, rather severe face relaxed, was transformed by its grin. 'Take no notice. I'm just bomb-happy, I guess. You sound pretty keen to get back. Somebody special waiting for you, eh?'

'Not me!' Was there was a shade too much emphasis in the reply? She felt herself pinking a little. 'Just family and that. A few mates.'

'You're from up north.' It wasn't a question.

Alice grinned. 'And you're not! You don't have to be Sexton Blake to find me out! Margrove. You've probably never heard of it. Up on the north-east coast.'

'Yes, I have. So you're a Geordie, eh?'

'Don't let anybody back home hear you say that! We're a good thirty mile away. We talk completely different!' She hesitated, then went on, 'I haven't let any of them know yet. They don't even know I'm coming home.' She might as well continue her effort to be friendly. Parish didn't seem quite as snooty as Alice had at first suspected, and she reprimanded herself for still being so thin-skinned under her veneer of confidence. Besides, two weeks could be a long time to be cooped up cheek by jowl on board ship.

'Hardly worth it now. Probably only put in at Gib. By the time a letter gets home, we'll be just about there ourselves.'

The Tannoy crackled overhead somewhere, and the loud, metallic tones broke in to their chat. 'Attention! Non-working personnel clear the upper deck. Sea dutymen close up. Prepare to darken ship.'

Despite the crowded conditions, Alice spent a convivial evening with the other non-coms in the mess, after she had carried out her far from onerous duty of seeing to the contingent of junior rank ATS girls, bedded down in a large, sectioned-off space which had probably been part of a lounge or dining-room for second-class passengers in peace time. 'You're lucky!' Alice answered the few generally good-humoured grumblers. 'You're near the fresh air up here. You should see our mess! We're two decks below, in some sort of glory hole. Where they used to keep the coal, I think!'

'My heart bleeds, Sarge!' a short, chubby girl called out. 'I bet you don't have to sleep in these things, though, do yer?' She gestured in disgust at the hammocks, which were already slung, in long rows, so close that the occupants would be almost literally rubbing shoulders. 'I'm buggered if I'll ever get the hang of rigging one of these things, no matter how many times they show us!' She grinned lasciviously. 'It's a good job we've got them matelots to come and show us how to do it, isn't it, girls?'

'Aye, and that's not all they'll show us!' someone called out, to a burst of laughter.

Alice watched the girl scrambling to climb in. She clung precariously to the narrow, swaying canvas, and rolled in, revealing a comprehensive and inelegant display of bare limbs, and solid backside clad in the light-cotton regulation knickers. 'I hope you're not intending to sleep in your underwear,' Alice said, glancing about her, her comment intended for the general company.

'Nay,' the chubby girl answered, 'but I want me vest and drawers in here with me.' She was already peeling the singlet over her head, before dragging on the short nightshirt. The hammock swayed dangerously, and bumped its neighbours on either side. She squealed and swore profusely. 'Sorry, Sarge! I'm wearing this bugger an' all!' She held up the life jacket and wriggled it over her shoulders. She looked about her with a hint of defiance. 'Imagine what a carry-on we'd have trying to get out of here in a hurry!'

The light heartedness was forced, and there were more than a few serious faces nodding in response. 'Don't be daft, ladies!' Alice's voice was firm and jovial. 'Jerry's got far too much on his plate to bother about us these days. Be like one of them luxury cruises, will this trip!' She turned to go. 'Don't forget. Parade on upper deck, starboard aft – that's right hand side at the back, facing the pointy end!' There was another burst of laughter, and a few groans. '0-seven-thirty. You're still in the army!' She turned at the foot of the wide companionway, her feet on the bottom step, and gazed at the sea of faces. 'And also don't forget. I don't care how friendly the matelots are. Only one to a hammock, all right? You'll probably break your bloody neck or hang yourself if you try owt!'

The 'micks', the crew's familiar term for the hammocks, might be difficult to rig in the evening and stow in the morning, but they proved far less uncomfortable than the two-tiered metal bunks in the NCOs' messes or the berths in the officers' quarters when the ship hit a passage of rough weather during the afternoon of the second day's voyage. It lasted almost forty-eight hours, while the ex-liner reared and bucked and rolled and thumped through the fifteen-foot waves and the rain driven horizontally on the fierce gale. It belied the popular image of the sparkling Med, but was not at all unusual for the time of year, the crew members assured them. 'Never mind, girls! Keeps the dive-bombers away, eh? And even the U-boats go down deep to ride these bastards out.'

But below decks the crowded accommodation became a claustrophobic, evil-smelling torment, as the heads (toilets) filled up, and the round, shallow metal containers known as 'spitkids', and buckets, received the eructations of those unfortunates unable to make it to the lavatories. Alice was comparatively lucky in that she was not throwing up, but she had little appetite for solid food and suffered from a headache, as well as aching muscles from constant tension against the violent rolling and pitching movements of the vessel. She felt a great deal better when she was allowed to get up into the open air of the grey day, where a portion of the deck had been roped off for their use. She held her face up gratefully to the slanting rain and the spindrift, and huddled in the lee of one of the lifeboats high on its davits. The tarpaulin cracked and threshed in the wind. Alice's mood lifted a little at the sight of the white-tipped racing waves. The inclement weather gave her a further excuse for delaying correspondence home. Only three more days and they would, God willing, be docking in Gibraltar. And, as Joan Parish had said, a letter posted there might well take as long to reach home as the voyagers themselves.

She wasn't much good at letter writing, she was the first to admit. Mind you, her family were no better, except for her sister, Doreen. Alice looked forward to receiving the neatly scripted pages from the thirteen-year-old. They read like a book and always made her grin, with their comical stories of the doings of Howbeck, the dales village where Doreen lived with the posh spinster, Miss Elizabeth Ramsay, now officially described as her 'guardian', where she had been staying for more than three years now, ever since the first day she had arrived in the village as one of the batch of evacuees from Margrove. She had looked suitably winsome and waiflike, a delicate little rose among such coarse weeds, batting her big dark eyes at the well-heeled, snobbish and distinctly lonely old maid with calculated craft quite unnerving in one of such tender years. It had certainly worked. Al could not help but admire, reluctantly, the scheming little madam. Miss Ramsay had, literally, purchased the youngster from the parents, and Doreen was already a young lady, attending the grammar school for girls in Whitby, looking and speaking, and writing like a genuine toff. Al's father, Fred, had justified selling off his daughter as 'doing what's best for her', and her mam went along with it, though with many private misgivings and much pain, Alice knew. Maybe they had done the right thing after all, though in Fred Glass's case and despite his righteous trumpetings not for the right reasons; Alice was equally sure of that.

Doreen's letters were a rare enough treat. Al had received no more than three or four in the year that she had been abroad. More from mam, but Alice could recite almost word for word the laboriously scripted one-page notes before she opened them. Not a word from any of the others, except for her youngest brother and favourite, little Algy, who had once sent her 'love' and three crosses, under a suitably martial picture of tanks spitting fire, with bombers overhead which looked like big black birds crapping on those beneath.

And nothing from the one she most longed to hear from, apart from the letter which had been waiting for her when she arrived in Egypt, telling her of the pregnancy and the hastily planned marriage to Arty Clark, and the even shorter note, informing her of the birth of Elaine Ruth six months later. Alice had struggled to pen a suitably enthusiastic reply, without saying any of the things she really needed to, and ended up with a stiff little message which sounded more like – what was that phrase Beth had introduced her to that always made her grin with delight? 'sour grapes', that was it – yes, sour grapes rather than congratulations. What would the new husband make of Beth's friend when he read it? See her for the rough diamond she was, no doubt. One thing was sure – he wouldn't know anything of the truth about their relationship, Beth would make sure of that. But then why should she confess to something so shocking, especially when it was all over and done with, pushed behind her? She was a wife and mother now, back among her own kind. And good luck to her.

It was only idiots like Alice who stuck to the truth, and were daft enough to mention the unmentionable. And that brought her thoughts on to the only other person she had ever felt really close to, whom, in a way, she loved, too, but not in the same way she loved Beth. Davy Brown had been deeply shocked when she had blurted out her tortured confession to him. Shocked rigid, he'd been, she'd seen it at once on his honest face. No getting round it, even though he'd tried to make up for it in the brief time they had left before Alice had departed to join the ATS.

Poor Davy! How many times she had wished since that evening in York that she could have taken back that outburst. How could she have dreamt that even her lovely, loyal Davy would be able to accept that wild confession? And she'd timed it so wonderfully, too: just when the lad had asked her yet again to marry him. How could even she have been that stupid? But then, like most confessions, it had been torn from her, in unthinking desperation, to ease the pain of what she was going through, the loneliness of it. She often wondered, kept returning to it, over and over, what her life would have been like if, instead of that erupting bombshell, she had been able to turn her back, the way Beth had, on their love, and had accepted Davy's heartfelt offer. Could she have made him happy, could she have found happiness herself, the way Beth had, in turning away from their 'abnormality'? Even at the wonderful height of it all Beth had found it difficult, even distasteful, to talk about their love. 'We don't need words!' she'd say, pleadingly, clinging to Al in the haven of their room and the old bed above the stables at Howe Manor, stopping her mouth with kisses to stem the words. And in the end the world had won. Beth had run away from her, and denied what they had shared. Could she have done the same, turned to Davy, who she was sure would have given her love?

They still corresponded. His letters were warm and tender, full of good things, gossip and news about York, hopeful comments on the world that lay ahead, the chance to reform it, his continuing care and concern for her. Perhaps she read too much between the lines, but she felt that concern was now as much for her soul, her spiritual as well as her material well-being. He didn't preach to her. He never mentioned directly the shocking thing she had admitted to him that evening on their walk out towards the racecourse, but still she felt that sense of burdensome morality. Guilty conscience on her part, she would acknowledge in more generous moments. He was her best friend. But could she face seeing him again? Part of her answered with an immediate and vigorous yes. She wanted him, the special warmth of his friendship, very much.

His last letter had arrived just over a month ago, full of greetings and best wishes for the approaching Christmas. She hadn't got round to answering it properly. She had sent him one of the cheap forces' Christmas cards, on that coarse paper: the photograph of the entrance to the Bethlehem stable/cave where Christ had been born, the most popular of several sites claiming to be his birthplace. She had not, of course, known then that she would be leaving for home so soon. She should scribble him a line, catch the mail drop at Gib to let him know she was on her way. Though she was taken with the idea of just turning up in Dubry Street, at his digs, out of the blue, out of a cold and dismal January day. She pictured the shock on his face – a pleasant one this time, she hoped, instead of that incredulous and then stunned expression she had put there the last time she had surprised him. She hoped she was right.

CHAPTER THREE

Who was it who had described life as ODTAA? Davy Brown couldn't recall which writer it was who had coined the acronym, but it certainly seemed to be true in his case at the moment. His life really was one damned thing after another. He gazed bleakly at Detective Inspector Holden as he came across to the small corner table, carrying the two glasses of dark bitter. 'Here you go, lad. At least they haven't drunk the barrels dry yet.'

'Thanks, sir.' Davy took a long pull and put the glass down on the dark wooden surface. 'Is it because of my background?'

His superior stared candidly at him before he spoke, accompanying his words with a small shake of his head. 'I don't think so, Davy. But I can't swear to it. Chief Superintendent Rush assured me it isn't. It's just the fact that you're still officially a special, and that you can't be regraded to regular status yet. Your medical category would have to be reclassified as well. Sorry, lad. You'll just have to be patient. Things could soon change.'

Not with *my* luck, Davy thought, then made an effort to shake off his moroseness. It wasn't the DI's fault. Mr Holden had always done his best for him, since they had first met nearly three years ago, in Howbeck. The inspector had been responsible for Davy's joining the constabulary, had been largely instrumental in enabling him to do so, given his chequered background. 'You're all done with your past,' he had said firmly. 'There's no need for folk to know all the ins and outs. It's confidential, and it won't stop you getting into the force, believe me.'

Davy could have sat out the war he didn't agree with safely at Howe Manor, working on the land, but he had never rested easily there, in spite of meeting Alice, and all the happiness that that had brought him.

Joining the police force had revitalized him; it was a kind of resurrection from the hideaway he had sought in the dales, and he had no regrets. Far from it. He felt he was achieving something solid, doing something he could be proud of, helping to keep the peace, and law and order, even in wartime. When DI Holden had secured his transfer to the detective branch, he had been even more enthused, and eager to contribute. In the year since the blow of Alice's revelation and her swift subsequent departure, the job had become even more important to him. He had little else. Which was why his request to be entered for the training course and examination for the rank of sergeant had meant so much. Though the refusal of his submission had not come as any great surprise, it was still a bitter disappointment. 'I could ask to take another medical. I'm sure I'd be passed A1 now. I'm fully recovered . . .' his voice faded. It was still hard for him to refer to his breakdown, even though it had happened more than three years ago.

'Just hold fire a while,' DI Holden said kindly. 'You'll make it. Things are going to start changing soon. We're going to win this war. It's just a question of how long it's going to take. It might happen sooner than we think. These thousand-bomber raids. Their cities are getting hammered day and night, with us and the Yanks. They'll not stand up to that much longer. Stands to reason.'

'Didn't work on *us*, in forty.'

'Aye, but they're getting it back tenfold. The Yanks are making all the difference. Some of us might not like it but it's true. The Yanks have come and they're here to stay, till we've seen it through.' He put his hand on Davy's knee in a brief grip of encouragement. 'Be patient. You're staying with us, on the team. Acting DC. They won't shift you back to uniform, I can assure you of that. Chief Superintendent Rush knows what a good job you're doing. And he knows what I think of you.'

Davy felt himself reddening with pleasure, and with shame at his parade of low spirits. 'Thanks, sir. I really appreciate it. All you've done for me. I'm very grateful.'

Holden grinned. 'I should think you are, lad. Now then, I'd better sup up and be on my way. Late for supper again. My missus'll be on the warpath. You want to thank your lucky stars you haven't got a wife ready with the rolling-pin. You stay married to the job. That's enough to be going on with!'

The mention of the uniformed branch had reawakened Davy's sense of grievance at the recent accumulations of misfortune life seemed to be throwing at him. Bob Noone, his roommate at the lodgings in Dubry Street, was also a special constable with the York city force. Bob was a year or two younger than Davy, a happy-go-lucky sort, and though his habits and attitude riled Davy at times, they had got on well enough together in the two years and more that they had known each other. Until recently, that is. Just as well then that Bob had only just moved out, having been granted the transfer to the West Yorks constabulary at Leeds, which he had been pushing for since he had met a girl from there who had transformed his former unattached, carefree bachelor existence.

He and Davy had not seen that much of each other, despite the shared room, once Davy had transferred over to the detective branch a few months after his arrival. Different duties and different shifts had made them something of 'ships that pass in the night', or noontime, though Davy had sensed a while ago that Bob's mateyness had cooled a little since Davy's switch to plain clothes. It might well have been Bob's own strenuous efforts, and the initial resistance he had encountered, that had caused him to stir up the muddy waters surrounding Davy's history before he had joined the police – a history Davy had hoped would remain securely hidden in the confidential records, with severely restricted access, according to DI Holden. 'Don't you worry,' the inspector had confided. 'No one at the station will know anything of your past. Beyond what you tell them yourself,' he had added, with a significant look. 'And that's up to you.'

There was only one part of that past which Davy felt shame at, and no amount of reasoning and rationalizing with himself would ever alter that. Certainly he still had no doubt that the stand he had taken against the war which broke out in September 1939, was the right one. It had nothing to do with his Quaker background and upbringing. He had rebelled against that from his schooldays at Bootham, had demonstrated his rebellion by leaving home at the earliest opportunity, and by the active part he had played in the Spanish Civil War, enlisting in the cause of the republicans against Franco's forces. It was that fighting, the sights he had witnessed in Spain, which had brought home all the horrors as well as the futility of war as a means of settling anything. He could appreciate full well the irony of his case. Even his father had served in the Great War, witnessed the horrors of the Western Front in his service as a stretcher-bearer, and now the son, fresh from the Spanish battlefields, refused to play any part whatsoever in the second world conflict, to the extent of being prepared to go to prison for his new and hard-won beliefs, with the label of conchy hung round his defiant neck.

Pride goeth before destruction, and an haughty spirit before a fall. The Biblical proverb had got it right. His spirit had been broken, and quickly enough. He could never tell anyone, not even Alice or his own loving parents, about the full horror of the brutality and the abuses he had suffered in gaol. His scarred mind shied away even from recall, in dark panic striving to shut out the memory of their violence and degradation. It had only taken three months. Only! An eternity, from which death seemed a logical route to escape. His breakdown was complete, physical and mental. He would always owe an immense debt of gratitude and love to his father, who had fought valiantly and unflaggingly to save him, challenging authority, moving higher and higher through its ranks until finally he prevailed, and Davy was released into his care, and the rest of his sentence suspended.

After bidding DI Holden goodnight, Davy walked down from the Duke of Wellington, past the old city walls at the end of Nunnery Lane and headed up towards Clementhorpe's rows of terraced houses. The winter darkness had long fallen, though the weather was amazingly mild for December, almost humid with the amount of moisture in the air. The low cloud cover made the blackout seem even heavier, and Davy resorted to the pencil beam of his torch, in spite of his familiarity with the neighbourhood, and the white daub of paint on the lampposts. He should be able to find his way blindfold after more than two years at 25, Dubry Street. He thought of it almost as home now, rather than simply 'the digs', and that was all down to 'Reeny' – his landlady, Irene Lumley: mum and big sister rolled into one, despite the fact that she was only four years older than he was. More than that, she was a close friend, and he was half in love with her, in a thoroughly decent, platonic way. She was married to Dick, an engine driver with LNER, and they had a son, Micky, who was nearly six years old. It was a happy marriage. Davy hoped fervently that Dick fully realized just how lucky he was to have someone as sweet as Reeny for a wife.

But even that friendship, which he so valued, had been threatened by the spectre of his past. Bob Noone had been like a sore-headed bear when his efforts to transfer to the Leeds force had run into difficulties, so when he had appeared in the kitchen of Dubry Street grinning like a pools winner, Davy had been relieved as well as pleased on his behalf to learn that his efforts had at last been crowned with success. There was a sting in the tail of Bob's departure, however.

'You're a bit of a dark horse, aren't you?' he had announced, making sure that Reeny was present to hear it. 'By heck! You must have some powerful friends in high places, apart from DI Holden and that lot! I bet it isn't often that an ex-jailbird has ended up working for the police himself.'

Davy could feel the hot tide of redness sweeping up into his features even as Reeny Lumley stared in incomprehension. She could sense the malign pleasure behind the words. 'What the devil are you on about?'

'His nibs, here! Only done time, has our laddo. Isn't that right, Davy? Armley, weren't it? We've had a real live conchy in our midst. Isn't that right, Davy?' He met Reeny's disbelieving stare. 'Go on then! Ask him if you don't believe me! What have you got to say for yourself, Constable Brown?'

'How did you find out?' Even to his own ears, Davy's croak sounded riddled with guilt, and shame.

Bob gave an ugly laugh, laid a finger along the side of his nose. 'Ah-ha! You know what they say about guilty secrets. They always find you out. Never you mind! I bet you thought you'd got away with it, eh? All this time! All this time we've been sat here—' he jerked his head up towards the ceiling – 'I've been living with a blasted conchy! Not a bloody word! Mind you, not surprising, is it? I mean!' His face wore a sneering expression of appeal as he turned his gaze towards the pale-faced landlady. 'I don't blame you for being shocked, Reeny, love. So was I, I can tell you! I'd have the bugger out on the street right now, if I was you.'

'Shut up, Bob!'

'Eh?' He blinked at her, in affected surprise. 'What have *I* done?' Then he glanced from one to the other. 'Oh God! No! Don't tell me . . . you never knew. . . ?'

'No, of course not! Don't be so daft!' Her eyes were still on Davy as she spoke, and his held hers. 'Just go on up. Give us a few minutes.'

Bob was disconcerted, angry at somehow being made to feel in the wrong. 'Right-oh. Dunno what the lads'll make of it down at the station, though.' And with this parting shot, he went out, and they heard his heavy tread up the stairs, the loud closing of the bedroom door.

Davy waited tensely, his gaze never leaving her face, which showed now the full force of the shock she had received. 'Why?' she whispered. 'Why didn't you tell us?'

'I couldn't. I was warned not to say anything. When I first got the job. It's . . .' he shrugged hopelessly. There was a brief pause. 'I'm not ashamed!' he went on, almost fiercely. 'Not about being an objector. Not about refusing to fight. I still believe in what I did, that it was right.' All at once, his shoulders dipped, his body slumped a little. His voice was changed, deadened when he continued, and he half-turned away from the long table across which they faced each other. 'You want me to go? I can pack now. I'll find somewhere. If I could leave just a few things. I'll send for them '

'I want you to tell me! Tell me everything. *Why* you did it! Just explain – everything!' She gestured towards his chair. 'Sit down. I'll make a fresh pot. Tell me all about it.'

Her voice was low and gentle, and he felt a great wave of tenderness for her. His eyes filled, and he blinked away the forming tears as he watched her slim figure in the drab blouse and skirt, the apron strings at neck and waist, as she crossed towards the range and bent to carry out the task of making tea. When she sat opposite him, their troubled eyes met once again. After she had poured out the tea, she reached across and laid her hand over his; he felt the coolness of her light touch, its intimate reassurance, and he told her everything: the violence he had witnessed in Spain, his complete conviction that warfare could never be the answer to any problem. He even told her of his time in France, and of Lou Varron, and the strange religion of hers, Baha'ism, which, too, advocated non-violence. His voice unsteady, his hands hidden beneath the table to hide their unsteadiness, he even spoke about his time in prison, with painful brevity 'I had a bad time – I had a breakdown. My father saved me – he got them to release me. I was at home quite a while. Then I took the job in Howbeck. Working on the land.' This time there was a longer pause, and he gave a shuddering sigh. 'I'm so sorry, Mrs L. I didn't mean – didn't like deceiving you. It's just – nobody knew. When I got the job as special constable, they said it was best to say nothing.' He glanced towards the ceiling and pulled a bravely comic face of resignation. 'I guess I don't have to worry about that any more.'

He felt Reeny Lumley's hand rest once more on his own. This time the grip was much firmer. Her fingers curled, pressed hard against his, and she kept her hold, shaking his hand a little in encouragement. 'No more talk of moving out, you hear? I thought that was supposed to be one of the things we're fighting this war for – freedom, the right to choose for ourselves how we go on. Don't pay them any mind, Davy! You've paid for your beliefs – and you're doing something worthwhile now. Look at that terrible bloke you helped to catch, harming all those poor women. You're staying right where you are, all right?'

'Yes, Mrs L. You're the boss.' He managed a slightly lopsided grin, and swallowed hard, his throat thick with emotion.

'You bet I am!' She stood and moved swiftly round the broad table, before he could rise, and came to stand close behind him. She put both hands on his shoulders, and pressed down hard, forcing him down into the hard wooden chair. He felt her upper body resting against him as he turned his head back and sideways, smelt the warmth and sweetness of her, as she bent, until her breath was warm against his face. He saw the pinkness of her lips as they approached his uplifted face, then rested against his own in a soft but unhurried kiss.

CHAPTER FOUR

Doreen Glass stretched her feet down to the bottom of the bed, revelling in the warmth under the covers. She arched her thin body, savouring the pull of muscles and joints. The bliss of solitude swept over her, and with the blankets still up to her chin, she let her eyes rove possessively around the room, the familiar furnishings in the deep gloom, with just the faint edges of light filtering round the curtains and the blackout drape. She heard Aunt Elizabeth's soft tread on the carpeted stairs, the affected shrillness of her voice as she called out. 'Come on, lazy bones! It's nearly nine. You've had your first holiday treat. I've let you lie abed long enough.' As she swung the door open and entered, Doreen's dark head turned on the pillow, and she screwed her face up in a theatrical sigh, let her mouth gape in an exaggerated yawn. She lifted her arms from the warmth and stretched them overhead, her eyes narrowing against the spill of pale light when Miss Ramsay dragged back the heavy drape, on its own wooden pole, then swished the curtains back. 'Another dull day, but then what can we expect at Christmas-time? Here's your milk. Drink it up, then wash. Mrs Addis has already started work, but I dare say she'll make you some breakfast. Maybe a boiled egg after your porridge. Another treat, as it's the first day of your holiday.'

Obediently, Doreen sat up, reached for the glass and drank off the milk in several great gulps, enjoying the bite of its coldness flowing down her throat. Miss Ramsay unhooked the dressing-gown from the back of the door and let it fall across the foot of the bed. 'And I think you could spend a bit of time sorting out your things,' she said, glancing round. 'I'm sure Mrs Addis would appreciate it, now that she has to manage everything on her own.' Milly, the girl who used to do the cleaning at Northend Cottage, had departed last month to join the ranks of those doing the much more patriotic, and lucrative, 'war work', in one of the Teesside factories.

'I will.' Doreen threw back the blankets, swung her legs out and shivered as she felt the chill round her bare ankles and feet. The sprigged pyjama pants had ridden up nearly to her knees. Her toes groped for the felt slippers, and slid gratefully inside them, like nesting birds. Miss Ramsay picked up the glass, was turning away. Doreen cleared her throat. Her voice was husky, a soft, pleading murmur. She shook out her long brown hair, letting it fall about her face in what she hoped was an attractively framing disarray. 'Aunt Elizabeth! About my going home.' She tried to stop short of a whine. 'Do I really have to? I mean, couldn't I just pop through for the day? Maybe after New Year?' Arrangements had been set in place, much to Doreen's dismay, for her to travel to Margrove by train next week, on Thursday, the twenty-third, and to stay until Tuesday, the twenty-eighth: an inordinate length of time, the thought of which filled the thirteen-year-old with shuddering repugnance. She reflected resentfully that if Miss Ramsay's brother, Gordon, and his wife, Esmé, had not been coming to Howbeck for the holiday period, her guardian would not have been so eager to let her go. 'I could help Mrs Addis,' Doreen pursued, the plea growing stronger and more urgent. 'Help her to get the place really spick and span for Uncle Gordon and Aunt Esmé.' Another pause, the pathos turned up to place a catch in the voice. 'I'd love to spend the holiday weekend with them . . . and you.' The voice was a whisper now, carrying a strong hint of near tears. 'I'd like . . . I'll miss you.'

'Good heavens, child! It's only five nights away. And they *are* your family! You haven't seen them since the summer. More than four months. And even then you didn't spend the night there, did you? You've hardly seen them for more than a couple of days in the whole of this year!'

You bloody old hypocrite! Doreen liked to swear in her head, delighted in imagining the shock and horror she would create if she voiced such sentiments out loud. Instead, she looked woebegone and crushed. There was nothing duplicitous about her feelings of distaste at the thought of returning to the family bosom of 19 Maudsley Street. She felt she had never truly belonged there, even as the scruffy and unclean ten-year-old with label and gas mask, who had looked on the journey from Margrove to the alien Yorkshire dale as an escape. The sight of that smartly dressed, fox-furred spinster, wrinkling her nose at the whiff of those unwashed urchins from the mucky coastal town, had been the lifebelt the wide-eyed youngster had been seeking. And instinctively Doreen had seen it; had clutched at it and refused to let it go.

Now she opened her eyes as wide as she could, gazed unblinking until her vision blurred, and she felt the moisture gather, pictured the shine of tears in the tragic brown orbs. 'I'm sorry,' she muttered, let Miss Ramsay catch a glimpse of her disconsolate features before she lowered them, and managed a hiccup of a sigh. 'I know I should . . . it's just . . . I feel so different there now. Not a part of them.' She gave a dramatic shudder, which transmitted itself through every part of her body. 'I can't help it. Last time – I was all itchy, and then I had these lumps all over and I couldn't stop scratching. I found a flea in my . . . inside my clothes. It was horrid. They made me sleep with Algy. He was all . . . smelly!' She sniffed, then again, heaving her drooping shoulders, and the tears came. She kept her head down. Her hands lay in her lap, the fingers twisting together. She was gratified to feel a teardrop splash on to her skin.

'Oh, darling! Don't upset yourself.' The bed creaked. She felt the settling weight of Miss Ramsay, the touch of her hip against hers as she sat beside her. An arm came out and cradled her into her sweet-smelling side. 'Come on! It's the first day of your holiday. Over a week to go yet before you need to worry. Tell you what. Maybe we could arrange for you to go just for the weekend. Perhaps go down on Christmas Eve. And come back on the Monday. We'll see if there are any trains running. You must be able to get to Whitby, surely? We can arrange for Mr Walker to pick you up from there. How would that be, eh?'

Doreen turned towards her, buried her head in the fragrant shoulder and wrapped her arms round her. 'Oh, Aunt Elizabeth! You're so good! I'm sorry. I know I shouldn't – they're my family, my flesh and blood.'

Elizabeth Ramsay's hand moved up, cupped the brown head, and her lips pressed against the soft brown locks. It was still rare for her to display such powerful emotion, and to make such physical contact, but she realized how thrillingly her body, her whole being, responded to it. Another smothering squeeze and she released the young girl, her own eyes damp. 'Now come on, young lady! This really won't do! Off you

go to the bathroom and then get yourself down those stairs. Skedaddle!'
She even aimed a friendly swipe at the scampering, revitalized figure,
who giggled as she fled at the unlikely expression the refined spinster
had just used.

Maggie Glass looked up from the single sheet of paper she was holding
in her hand. She had recognized the neat script on the envelope even
before she had seen the postmark. 'Our Doreen can't come till
Christmas Eve.' The disappointment on her sharp face was obvious,
though, to be honest, she had feared something worse when she had
seen her daughter's handwriting.

'That's only a day after she was supposed to be coming in the first
place!' Ethel Glass observed dispassionately. Her hair, much darker and
thicker than her younger sister's, stood up in unruly spikes as she
pushed it back from her brow. She was still in the shift she wore for
night-attire, with the ragged shawl draped round her shoulders, as she
lolled at the kitchen table, over her second cup of tea from the large
brown enamel pot which stood on the round black metal hob over the
glowing fire in the range. As far as she was concerned it would have
been better news if Miss lah-de-dah Doreen hadn't been coming at all.
With a week to go to Christmas, angry words had already been
exchanged across this very table about the proposed visit. 'It's not the
bloody princesses coming to stay!' Ethel had snarled, when Maggie had
announced it. The sixteen-year-old had anticipated what was coming
next, and had jumped in to try and forestall it. 'And I am not having our
Algy in with me so Miss Fancy Drawers can have a room to herself.
Bugger that for a game of soldiers!'

'I'll wash your bloody mouth out with soap!' her father had threatened, with vehement but illogical indignation at her language.

'But what if our George gets some leave an' all?' Maggie had asked.
Their son, George, two years younger than Alice and three years senior
to Ethel, was still doing basic training in the army four months after his
call-up. 'He'll have to have his room back. And you'll have to go in to
the back room with Doreen *and* our Algy, so stop mithering.'

'God! It'll be no hardship having to work Christmas Day,' Ethel
grumbled. 'They want us in till after washing-up at dinner-time.' She
worked as a domestic in a guesthouse with delusions of grandeur
named The Groves Hotel.

'Well, I just hope they pay you overtime for it!' her father commented. Fred Glass was not only collarless but shirtless, his canvas braces slung over his sleeveless, ragged singlet. His pale arms had the stretched, long muscles of a lifetime of manual labour. The black hairs stood out thinly against the skin of his forearms.

I'd do it for nowt to get away from this lot! Ethel thought, but wisely did not say. Not when she was sitting so close to those wiry arms, which, after years of wielding a shovel on various building sites and then, for the past ten years, at the Margrove Steel and Iron Co., could lash out with swift and stinging retribution at any 'lip'. Her eye caught the exotic card standing on the high shelf above the range, in isolated splendour so far, with its picture of Egyptian pyramids, complete with camel and palm trees. It looked like something off one of the films they showed at the Lex every week. She spent a lot of her time at the pictures, crowding in with all those others, puffing away in the blue-smoke, flickering dimness to escape the stultifying reality which waited outside for them. Well, Alice, lucky bugger, had certainly done that all right. Ethel felt almost despair at the thought of how much longer she herself would have to wait before she could escape the sheer dreariness of her life. She would give anything to be able to wish the next year and a half away. There were places that would take on girls at eighteen, factories and munitions works all over the country, even though the official age for registering for war service was still twenty. But it would be just her luck the war would be over even before she attained her eighteenth birthday, in August, 1945. Probably before next Christmas.

Another wave of bitterness swept over her as her thoughts returned to young Doreen. Trust her, the smarmy little get, to find a way out of this dump, and her not even fourteen yet! It just wasn't fair! Talked like a lady, dressed up like a toff in that posh uniform of hers, swanking away with her new friends. And not only her. Al had made it, an' all. Sergeant now. Her mam talked about her as though she was a bloody general or summat, winning the war single-handed out in Egypt. But Ethel couldn't help burning with envy of her, too. She didn't count her brother, George. He was a lad. Lads had it easy. When the war ended and he came out the army, he'd probably go back to the steelworks, booze and gamble his wages away till he got some poor cow up the duff and had to marry her, the way dad had had to when mam fell with Al. So he'd get his own personal skivvy to run round after him and have a houseful of kids to wait on him hand and foot. No. She didn't count George at all. . . .

So. Two of them had made it, and it was all so unfair. She was the bonniest by far. When she got the chance to take a good look at herself – not round here, but the missus at work let them have a bath once a week, in a proper bathroom, mirror and all – Ethel stood staring at herself in the glass for long, dreaming, private moments. She stared at her slim body, her delicate face. She could be as good as any of those glamourpusses in the magazines, or up on the screen at the Lex. All she needed was the chance, like young Doreen, or Alice. Maybe not like Al. She was weird, that one. Not a bit interested in making the best of herself, or in the lads. There was that lad, Davy, the one who was a copper in York. Doreen had told them he was mad on her. And real posh, too, like that mate of hers, that stuck-up Elsbeth Hobbs. But had Alice grabbed him? Not on your Nelly! Still, she'd done all right, fair do's. And Egypt wasn't bad as far as getting away from this dump went. If she had any sense, she'd stop out there for good, never come back to stinking old Margrove again.

She'd heard her dad going on about the war, like he was one of them clever dicks off the *Brains Trust* on the wireless. 'All be over before next Christmas!' Fred had declared confidently, like he'd just been having a chat with old Winston. 'Yanks come in late again, just like last time, but they've made all the difference.' He'd glowered at Ethel as though he could read what was on her rebellious mind. 'Then we can get things back to normal again. Blokes back home, back in their jobs, and the women back where they belong an' all!' Oh God! Ethel had prayed silently, but with equal fervour. Don't let it end too soon. Just another couple of years, that's all I ask!

Doreen stood in the narrow back yard, glanced up at the low uniform grey of the sky. She shivered, despite her warm woollen underwear and the long black woollen stockings under her school uniform of white blouse and grey skirt, and the maroon- and-grey striped tie, and the thick maroon sweater. She was not simply reacting to the damp cold. Her sensitive nose wrinkled as she thought of the disgusting smell in the outside toilet, the 'netty' – a word she hadn't used in years, she reflected sorrowfully – on Friday night, her first night 'home', after her father had been there, following his loud, triumphal, slobbering return from the Black Horse, bearing gifts of greasy fish and chips and bottles of stout and lemonade.

She shivered anew. She would have preferred to hang on, to remain constipated until she got safely back to Northend Cottage on the morrow, but needs must. She steeled herself and went in, slipping the catch on the inside of the wooden door, with its gap of a foot or so at the bottom and an even bigger one at the top. At least it meant that *fresh* air, if the adjective could be applied to the atmosphere floating around the environs of Maudsley Street, circulated more freely. She would have sighed, except that her lips were clamped thinly together as she stared at the wad of square newspaper clippings held by the looped string attached to the nail in the door. Fastidiously she tore off several sheets and carefully balanced them round the rim of the wooden seat. Better to have imprints of the racing results or images of Jane's scantily clad form on her bum than allow it to come into contact with that well-worn surface. With a martyred expression she hoisted and lowered her clothing, then herself, and sat. She waited humiliatingly for nature to take its course, reflecting how everything seemed to be conspiring against her to make her sense of suffering complete.

She managed to escape soon afterwards to take a solitary hike up the appropriately if unimaginatively named Park Road, one of the longest roads in Margrove, up to the municipal park itself. Despite the unpromising weather the wide expanse of grass and trees and black flower-beds and winding paths was well populated on this Boxing Day morning, mostly by mums or big sisters and toddlers, and noisy gangs of older boys. Doreen was just a little nervous but mainly proud of her smart school outfit, which so distinguished her from the packs of scruffy youths. She was comforted by the suspicious glowering looks some of them cast at her as she passed by them, striding out purposefully. Those looks told her how different she was from them, how far she had moved from their background. However, she was a little disconcerted when two of them, louts around her own age, detached themselves from their group, who were kicking a small rubber ball about on the grass, in defiance of the notices and the absent 'parky', and began to call out to her in mockingly insulting tones. She turned her gaze pointedly ahead of her, away from their loutishness, her head held high, her cheeks red and her heart racing a little.

'Clear off!' The firm voice startled her. A young man on a bicycle had appeared suddenly on the path behind her. He was fair-haired, nice-looking and well-dressed, in a belted waterproof jacket with a high collar, and with a blue-and-black college scarf wrapped round his neck. His face was pink from the cold and exercise, and grew a little pinker as he smiled and addressed her. 'Those tykes bothering you?' They had retreated, though they flung a few crude curses as they made off back to join their fellows.

'A bit. Thanks very much.' Doreen's face reddened, too, much to her chagrin. She was quite used to the boys on the train from school, and in Whitby, chatting to her and her companions, in spite of the school's stern injunctions that they should not mingle. He fell in step alongside her, wheeling his bike along on his left-hand side, and her heart beat fast again, for a different reason this time.

'I'll just walk a little way with you, if that's all right?' He glanced back over his shoulder. 'Just in case those oiks try it on again. I'm Robin Hobbs, by the way.'

'Oh. Thanks very much. Yes, that would be fine. My name's Doreen Glass. How do you do.' She laughed, a little gushingly, and suffered a flash of self-fury at her gaucheness. For God's sake! Get a grip of yourself, girl! The first halfway decent chap that looks at you and you turn into a giggling school-kid! He probably thinks you're grown up. Fifteen or sixteen. He could be a college boy himself. Then the surname registered. 'Did you say Hobbs?'

'That's right. Most people call me Rob, by the way.' Similar thoughts seemed to be striking him, in relation to her name. 'Glass? That's quite unusual. Are you from round here? Only my sister – Elsbeth – used to know a girl—'

'Good heavens! Yes! I know her! We were at Howbeck. In the dales. My sister's Alice. They shared a flat.'

'This is incredible!' He was grinning delightedly. 'Look, have you got a bit of free time? We live just nearby. Elton Grove.'

'Yes, I know. I met your da – father. He gave me a lift once.'

'Come back for a cup of tea, will you? We're practically old chums.'

She nodded enthusiastically. 'That would be lovely!' Steady, she urged herself. Where's the poise, the perfect young lady? 'How is Elsbeth? She's married now, isn't she? With a baby?'

'You can find out for yourself. She and the infant are up home for the holiday. She'll be over the moon to see you!'

37

CHAPTER FIVE

Rob was naïvely optimistic in his estimation of his sister's reaction to the sudden reappearance of Doreen Glass in her life. The flustered young mother was still in her housecoat and her curlers were partly concealed by the green headscarf knotted about them, from which strands of the corn-yellow hair escaped – more hay-coloured these days, Doreen would cattily amend later in her own reaction to the initial dismay stamped upon those pretty features, which was clumsily disguised, far too late to fool the young visitor. Doreen, however, completely misinterpreted the reason for Elsbeth Hobbs's response to seeing her again. Partly through her unworldliness, and partly through her innate self-centredness, the adolescent assumed it was the social gulf which the ex-teacher still felt divided them that was responsible for that instinctive, shrinking flash of unwelcome. It was lucky that Elsbeth's father was on hand, ably supported by his wife, to welcome her over the threshold and into the festively hung living-room.

'My word! Who's this smart and sophisticated young lady come to see us? Why, if it isn't little Doreen! Except she's quite grown up!' She had removed her woollen gloves, and he held on to her cold hand, drew her forward without releasing it. 'Come in and get yourself warm. It's grand to see you again! How is everyone? Miss Ramsay, your family – your Alice? It's ages since we've had news.'

Because of Elsbeth's instinctive response to seeing her, Doreen hastily and volubly backed up the unsuspecting Rob's account of how they had met by accident. When she was ceremoniously installed in a place of honour on the settee, near the warmth of the cheerily burning fire and the festive hearth, a glass of home-made ginger wine in her hand, she answered Mr Hobbs's jovial interrogation. 'Alice is doing really well out in Egypt. She's been made sergeant now.'

'I'd better go and get dressed,' Elsbeth said. 'Elaine's asleep at the moment. I won't disturb her. She's so grumpy when she's woken.' She was already half-way through the door by the time she finished speaking.

Rob had quietened, too, and retired into the background. He seemed suddenly rather embarrassed. Was he a snob, like his older sister, Doreen wondered bitterly? but then deduced that his sudden withdrawal had more to do with the fact of Mr Hobbs's innocent exposure of her age. 'You're what? How old now? Thirteen! My word!' Rob, she had already learned, was a seventeen-year-old sixth-former and prefect at boarding school. For a very brief instant Doreen wished she were her sister, Ethel, who would, in her own vulgar parlance, 'have him for breakfast'. Give her another couple of years and she, too, would have lads like Rob running after her, hanging on her every word.

Upstairs, Elsbeth listened to the buzz of voices drifting faintly and unintelligibly up to her. It had been such a shock, seeing her, looking so charming in that uniform. And sounding so well spoken, too. She recalled the snivelling little runny-nosed urchin she had first met at Lister Road school: the girl who had meanly been bullying that other lardy creature, forcing her to hand over her pennies. That's really how Beth and Al had got started. It had brought them together for the first time since their own childhood. Elsbeth had helped to smooth things over, with Alice's co-operation. That was the beginning. Beth had suggested Alice apply to come with the school to Howbeck, to work as a general assistant – cleaner, cook, and invaluable surrogate big sister to all the young evacuees. And that had led . . .

It was still too painful for her to think about. She had got used to pushing it away, though not before that anguish, that fierce, scalding pain, and shame, each time she was forced to remember. She *mustn't* remember.

She stood staring at her reflection in the mirror over the washbasin. Without make-up her face looked worn, her skin patchy, her eyes tired, and lined. She was still only twenty-one, for God's sake! Another three months before her twenty-second birthday. Alice would have celebrated hers less than two weeks ago. She hoped it had been happy. She had thought about her that day. She couldn't help it. It had been such a bad day for herself, one that ended in tears, lying on the bed entirely conquered by those great, heaving sobs, washing over and racking her, so that her face had swollen up like a battered prize fighter's, slit-eyed, and little Elaine had howled, probably terrified by the sight of this awful, blotched stranger who clutched her and tried to soothe her while the tears streamed down endlessly. Beth had been forced to think of Al that day, to remember until every part of her ached with fierce and shameless desire for what she had lost.

Arty had been perfectly beastly, storming out of the flat, walking out on her in the midst of her tearful tirade, so that rigid with fury she had screamed at the slammed door and flung the teacup at the shabby, tiny kitchenette wall. The dregs had left a dark stain, with rivulets dribbling down to the chipped skirting-board, and the leaves clinging to the cheap, sick-yellow paint. Her abandoned violence shocked her. She stood for maybe a minute, staring at the mess and the shards of crockery scattered round her feet, while Elaine sniffled and whinged in her cradle. It was such a wild and uncharacteristic thing for her to do that it frightened. her. Then the tears restarted, and flowed non-stop as she fed and bathed Elaine, wrinkling her nose and pursing her lips at the ammoniacal stench of the soaking nappy, which she carried held fastidiously at arm's length to drop into the soak-bucket in the equally tiny bathroom.

How dare he just turn his back, walk out on her like that? How could he be such a brute? But her precipitate action in hurling the cup seemed to have drained her of her rage, leaving only the smothering misery, the rolling, silent tears in the electric gloom. Arty – her sweet, lovable, faithful knight, Arty. What had happened to him, that gentle, selfless lover, who had eased away her fears, brought her such bliss, helped her to overcome even her terror of being pregnant, and the bloodiness of birth?

And she *had* been afraid, more than she could ever tell him, not only of having the baby but, before that, of being lovers, of committing herself so completely to him. She could not share, even with him, the real fear and shame – that she was running away from Alice rather than towards him. And she had done so well, she thought, though without him, without his unique love and devotion to her, she would never have achieved all that they had together. There were times, when he lay sleeping beside her, that she wished fervently that she could tell him, share everything with him: Alice, and even the trauma of Luke Denby, the only other man who had made love to her. Her mind screamed recrimination at her for the lie that lay in that phrase, 'made love'. It had been nothing like that. There were other, cruder, obscene words to describe their act together, the nightmare it had been for her.

She could scarcely analyse her own behaviour even now. Why had she allowed the son of the squire of Howe Manor to seduce her? The plea of ignorant, uninformed virgin would not hold. Was it guilt over the secret, shocking feeling she was already experiencing for Alice Glass – a feeling so passionately realized in the haven of that little flat? Certainly it was the news of Luke's death in the skies over Germany which had driven her away from the sanctuary she and Alice had found. Illogical or not, Elsbeth saw his death as part of some divine judgement for her deviance. She had fled Howbeck to join the Wrens, but she had taken her tormenting thoughts with her.

Arty had saved her from all that, without knowing it. How could they have come to this, trading insults like blows, shouting, hurting each other, while their six-month-old daughter lay between them? Their first wedding anniversary was only four days away. How could he do this to her, be so shockingly unfeeling, be so un-Arty? Total honesty could be so painful, as she well knew, but the lonely, weeping quiet, made all the worse by baby Elaine's unconscious burbling, post-fed, post-bath placidity, forced Elsbeth to admit to her own complicity in the present sad state of things. She had a beautiful baby, a devoted husband. What right had she to be unhappy? But the truth was inescapable. For the past few months she had felt the weight of depression, the moods hovering, sometimes like vague shadows in the background, then closing blackly around her. At first she ran from them. She would get Elaine ready, hurry her out in the pram, into the busy city sunlight, walk in the small park up the road, with its scuffed grass and bright flower-beds, the larches and the holly bushes. Traffic would be roaring by, people hurrying past, but others, with infants, would stop to chat, to admire, and it made Elsbeth feel better, calmer: a pretty young mother, in her smart costume, with her smart perambulator, her lovely child. Sometimes her handsome husband would be at her side: warrior and gentleman, serving king and country, fighting for his loved ones.

Fighting from a desk. The painfully disloyal thought would sneak up, jab her like a splinter suddenly. While her brother, Bill, was across the world, risking his life on the Burmese frontier. And even Alice was away out in the desert, facing all kinds of dangers. Luke Denby, her seducer, had already made the ultimate sacrifice, blown or burnt to death in the wrecked remains of his bomber in Germany.

Did she want her husband to risk such dangers? Of course not! She should pray each night, thank God that he travelled no further than the War Office, or that place in the country, that secret mansion where all the boffins were secreted and dreamed up new and vital ways of winning the war. As if somehow attuned to her disloyal thoughts, Arty had begun to talk of playing a more combative role. There was a great deal of liaising with the Americans now – London was full of them, in their glamorous, well-cut, expensive-looking uniforms and their carelessly displayed rolls of banknotes. He began to travel much further afield, and to be away for several days and nights at a time. He talked of this 'second front' more and more, and it irritated her more and more. Then he confided, still in that shy, diffident way of his, that he might well have to go overseas when the cross-channel assault took place.

'No! You can't!' She almost added ridiculously, *I won't let you!* 'I couldn't bear it. You must promise me! You mustn't leave me!'

And he had laughed, and she heard, for the first time from him, that condescending, masculine tolerance in his tone that infuriated her. She was startled by the force of her feeling. 'I'm low enough as it. is! You're away half the time now. I'm left alone, stuck in this flat with the baby. It's no joke, believe me.'

They began to quarrel. She snapped at him now, she couldn't help it. He wouldn't retaliate, just had that miserable, hangdog look about him, which made her worse, because she felt so bad about causing it. But she was unable to stop herself from doing it, her voice growing shriller, sharper, more self-righteously plaintive, until even poor compliant Arty was drawn to hit back.

She had suggested that she might well go back home, to her parents at Margrove. 'I hardly ever see you as it is.' She knew she was exaggerating, was ashamed to recognize that she had voiced her thoughts of returning home with Elaine almost as much from a shameful desire to hurt him, to draw a wounded response, as a serious consideration of the move. He had picked up on it.

'*Home?* Surely this is your home, with your husband?' Then he had added, with such uncharacteristic cruelty, 'Surely you can't be afraid of the bombing any more? We haven't had a raid for ages.'

And she was stung to continue the argument, until it built up, ran on, rising into a nasty, sniping engagement. 'I'd have help with Elaine. I could get out now and then, see some of my friends. Without pushing the pram everywhere I go. It's no fun being stuck here. London's a pretty lonely place when you don't know anyone.' She hated the whining quality of her own tone, the petty selfishness of it, but she couldn't stop. She continued to snipe vindictively at him. 'You're away more and more. You said yourself you're going to be more and more involved with this hush-hush stuff with the Yanks. Anyway, supposing you had been posted overseas, like Bill, say, or Alice. We'd have had to put up with being apart then, wouldn't we?' She saw the hurt, the withdrawal on his youthful face, its reddening. When they first got to know each other he had been so embarrassed, even dejected, at his special chum Bill's being posted to the Far East, and his own home posting.

'P'raps you'd have felt better if I *had* been! You could have stayed in the Wrens. You might even have got overseas yourself, like your chum, Alice!'

'What do you mean?' Her voice shrilled piercingly, and she felt the hot flood of colour, the sting of tears. Chum? What did he mean by that? Was he trying to say. . . ? But he couldn't know. She hardly ever mentioned Al nowadays, even though he knew they had been so close. No one knew the truth. She let the tears come, turned away from him, *ran* away, to lie weeping on the double bed in that dark, damply dismal bedroom gloom.

The creaking bed itself was an accusation in her bitter mood. It was the place she had been most afraid of, when they had first confessed their love and she made the momentous decision to commit herself to him body and soul. But the sexual aspect had proved to be nothing like the nightmare she had feared and anticipated. His loving was inevitably gentle, diffident even, in its approach, except for the briefly wild culmination of his passion, and then he would strive so selflessly to ensure her own satisfaction that she wept afterwards with sheer gratitude and love for his devotion to her needs. There was nothing of the brute, the force of taking, which had so shocked and revolted her with Luke Denby. 'I love you! I love you so much!' she would sob, after her climax, clinging fiercely to him as he lay holding her tenderly.

One of the visiting nurses in their first Bermondsey room had said, when she came to see the month-old Elaine, 'Have you had your fit of the baby blues yet?' And Elsbeth had shaken her head, wondering at this old wives' tale, for she had never, she swore, felt happier, with the baby at her breast and Arty lying adoringly at her side. Of course the sexual side of the marriage had been suspended, naturally. She was content, absorbed in the baby, with Arty devoted beside her, sharing night vigils, when he was not on duty, helping about the flat, with the cleaning and the washing, the rinsing of those smelly nappies, even helping with the feeding of Elaine when it became necessary to supplement Elsbeth's dwindling supply of milk with the powder formula.

One chilly autumn evening, when Elaine had settled for her sleep after a six o' clock feed, and Arty was home, he and Elsbeth had nestled on the sofa. 'She won't wake up till eleven or twelve,' Elsbeth confidently predicted, and lay back, savouring the intimate luxury of the quiet and her husband's arms, and the wireless playing softly in the background. She was drifting off to sleep, her head on Arty's chest. She enjoyed his lips nibbling at her ear, his fingers toying with the tendrils of her golden hair, even a hand gently stroking at her still tender breast. She was rather proud of their ripe fullness, and of his appreciative gaze when they were revealed. But suddenly the hand playing with her hair was withdrawn, then she felt it light on her knee, and sweep up under her dress, to the smoothness of her stocking, then beyond, to the skin of her thigh, and on again. Her body stirred, and stiffened, and before she had realized what she was doing she had seized his thin wrist, thrust it down, away from her. 'Don't!' She spoke sharply, instinctively, and felt a hot flood of shame. 'Please, darling,' she said. 'It's been . . . I don't think we're ready, yet.'

'It's been over three months – since Elaine was born. Twice that time since . . . we made love.'

She had turned into him, hugged him closer, winningly, soft with reproach, as much for herself as for him. 'I know, my darling. I know . . . how long, how bad it must be for you. But it's been hard for me . . . I feel . . . if you can just give me time, be patient, and gentle, with me. The way you always are.'

It was a shock for her to realize she no longer wanted him to make love: not even to touch her the way he had, with his hands and mouth, to make those wonderful things, that release, happen for her. A few weeks later, she had steeled herself – it shamed her to acknowledge that that was the word that came to her mind – to offer him her body; when he came eagerly towards her, and his hands and lips began to carry out those soft caressing strokes to arouse her, she had stopped him. 'No, please. Let's just . . . you do it to me, now. Come on, darling.' She had lifted her nightdress, not removing it the way she always had before, and moved, spreading herself beneath him, and it had hurt, abominably, and she had set her lips grimly, hidden beneath his rutting shoulder, clung to him like a samurai or a noble Roman falling on his sword and endured it, shuddering with both relief and a shameful disgust, when it was swiftly over.

CHAPTER SIX

'It *is* all right if I stay up here for New Year, isn't it? Or are you sick of us already?'

Mrs Hobbs looked at her daughter with wounded and righteous reproach. 'Elsbeth! You know we love having you here! As long as you want to! It's made it a wonderful Christmas. Helped to make up for not having Bill with us.'

Elsbeth heard that catch in the voice as her mother mentioned Bill's name, and was ashamed at her own reflex of jealousy, the age-old sense of her inferiority that it always sparked, like the twitch of a nerve in a sensitive tooth. Stronger still was the acknowledgement of her impulse to make such a hurtful and totally unjust accusation, even in disguised jest. It showed how weak she was still, how she could be so vindictive, simply to alleviate the pain of her own hurt.

'Will Arty manage to get up at all? The poor lad must get a break from all that work, surely? Even if it's only a couple of days?'

Underlying the tentative tone, there still seemed to Elsbeth a hint of criticism, as though she were somehow responsible for Arty's absence throughout the festive period. It did not help that she was suffering from a bad case of guilt on that very score. If she had not headed north with Elaine for the holiday, she and Arty could have been together, for the night of Christmas Eve – Arty would have been off duty eventually, and probably for the majority of Christmas Day, if not for the whole twenty-four-hour period. The baby's first Christmas, the three of them could have been sharing it, a cosy family trinity; sharing the humble little Bermondsey flat, transformed by the decorated tree and paper-chains and candlelight.

But she had put paid to that, with her whining and bitter tongue,

46

with Arty reacting, as he had lately, with his own brand of sullen, sarcastic defence. The worst of it was, Elsbeth could hear how selfish and self-centred her complaints were, was helpless against that rising tide of misery that turned her into such a carping, unpleasant creature. Part of her was revolted, stood by helplessly as she slid into those moods of blackness, until poor, wounded Arty was striking back, hurting in his turn at her attacks. He hadn't even come to King's Cross to see her on to the train, thereby managing to sting her conscience yet again at her unpatriotic selfishness, that she should imagine he could just leave the office (or wherever he was these days – she hardly knew any more), holding up the war effort until Mrs Clark and infant daughter were settled into their first-class carriage. The taxi driver had had to come into the dingy flat and help her down the steps with the luggage, and all the extra paraphernalia necessary to move a six-month-old child. Then she had endured cold and lonely hours in a train packed with servicemen beerily jolly at escaping to home and loved ones for the holiday; a journey that should have taken six hours but was nearer ten, blinds down for most of it, darkness to add to the numbing cold that worked upward from the feet, so that she cursed herself heartily for the vanity and foolishness that had made her put on silk stockings and underwear, despite (or because of?) Arty's soulful admonition to 'wear your winter woollies'. The dreadful dim blue lights that came on when the blinds were fastened down only seemed to add to the chill and the gloom. The baby food in the flask was too hot, and Elaine had grizzled and then bawled while her increasingly flustered mother jiggled and patted her and squirted the sickly smelling, still-too-hot liquid on to the back of her wrist to test it, and the rest of her fellow travellers, all males, sighed ever more noisily and crossed their legs and gazed heavenward and crackled their papers ever more fiercely.

She forced herself to reply to her mother's question. 'I really don't know, Mam. He hardly seems to know what he's doing himself from one day to the next. Probably not. He might just have twenty-four hours off, so he wouldn't be able to get up north. Not that he'll be lonely,' she couldn't help adding or allowing the bitterness to peep through. 'I'm sure he'll be celebrating in the West End somewhere if he is off. Probably glad to play the bachelor gay again!'

'Elsbeth?' Her mother's voice was even more hesitant, and Elsbeth waited in dread. 'Everything's all right, isn't it? Between you and Arty?'

'Of course! What on earth do you mean?' The answer was shrill, and sharp with aggression. Careful! Careful! The alarm bells sounded in Elsbeth's mind as she felt the rise of emotion.

'It's just . . . well, you've seemed a little bit on edge since you got here. When that young Glass girl called on Boxing Day you weren't very friendly. She wanted to see Elaine. You were such good friends with her sister, weren't you? You used to be full—'

'For God's sake! That was ages ago, Mam! I've grown up a bit since then, I hope! Maybe I'm just not cut out to sit at home producing babies one after another, like . . .' It was too late to stop herself. She saw the stricken look on her mother's face, the dark flush of pain and recognition of the jibe behind her words.

'I'm sure you were all very much wanted – and loved. I never – we never thought of any of you as a burden. And we've always been proud of you. *All* of you. We've done our best for you. It's nothing to be ashamed of, bringing up a family. I say my prayers for you, every night. You and Rob . . . and Bill.' Her voice trembled, and she swallowed hard. 'That he'll be brought back safely to us.' The voice failed and with a soft gasp, Mrs Hobbs turned and hurried from the bedroom.

Elsbeth wanted to cry out to her, her hands rose automatically, as though she would hurry after her, but she stayed still, staring at the doorway, hearing her mother moving downstairs. That engulfing sense of misery rushed over her once more, and she sank down weakly on the side of the creaking bed, then fell back, drawing up her knees and curling up, putting her hands over her face to close out the grey daylight as the tears welled up and her body shook with the sobs she muffled in the dampening pillow.

The day after Doreen returned from Margrove she met Becky Aygarth in the village shop, which was perched on the high bank of the beck, as the shallow, fast-flowing River Howe was known in the district. Doreen had just come over the humpbacked stone bridge, refusing to use the stepping-stones across the water and the narrow muddy path that led up along the side of the building which was home and shop combined for Mrs Floyd. Doreen was wearing one of her best outfits, pale-mauve jumper and tartan kilt, under her red winter coat, and her smartest pair of shoes, of shining patent leather, with the heavy silver buckles, over a pair of spotless white knee-stockings which she was determined should remain immaculate, despite the wet surface of the road and the lane she had to traverse. Anyway, the stepping-stones were for kids or heavy-booted farmhands. Adults, certainly the womenfolk, always used the bridge rather than save the few extra yards the stones avoided.

She was dressed in her finery because it was still the holiday, and they still had their visitors at home, Uncle Gordon and Aunt Esmé, Aunt Elizabeth's brother and his wife. And Doreen felt very much in the holiday mood, rejoicing in the fact that she was back where she belonged, safely delivered from 19 Maudsley Street and the horrors she had been forced to endure there: the outside toilet, the chipped sink out in the back kitchen, or the humiliations of the zinc bathtub in front of the fire in the kitchen proper, with only a clothes' horse draped with towels to hide your nakedness from anyone who cared to enter the room. And there was always *someone* who did. And, worst of all, the horror of having to share a bed, either with smelly, unsanitary Algy, her eight-year-old brother, or her elder sister, Ethel, or both. Still, that was all behind her now, for at least another three or four months or however much longer she could put off the prospect of another visit home.

She had no shame about the feelings of disgust returning to Maudsley Sreet gave her. Her father and mother couldn't wait to get rid of her. They had sold her to Miss Ramsay − one day she would make it her business to find out how much she was worth. Not that she harboured any sense of betrayal at their mercenary act. It had been the best thing that could ever have happened to her. But she was not fooled one jot by the plea put forth by her often drunk father that they had done it for her sake, to give her the opportunities they could never give her. It had been calculating and selfish, and soon da would probably start regretting it. After the war ended he might well start angling to get her back, as she became old enough to earn a living and to provide another pair of skivvying hands around the house. She must make sure that that could never happen, and that meant sticking in at school and making the most of the chance to get a good education − and making sure that Aunt Elizabeth loved her far too much and far too fiercely ever to contemplate letting her go. Until, of course, Doreen herself was equipped and ready to flee the nest, like the cuckoo she had so blithely become.

As she approached the two small bow windows of Mrs Floyd's shop, she saw the stocky figure of Becky Aygarth emerging and heading towards her. There was no way of avoiding her, so she fixed a spreading smile of conviviality on her delicate features, much like the grin mirrored on the face of the girl before her. Becky was a year younger: twelve and still at the village school where Doreen and the other Margrove exiles had come more than three years ago. The others had returned home over two years ago. And big sister Alice had been gone almost as long. All part of the world Doreen had left behind, just as they had left her behind; and she had no intention of ever joining them again.

'Hello, Becky!' Doreen said brightly. 'Did you have a good Christmas, all of you? Everyone all right?' The Aygarths were farmers. Alice and Algy had been billeted there during their time in the village, and had become very close to Eileen and Malcolm Aygarth and their family. Doreen knew they would have welcomed her, too, had she wished to become friendly. But she had made no effort to maintain any intimacy. Becky was the one she had been closest to, because of school in the village, but even there no real friendship had developed. In fact, Becky had been wary of her, and that wariness showed now behind the smile, and in the heightened colour in the homely face.

She answered Doreen's query politely, then made her own. 'You been home for the Christmas? How's your Alice? Have you heard lately? We got a card from her, from Egypt.' There was pride in the voice, heavy with the local accent, in great contrast with Doreen's more refined tones.

'Yes. We got one, too. Sergeant Glass, eh? I can just imagine her, can't you? She always was a bossyboots.' She laughed, inviting Becky to laugh with her, and the girl obliged. Her face turned a shade redder, and she scuffed her Wellington boot among the small-grit stones of the lane.

'You'll have heard, have you? Bob Symmonds is back home. He's out of gaol.'

Symmonds had been the tenant of a dilapidated sheep farm up on High Top, on the moor, and had been imprisoned largely through the efforts of Alice's friend, Davy Brown, for being part of a ring of black marketeers and sheep-stealers operating in the area. His partner, and the real ringleader locally, had managed to escape. Gus Rielke had been known to the villagers as the Big Swede, even though he was Norwegian. He had started working for Vera Rhodes, the landlady of the pub, the Oddfellows, whose husband had been taken prisoner of war after Dunkirk. Gus had done more than work for her behind the bar, so the accurate rumour had run. Despite the whiff of scandal, he had made himself quite popular with many of the villagers, because of work he would undertake for them (he had been for a time the much appreciated odd-jobbing gardener at Northend Cottage) and not least because of the little 'extras' he could get for them from time to time. He was always cheerful, and friendly to everyone. Alice was one of the few with whom his charm failed – Doreen still sniggered whenever she thought of the tale spread round the village of the day he had handed her sister a present of a pair of beautiful frilly silk panties, over the bar at the Oddfellows. He was a rogue all right, as Doreen well knew. He used to give her threepence to do a handstand against the wall of Miss Ramsay's garage so that he could catch a glimpse of her own far less fetching drawers, a fact and a secret neither of them ever acknowledged.

Doreen was well aware of Becky's keen-eyed stare to observe the effect of her news on the older girl. No doubt she was anticipating and hoping for some sign of anxiety or alarm at the announcement of Bob Symmonds's return. It had been through Alice's curiosity and at her instigation that the large cache of petrol and stolen black-market goods had been found up at High Top, as well as the sheep which had been rustled, to pass on to the crooks Gus Rielke and Symmonds had dealt with. And it was through Alice's persuasion that Davy Brown had agreed to let himself be used as a would-be accomplice and thus help to set the police trap.

Doreen was not wrong in her assessment of a certain amount of malicious pleasure in the passing on of the latest information about Bob Symmonds. Becky had always been a little afraid of Doreen's sharpness of mind, and her ability to command or influence her peers. It was all part of a general feeling among the village children that they should beware of these invaders from the alien world of the town, to which most of them had seldom or ever travelled, the home of so much trickery and deception. 'You've got to watch them vaccies!' Even their elders said so, regularly.

When they had first arrived, in the autumn of 1940, and Doreen's grown-up sister and little brother, Algy, had come to live with them at Beckside farm, the nine-year-old Becky had naïvely assumed that this gave her some kind of advantage over her Howbeck contemporaries. Alice was so nice, and five-year-old Algy had been so pliantly ready to be taken under Becky's and her younger sister Maureen's wings, that Becky believed this would give her some kind of special status, an entrée to the exclusive little circle Doreen had swiftly gathered about her. She was all the more hurt when this proved not to be so. For one thing, the year's difference in their ages was a formidable obstacle. Doreen was in the class above her, standard five, the senior class, and sometimes the gap seemed enormous. Doreen encouraged the exclusivity of the 'top class', and her classmates were quick to follow her lead. For another, Doreen also created division even within her class by emphasizing the difference between the evacuees and the village children. She startled the girls by choosing as her intimate not one of their number but a boy: Alfie James, one of the toughest and roughest of the Margrove incomers, who was billeted with his brothers up at the Symmonds's run-down farm at High Top, and who, it was subsequently revealed, had helped Bob Symmonds and the Big Swede with their various and nefarious activities.

It was a big scandal. Bob had been sent to gaol, and the foreigner, Mrs Rhodes's 'fancy man', had disappeared. It was just as well that the Margrove vaccies had departed themselves around that time, otherwise goodness knows what might have happened to the notorious Alfie. Remembering the incident now, it made the slightly more worldly-wise Becky smirk inwardly at the notion of this transformed, ladylike figure, with her posh new voice, and clothes, and friends, being mates with ragged-arsed Alfie; there were other secretly whispered rumours of just what the pair had got up to for the presents Alfie lavished on his 'girlfriend'. This dainty, delicate creature, with her white socks and her gleaming buckled shiny shoes would recoil with horror if the likes of Alfie James came within ten feet of her nowadays.

But Becky was disappointed in her hope of seeing some flicker of disquiet on those perfectly controlled features. The dark eyebrows were only slightly raised, and the delicate face took on an expression of supreme indifference. 'Really? No, I hadn't heard. Let's hope he's learned his lesson at last, eh? I shouldn't think his family will welcome him with open arms. His boys have made a better job of running the farm than he ever did. I don't suppose his wife will be all that keen, either. She was just about ready to have their latest baby when the police got him. I suppose this means that number six – or will it be seven? – will be on the way soon.' She shook her head in almost perfect imitation of Miss Ramsay's amused despair, while Becky sniggered involuntarily. She moved around the stocky figure and reached for the handle of the shop door. 'Excuse me. I just popped out for some things for Aunt Elizabeth. We've still got guests staying with us. Enjoy the rest of your holiday.'

Becky nodded, and felt herself turning red. As usual, she felt somehow belittled, without knowing exactly why. Aunt Elizabeth my Aunt Fanny! Stuck-up little nowt! And she gave the stones an extra vigorous scuff with her wellies as she strode away.

CHAPTER SEVEN

No one was happier than the detachment of ATS aboard the *Empire Indus* to see the Rock of Gibraltar towering over them as they entered the crowded harbour a week into their voyage. Though the gregale had blown itself out after forty-eight hours, it left a legacy of choppy waves and driving rainsqualls, so that for those suffering most acutely from seasickness their misery was only marginally alleviated, and there was still general disquiet below decks at the ship's buffeting movement. They took little comfort from the aggravatingly cheerful comments of the sailors who kept insisting they should thank their lucky stars for the weather that was making life difficult for any U-boats or dive-bombers to come after them.

It was ironic, or just their bloody luck, as the girls more prosaically put it, that the sun should emerge and the clouds rapidly disappear just as they began to negotiate the outer defences of the harbour. They were even more disappointed to learn that they would be anchoring several hundred yards from the shore rather than berthing alongside one of the quays, and that there was little prospect of anyone getting ashore, except for those with pressing official business. But at least the floor had stopped rolling and pitching beneath them, enabling their guts to stop heaving, and when the engines were stopped, so was that pounding thump that had become almost as natural to them as their breathing, to be replaced by the gentle, almost indiscernible hum of the generators. The sun was shining again, and they had almost unhampered access to the upper deck. 'Stop your dripping!' Sergeant Glass told them humorously. 'Make the most of it. Get up top and start getting your sun tan back.'

'That's right,' one of the seamen of a nearby working party advised them when their sergeant had departed. 'You wait till we get round the corner, and into Biscay. Then you'll know what roughers really is!'

Alice's conscience was stirred by the voice over the Tannoy, preceded by the already too familiar piercing whistle of a bosun's pipe, which announced, 'D'you hear there? The mail boat will leave at 0-eight-thirty tomorrow. Mail will be collected for censoring at nineteen hundred hours this evening.' She took her pad and pencil and made her way up the companionways which led to the former sun deck, part of which had been allocated to NCOs and part to commissioned ranks. The pre-war windows and deck head (ceiling) had been removed, leaving the ten-foot-wide thoroughfare down the port side of the vessel open to the elements; no disadvantage on this now sun-filled day. Alice was comfortable enough in shirt and slacks, though she noted that many of her fellows had stripped to singlets and shorts. On the other side of the roped-off enclosure, she could see that some of the officers were equally casual in their dress, or undress. They had deckchairs to recline in, while the non-coms had to make do with palliasses. Alice placed one against the drab grey bulkhead of the upperworks and folded it so that she could lean her shoulders against it to protect them from the hard metal behind her and still have enough room to fit her buttocks on the rest of the thin mattress. She rested her pad against her drawn-up knees and stared at the blank lined page, while chewing at the end of her pencil.

Who should she write to first? She still didn't know when she would get an opportunity to see any of her family and friends. She was due for some foreign service leave. She was sure of that. But when would she be able to take it? She supposed she should let her family know first that she was coming home, even if she was already on English soil when they got the news. It would be wicked of her just to turn up on the doorstep of 19 Maudsley Street without a word of warning, when they were still thinking she was halfway across the world from them, however strongly tempted she was by the idea. In any case, there was no need for her to go into any great detail. They would not appreciate her description of her trip to the pyramids, or seeing the boy king's treasure, or the voyage on *Empire Indus*. She couldn't help a stirring of pride, though, as she scribbled at the top right hand corner of the page, *Troopship Empire Indus*. Unless brother George had already been posted overseas, she was the only one of the Glass family within living memory, as far as she knew, who had been beyond the shores of Britain.

For the first time in quite a while, she found herself thinking ahead, and wondering what would happen once the war was over and she was out in civvy street again. One thing she was determined about. She would not be going back to Margrove and Maudsley Street. She felt a pang of sympathy and regret for her mother, who seemed to live for the time, never to be realized now, when she would have all her children back under her roof once more. Ma had this sentimental, rose-tinted dream of family harmony, a simple belief in the myth of family life and love, which had never in reality existed. It was an ideal as far from truth as the *True Romance* and *Woman's Weekly* stories which she would plough through at the kitchen table, over a well-stewed pot of tea, like as not one work-worn finger tracing the narrow, small lines of print, her lips just visibly moving. The thought made Alice's heart ache with compassion. At the same time she felt an altogether new understanding of Doreen's fierce determination to make her escape, even though the youngster's seemingly ruthless disregard of her roots would cause such pain.

Alice scribbled the brief note to her mother as swiftly as possible, closing with the kind lie: *no time to add any more, must get this in the mail to go ashore in Gibraltar, will be in touch as soon as possible, Luv, Alice xxx.*

Davy. Now there was someone who *would* be interested in hearing all about Giza, and the museum, and any and every aspect of her life on land and sea. But how would he feel about the news that she was returning to Blighty? Would he be delighted, or would he be filled with dismay at the thought of seeing again the woman he had declared himself to be in love with, whom he had asked to marry him, and who had shocked him to his core, bless him, with her confession at one of their last meetings?

His last letter, which she had received nearly a month ago, written from the depths of a murky English November, had been a kind of early Christmas greeting. She still had it tucked along with other correspondence from home, in the back of her writing case. She dug it out now, slipped it out of its flimsy envelope and unfolded it. He had never referred to his personal attachment to her in any of his letters – except at the end, she guessed, when he always signed off with, *All my love,* and followed his name with two crosses. Not that they had shared many passionate kisses – not even though they had once slept together, in the same bed, in her flat over the stables at Howe Manor after Beth had left her. She recalled now, with a vividness that aroused an embarrassing physical response as she did so, how she had watched him sleeping in the dimness of early morning, and how she had imagined offering herself to him, flinging aside the pillow she had carefully placed down the middle of the old bed before inviting him to share it – a barrier which, as she knew he would, he had respected faithfully.

As always, thoughts of Davy and his love for her were inextricably bound up with thoughts of Elsbeth, from whose lovely and beloved body there had been no barrier at all during those golden months they had spent together. Just as he had never written of his own love for Alice, so he had never mentioned the shocking truth which Alice had revealed to him about her feeling for Beth. At times she wished he would. Better to bring it out into the open, as she had at last in that abandoned outburst to him not long before they parted. He did mention Beth. Alice had told him about her marriage and the birth of Elaine Ruth, and he had commented politely on his pleasure at the news, asked her to pass on his best wishes and congratulations *when you write to her*. Did he really think they kept up a regular correspondence, given how they had parted, and the pain of loss Alice had revealed to him? Probably not. If he knew anything at all about Alice, he must know how impossible it would be for her to maintain such a level of falsehood, of cosy girlfriend chat, after all that had happened between them. He was just observing the conventions, perpetuatmg the lie.

But then, wasn't that what he was doing with Alice herself, and she with him? Not only had he stopped pleading his love for her; he had never once referred to the relationship between her and Beth that she had confessed to. And Alice was the same. She replied to his letters with the same note of friendship, the easy, innocent familiarity she and Davy had shared in the early stages of their acquaintance, as they had got to know each other during those first months in Howbeck. Were they both being dishonest, hypocritical? Or did it mean that they both valued their friendship, could still maintain it in spite of all that had happened to them and between them?

Certainly this last letter of his displayed still his deep concern for her, as well as his moral and even religious conviction. She found again the paragraph on the third page:

I hope you understand that you being out there facing the dangers of the war I didn't want anything to do with doesn't rest easily on my conscience. You remember the French girl I told you about? Lou? I still don't know what happened to her after the occupation, but I have managed to find out more about her religion. I managed to get in touch with an English Baha'i. There are a few of them, and there is a centre down in London, somewhere near the Houses of Parliament, I believe. They sent me a book of their prayers. What do you think of this?

'O Thou kind Lord; Let the religions agree, make the nations one, that we may see each other as one people and the whole earth as one home. May we live together in perfect harmony.'

Sounds pretty sensible to me. I include it in my prayers now, along with my nightly prayer that you will be brought home safely, and soon.

Sooner than you think, Davy! she thought, a smile tugging at the corners of her mouth. Yes, he would always be special to her, she would never want to lose his friendship, and she was grateful that even after her confession to him he still showed that he cared. But all at once, just as she was about to start writing on the blank page, she was overwhelmed by a rush of feeling that brought stinging tears to her eyes and a lump in her throat. The one person she really wanted to be close to, even if it could be only in her thoughts and on paper right now, was Beth.

Well, she was close in thought, true enough, just about every night and often during the day as well, and it damned well hurt. More so because she couldn't even communicate with her, not in the way she wanted to. Not in any way. She had answered the three short missives she had received from Beth: one that had been waiting when she had first arrived in Egypt over a year ago, telling her of the pregnancy and the hastily planned and executed marriage, the second an even briefer note in the summer announcing the birth of Elaine Ruth, and the last in September, an answer to Alice's own cheery, hearty congrats at the *wonderful news.* Alice had written her bubbly letter while the tears streamed down her cheeks. Beth's reply made her cry again, not so profusely but even more painfully, for Beth had made it plain that she had no wish for the correspondence to continue, even though she hadn't had the guts to say so in so many words:

*I'm afraid I won't have time for luxuries such as letter-writing now that I have
a baby and a husband to look after but I wish you all the very best for the
future, and a safe return home.*

No x's at the end of that note! As Al sat in the pleasant warmth of
the January sun, with the grey-and-green rock mountain rearing up in
the blue sky ahead of her, she wished more than anything that she
could pour out her heart on to the flimsy paper to express the ache of
love choking her for the blonde girl whose cold-hearted cruelty had so
stunned her.

It was frustrating for the corralled passengers to gaze across the short
expanse of water which proved an impassable barrier for the majority
of those on *Empire Indus*. It was a frustration which was heightened
when, on the second and penultimate day of their stay, the voice of the
duty quartermaster laconically announced, after the customary shriek
of the bosun's pipe, 'Liberty boat will leave from port aft accommodation ladder at 0-ten-thirty hours. Officers only.'

Above decks the guardrails were dark with the clustered figures of
the Other Ranks, and there was a sustained outburst of whistles,
catcalls and even a few boos as the privileged few hurried down the
wide steps of the ladder and stepped on to the MFV waiting to ferry
them ashore. 'D'ye hear there? Clear guardrails! Clear guardrails!' the
metallic tones screeched, backed by a number of non-coms moved to
step in for the sake of discipline.

The contingent of ATS girls was prominent among the jeering
multitude, and Alice dutifully played her expected role in maintaining
order, but with considerably less acerbity than many of her male
colleagues. 'All right, girls! You've had your fun! That'll do. Anyway, just
think how much better you'll feel when we sail tomorrow, without a
thick head or worse to feel bad about.'

'Speak for yourself, Sarge! I was hoping to climb up the Rock and see
one of them apes they got up there!' The chubby girl whose comic
efforts to get into her hammock Alice had observed on the first night of
the voyage grinned at her.

'More like a corporal or a two-badge stoker!' one of her companions
cackled.

'My word! You sound just like regulars yourselves, the way you girls chat. Got all the patter, haven't you?'

'Fat lot of good it does us, Sarge! Still one to a hammock down on our mess deck. How about you, Sarge? Anything taken your fancy? Nice chief petty officer with a stack of pay to spend when we get back home?'

'My mum told me all about sailors. Pity some of yours didn't do the same. I've heard about what goes on during boat drill. You should be ashamed of yourselves, letting down the good name of the ATS.'

'And that's not all we'd be letting down if some of them matelots had their way!'

There was a senior commander, the equivalent of an army major, who was the most senior of the ATS personnel on board, but she remained a distant and aloof figure, and was expert at delegating authority. Alice was the only non-commissioned rank above corporal, so that almost all the maintenance of 'good order and discipline' fell on her capable shoulders. She did not object. After all, she was returning to England in order to gain further promotion, which would mean, she presumed, even more responsibility. As far as she had seen, in her admittedly limited experience, an army marched not so much on its stomach but on its non-coms and she was determined to do her best. She was a little uneasy about the kind of authority she should establish with her little band on the high seas. They were a fairly disparate group of individuals, in a kind of limbo while they were on board ship. She wondered sometimes if she was perhaps being a little informal, too easygoing with her charges, especially when, after passing through the Straits and hugging the coast of Portugal as they made their way up towards Lisbon, there was a burst of almost tropical weather, and their portion of the upper deck was crowded with recumbent bodies making the most of the bathing sun. 'You told us to work on our tan, Sarge!' one of the more voluptuous girls exclaimed at Alice's crisp comment on the brevity of her attire. She claimed that her one-piece swimming costume was unsuitable for soaking up as much sun as possible. Instead, she was wearing brassiere and panties, definitely not of service issue. She had slipped down the shoulder straps of her upper garment and unhooked the three fasteners so that when she turned on to her front her back was completely bare to receive the sun's rays. Moreover, she had rolled up the legs of her panties to form the slimmest of cotton ropes, which all but disappeared in the cleft of her splendidly statuesque buttocks and, at the front, gave only the most abbreviated triangle of material to conceal her private parts.

Ashamed of her automatic thrill of approval at the generous, indecent display afforded her, Alice gazed down sternly and ordered her to 'cover up right now!' The girl wasn't the only one who was sunning herself in her underwear. The others were very soon disabused of the notion that the sergeant might be joking, and Alice barked at them until they scuttled, clutching towels and other gear to their bosoms, below decks.

Her desire for propriety was appeased a day later with a vengeance, when the more seasonal wrath of the Atlantic hit them full force, and, instead of stripping off, they dragged on extra layers of clothing as the winter gales washed over them. The mess decks became the unsavoury, unsanitary hell-holes they had briefly endured at the start of their voyage. They lay whimpering in their swaying hammocks, or leaned heaving wretchedly out of them, while everything that was not bolted down clattered, slid or rolled about the wet deck plates, and the vessel groaned more loudly than her suffering inmates. Four days of this was an eternity, so that the fog-shrouded calmness, and the icy chill that set brown frames shivering and teeth chattering were welcome as they crept up the Channel, past the invisible Needles and the Isle of Wight, to drop anchor in Southampton Water.

Alice stood with the nurse, Joan Parish, almost at the identical spot on which they had stood at the commencement of the voyage fifteen days ago. An impenetrable curtain of pale fog surrounded them completely across fifty yards of oily, slowly shifting water. Alice breathed deeply, and sighed as she felt the damp cold bite down into her lungs. 'Ah! Just smell it! That's Blighty, that is!' she said, with youthful optimism.

'That's sewage, that is!' the older woman answered, to prick the balloon of such naïve enthusiasm.

But Alice was not to be deflated so easily. 'Listen, mate! It may be shit, but at least it's British shit!'

CHAPTER EIGHT

Davy Brown had been dreading the reaction at Tower Street police station to the discovery of his 'guilty' past. For a short while it seemed as if his fears were being realized. He was not quite sent to Coventry but on his first shift after news of his history had broken he could tell at once how different things were. One look at the faces of everyone he had dealings with was enough for that. There was none of the easy, relaxed familiarity, the smiles and shared witticisms, or what passed for such among the station's inhabitants. Expressions were set in carefully arranged masks of indifference, eyes failed to meet his with their usual frankness. On the second day he found his locker had been daubed with yellow paint, and on the duty roster pinned up in the CID office someone had printed CONSHIE in heavy black ink over his name.

It hurt a lot. He had always got on so well with most of his colleagues. Dave Wilson, a fellow detective constable, was the only one he had found really hard to like, with Wilson's simplistic, bigoted and loudly trumpeted views on just about every aspect of life. It came as no surprise that Wilson was the only one who seemed to revel in the disclosures about Davy and to refer openly to them. 'You should do well at this job, then, eh? They say it takes one to know one, eh? You being an ex-con and all that!' He gave his trademark belly laugh. 'Take that any way you will. Con as in convict or con as in conchy!'

'I didn't notice *you* dashing off to join the colours when the balloon went up.' Len Potts, the desk sergeant who had come out of retirement at the outbreak of war gazed at Wilson with his usual, open smile.

Dave Wilson's face flushed and he bristled a little, his head lifting in turkey-cock challenge. 'If it had been left up to me I'd have been off like a shot, Len! You know me! *I'm* not afraid of a scrap!' he emphasized meaningfully, turning his gaze on Davy.

'Oh, aye. Broke your heart, getting Reserved Occupation on your ticket, did it? And it's Sarge to you, lad. Only me friends call me Len!'

It was largely through Potts's attitude towards Davy, which continued to be as it had been before his past had become public knowledge, that his colleagues' behaviour towards him began to thaw. That and the fact that the festive season of goodwill, if not peace, was upon them. On Friday, the last day of 1943, Davy finished his shift at ten. He had spent a profitless three hours sitting in the packed-out bar of the Punchbowl, watching its mostly uniformed servicemen getting as quickly and noisily drunk as they could on the rumouredly watered-down beer and limited supply of spirits. He nursed his two halves, telling himself that this was not a bad way to be serving king and country. His brief was to keep both eyes on a certain market trader and his cronies whose regular watering-hole this was, and in particular to look out for a new face or faces with whom they might become deeply engrossed in conversation. The usual tantalizingly vague murmurs of 'black market' supplies were circulating, on a somewhat more ambitious scale than usual. More often than not, these rumours were the result of professional envy or pure malice.

'It's a tough life but someone's got to do it.' He had grinned when DS Tommy Baxter had given him the assignment, but in truth he was glad when his watch came to its appointed end. The traders in question probably knew quite well who he was. In any case, a bloke in civvies, sitting on his own in this beery crowd of warriors, was a bit of a sore thumb. Still, at least he might be tossing a spanner in the works, if only by preventing their illicit dealer from making his approach. Until after ten! The bar would close at 10.30, New Year's Eve or no. The city council were disinclined to issue special licences these days. In any case, there was a good chance that the pub would run out of beer any minute. He eased himself out of his seat at the small table by the door, nodding at the friendly smiles and calls from strangers. 'All the best! Happy New Year!' with the condescension he always got, or always felt he got, from servicemen to a young chap in civilian clothes.

His mind easily and swiftly turned from professional matters to those of a more personal nature as he hurried through the cold darkness towards Clementhorpe and the pleasures that awaited him there. And the problems. Reeny was having 'a few people' round for drinks, to see the New Year in. She had been delighted when he said he'd be back home before midnight. He had been on duty over the Christmas weekend and then had gone on two days' leave, which he had spent with his parents out at Helmsthorpe, a village nine miles south-east of York, on the York-Hull line, so he had seen very little of Reeny over the holiday period. Part of him muttered, much to his discomfiture, that that was just as well.

It had begun with Bob Noone's departure, or, rather, just before, with Bob's announcement of Davy's notorious secret past. He had not known how his landlady would take it. Hurt? Wounded betrayal? Outrage? He should of course have known better.

'No, I'm not going to take anyone else in,' she told him, in answer to his query. 'I've told them at the station. You're more than enough for me to cope with.' She had laughed, but she had pinked a little as she spoke. 'We don't need it,' she went on quickly, and Davy had the feeling she was offering some sort of excuse. 'The amount of overtime Dick's getting in these days. He's away more than he's at home. We don't need the money. And I'm sure you'd rather have the room to yourself. It's a nice big room. You can do what you want with it, do it up how you want it, decorate and that. Maybe put a few pieces of furniture in, if you like. Make it your own place, eh? And I can concentrate on you. You'll have my full and undivided attention!' She laughed again. This time it sounded high and girlish, and embarrassed. And her face was redder.

It was strange having the room to himself. Bob Noone's bed was still neatly made up, on the other side of the room. 'You might want someone to stay. Friends – or family. This is your place, Davy. I'd like you to think of it like that. Your second home.'

'It's so good of you, Mrs L—'

'Oh, please! Don't call me that any more. Promise? Makes me feel ancient. And . . .' the becoming blush spread slowly up into the face and her gaze lowered briefly, and she looked very young and desirable, 'I'd like to feel we were much – closer than that. Real friends.' Her eyes met his, shy, appealing and very vulnerable, and his heart was beating faster all at once, and he thought how beautiful she was.

Today she had come up at 11.30 and woken him with the usual cup of tea. 'Miserable cold day again. but at least it's not raining. Fish for our dinner, all right? Cod, from the fresh fish shop. You've plenty of time for a bath.' She perched on the edge of his bed, facing him, and he tried valiantly not to look at her knees in the thick lisle stockings as she crossed her legs and they peeped from beneath her skirt and flowered apron. 'Dick's not going to get back till tomorrow afternoon. George sent a note up with one of the lads. He's got a goods to Preston, one to bring back in the morning. Can't grumble, eh? He *did* have Christmas and Boxing Day, after all!' She grinned and nodded, her eyes shone, and she paused briefly, waiting for him to join in. 'And there is a war on!' They laughed together, then their eyes seemed to lock. The smile faded from her and she put her hand out, cupped it very gently round the side of his jaw and neck, just above the striped, crumpled collar of his pyjamas. He felt its coldness against his warm flesh, was aware of his body heat, trapped in the cocoon of the sheet and blankets, made tighter by the pinning weight of her body against his thigh.

'Mm! You feel so warm and snug in there!' Her voice was a murmur, still teasing but sensual, too. He felt a tension between them, and the throbbing response of his body to her nearness, her fragrance. The bed creaked as she leaned forward close to him, and said softly, 'You *will* get back as quick as you can tonight? I'll need you to get the party going. I'm counting on you.' Her hand was still on his neck, her fingers moved softly on his skin. He watched her red lips closing in on his, felt them touch, then they were kissing, keeping contact, and her mouth opened, his hand came up, his fingers curled strongly in the dark hair, felt the ugly cylinders of the curlers hidden by that thin scarf. Their tongues flickered, he felt her wetness, the hard stir of his hidden sex, the jolt of his lust for her.

The kiss had lasted long seconds, and they were both panting when they broke. Their breath was warm and heavy, mingling, their faces still close. He dropped his hand from his hold on her, leaned back. 'I'm sorry!' he gasped.

'I'm not!' she whispered fiercely, and he saw her big eyes fill with tears, then she stood abruptly. 'I'm not wicked, Davy! I'd never do anything bad, you know that, don't you? I like you a lot. I'm very fond of you. You don't mind, do you?'

'No,' he answered inadequately.

'That's all right then!' She moved briskly to the door, called out over her shoulder, 'Now get yourself up, you lazy tyke! Let's hope I haven't boiled the fish dry!'

65

But that kiss was there, it lay between them, and he was reluctant to try to work out exactly what it meant, as he made his way through the black streets of terraced houses towards Dubry Street. It was not 'all right then', as she had said, and he had no doubt she didn't believe it, either. It was far too intimate an embrace. His body had reacted truthfully to it, if not his mind. And she must surely know, too, its sexual nature, the charge that had flowed between them. She was not innocent or ignorant in that sense. She was a wife and mother, and belonged to someone else, the way he had wanted Alice to belong to him, or, once long ago, Lou Varron, the French girl, in Paris. The ring of paint that marked the lamp post which stood at the corner of Dubry Street loomed palely before him, and he switched off the pencil beam of his torch. He could almost count the steps to the door of Number 25 from here. He heard voices and faint snatches of music from behind the blacked-out windows as he passed. People were gathering all over to mark the end of the old year and the start of the new. And with strong hopes and prayers that this might be the last year of war to be ushered in. Perhaps a little too eagerly he shouldered aside his disconcerting private speculations. There were bigger, more important issues to occupy one's mind with. I'd never do anything bad, Reeny had said, and he believed her. Neither will I! he determined. He turned, opened the front door and swished aside the heavy blackout curtain, entering the dim light of the long passageway to Reeny's shout of greeting, and the moist, fleeting touch of her lips on his yet again, with this time the heavy sweetness of port wine on her breath.

'Ah! Here he is! Sherlock Holmes himself!' George Mears, the rotund railway inspector, the Lumleys' friend, who had been instrumental in securing a job for Alice at the railways canteen, came forward, his face ruddily aglow with conviviality and alcohol. The spirit of celebration was well alight, as George's wife, Nancy came forward and hugged him, her nose nuzzling at his ear. In great contrast to her generously voluptuous size, he next found himself facing a figure of childlike diminutiveness, whose skinny arms had to reach up almost to full stretch to encircle his neck. Mary Douglas stood on tiny tiptoe and pulled his head down to meet her eager kiss, wet and blatantly mouth-to-mouth, and with the same wine-flavoured excess. It was New Year's Eve after all, he conceded as he held the frail form close.

'How do, Davy! Getting in early with me New Year's kiss! Haven't seen you for ages, luv! How's that bonny lass of yours? Have you heard owt from her recently? Never a word I've had, the wicked minx! Tell her to get her finger out' – he stared in surprise at her indelicate snort of laughter through her prominent nose – 'and drop me a line.'

'Now then, Mary. Good to see you. I've told you umpteen times, she's not my lass. Just good mates, that's all. And no, as a matter of fact, I haven't heard from her for ages, either, apart from a Christmas card.'

'Well, you're lucky to get one! More than I did!' She was grinning up at him brightly, still clinging round his neck, almost hanging from it. There was something in those dark eyes shining up at him, some message behind the brightness that he couldn't read, that made him feel uncomfortable.

'Now then, Mary! Put the lad down and let him come and get something to eat. You'll get your chance to ravish him at midnight. Come on. The grub's out in the kitchen. Come and I'll get a plate for you, and a drink. Anyone else ready? Help yourselves, while I see to our working man.'

The long table in front of the kitchen range was laden with an impressive variety of dishes. 'Who've you been sweet-talking for this lot?' Davy said admiringly. 'There's more than a month's rations in this lot.'

'Ooh! You're not going to arrest me, are you, Constable?' She grinned, held out both thin wrists to him. 'I'll come quietly.'

He could see she had been drinking by her heightened colour. It made her look more vivacious than ever. She glanced quickly at the doorway, then suddenly flung herself violently into his embrace. 'Here, before our little Mary gobbles you all up!' For the second time that day she kissed him, boldly, lipsticked mouth open and proffered, her slim body thrust against his, her arms dragging him into her. Her mouth was soft and sweet, then hard with aggressive challenge, he felt her teeth gnawing and clashing against his. She was gasping audibly when she let him go, and turned away, unable to look at him, her voice shaky, her laugh uncertain. 'There now! I'm just a bit tiddly, that's my excuse! What about you?'

'Stone-cold sober,' he answered, striving to ease the tension between them. 'But I'll do my level best to match you as soon as I can.'

There was another young couple there, engaged, the chap being one of Dick's workmates, his fiancée an attractive blonde girl who, apart from her hair, appeared to be doing her utmost to anticipate the married matron she was destined to become in the plainness of her garb and the decorousness of her manner. The Mears, already into advanced middle age, made a valiant effort to be jolly, in keeping with the mood and the season. The three men went outside just before midnight. 'I think Davy has to be our first foot,' Reeny ordered, passing him the requisite materials of coal and bread and salt for the ceremony. She managed to restrain an eager Mary Douglas from accompanying the men outside. 'You'll catch your death in that dress! You'll get your chance for kissing and cuddling when they get in.'

She made the most of it, too. Davy was surprised at the chaste peck on his cheek offered by a suddenly demure Reeny, and in a fit of wildness he seized her round the waist and dragged her to him, bending her supple back and planting a kiss in true Valentino style, to rousing cheers from the onlookers and her gasping protest. But at one o'clock the engaged couple and the Mears left together. Reeny made an attempt to persuade Mary to leave with them. 'George and Nancy can see you home,' but Mary brushed aside the half-hearted effort.

'I could find me way blindfold!' she laughed raucously, in that rasping voice whose huskiness was aided by her continual sucking on a Woodbine from the packet that lay near to hand.

She was clearly drunk, but also clearly unready for sleep. The atmosphere now was quiet and intimate. The three of them moved from the front room to the kitchen. Davy had slipped off his jacket, and now undid his collar and tie, and eased off his shoes, until they were all three sprawled in easy chairs, with stockinged feet propped on the high fireguard that Reeny still kept in front of the range, mainly for drying and airing clothes, now that her son was approaching his eighth birthday. Gazing at the red glow in the small, high grate, not looking at one another, somehow made it easier to converse in this new, reflective atmosphere. Mary's croaky voice matched the early hours' quiet. 'I really miss your Al, you know.'

Davy decided not to repeat, for the seemingly hundredth time, she is not my Al. He let her continue uninterrupted.

'She was ever so good to me. She's a lovely lass.' Her voice cracked a little, wavered, and the emotion was suddenly evident.

Davy felt a sudden prickle, like a shiver, of secret alarm, and a deep sense of shame at the shocking depth and deviance of his speculation.

He thought again of that summer evening walk, and Alice's stunning revelation, the shattering depth of feeling she had displayed.

'She kept me going, she did.' She sniffed, loudly, and Davy felt even more embarrassed and wretched at the sadness in the husky tones. 'I wonder what she's up to now, eh? I hope to God she's enjoying herself, and that she comes back safe and sound to us, eh?'

In spite of his racing mind and disturbing unspoken questions, Davy echoed wholeheartedly Mary's wish. They were ignorant of how successfully that wish had been granted, as at that moment Alice lay peacefully exhausted in a Cairo bedroom, in the loving young arms of Private Lynne Manning.

CHAPTER NINE

On 15 January, 1944, the day that the Allied forces in Italy fought their way over the Rapido River 'and found their advance halted by stubborn German defence at a place little known to the rest of the world, Cassino, Alice Glass sat on her kitbag in a huge draughty baggage shed at Southampton Docks and waited stoically, amid what she hoped was the organized chaos that was filling the vast building. She had seen places like this only on the films back in Margrove: heaps of hatboxes and expensive cabin-trunks, and fur-coated slender beauties like Claudette Colbert and Bette Davis, silk-stockinged, high-heeled, elegantly embracing their handsome men. Shots of Cunard luxury liners like the *Queen Mary*, with cheering crowds and bands playing 'Auld Lang Syne'. Well, they had the crowd and the bustle, but no bands and banners, only a distracted-looking RTO and his staff of red-faced bellowing non-coms, all dashing about with clipboards and armbands as though they had been taken completely by surprise at the docking of *Empire Indus* and her disembarkation of 2,000 personnel.

Alice's three stripes didn't seem to cut much ice in this set-up. Her little band of fellow ATS had been hurried off, with a few hastily called well-wishes, and she could no longer see them. The great flock of arrivals was slowly being divided into various sub-sections, lined up before the long rows of trestle-tables and marched away, each with its armbanded overseer, like a scurrying sheepdog with his little huddle. There was a troop-train standing at the adjacent Southampton Docks station, and it was in this direction that most of the files were being shepherded, to climb aboard, no doubt for more hours of waiting. Alice had anticipated she would be joining them, and was more than a little puzzled to be told to wait where she was.

The military life had taught her, along with many other things, to be patient. She sat, a minor rock in the swirl of activity all round her, until the shed was more than half-empty. Enough was enough. She stared, her keen eye picking out a khaki-clad female warrior, in fact several, one of whom bore the two pips of a lieutenant, or subaltern, as they were known in the ATS.

'Ma'am!' The officer turned, looking down her haughty nose at being interrupted, but mollified by the pukka salute and the click of heels, as well as the sight of the three stripes on Alice's sleeve. 'Sergeant Glass, ma'am.' She rattled off her service number, produced her pay-book and papers. 'Just disembarked. Discharged from transport pool at Burg-el-Arab. Listed for Staffs course?' She allowed her voice to rise in a suggestion of query, along with her eyebrows, on the last word.

The subaltern was young, and rather horsy, but proved far more pleasant than she looked. She searched diligently, and eventually located Alice's name somewhere on her sheets of papers. 'Ah yes. Bit of a change of plan, I think. Look, can you hang on a sec? I'll get one of my gels to take you across to our place. We have a cabin over the way, by the station. They'll get you sorted out.'

The girl chosen as guide was a short, bouncy private with figure to match her personality. She looked no more than sixteen, with red cheeks and nose that gave the look of a farmer's lass, and she had a broad Yorkshire accent. 'Is it always like this?' Alice asked, gathering her other luggage together, as the girl easily swung the bulging kitbag up on to her shoulders.

'Oh, aye. Every time a bloody boat comes in. Wouldn't think we'd been doing it for four year an' more, would you?'

In the 'cabin', close to the busy station near the dock gates, Alice was ushered into the presence of a junior commander, a figure with crimped iron-grey curls and a manner that reminded Alice powerfully of her old schoolmistress, Miss Laverton. 'Please, have a pew. I'm Junior Commander Holly. Prickly by name but not by nature, I hope. Welcome home. I expect you're freezing, eh? From desert sands to arctic slush in – what? Two weeks?' Alice dutifully laughed in acknowledgement. 'I suppose they told you over the way that things have changed a bit. You were down to do the Staff and Quartermaster's course, weren't you? I'm afraid that won't be possible.' She caught the look of dismay on Alice's face and went on hurriedly. 'You'll soon see, when you get out of here' – she waved one hand vaguely in the air – 'things have changed. The whole place is on the move, getting ready for the big push. You've quite clearly proved your worth over in Egypt. We need more of the same here. Transport pool, maintenance work. We're swamped with work and it's going to get worse – or better, I suppose!' She gave a grunt of ironic laughter. 'You're just the sort we need so desperately – and you don't need a course for that. Let's face it, you could probably run one. Probably find yourself doing so once you start work. You'll be made up to acting staff-sergeant w.i.e.' She grinned. 'Pay adjusted accordingly, and the rank to be substantive later on.' She glanced up from the papers in front of her, pushed them slightly away, as though the matter was closed. She leaned back, her fleshy face splitting in a broad grin. 'So, how does that grab you, as our Yankee allies say? You'll see a lot of them, by the way. In fact they'll probably be your best customers. Most of them are charming. Be warned!'

Alice's head was spinning. 'Er . . . yes, ma'am. Fine. Where. . . ?'

'Very close to here. Just outside town, believe it or not. And Southampton's a very lively place for a spot of R and R. Not that you won't be kept pretty busy. But first things first. Here's a chit. There's an RTO office in the station. And the pay wallah's next door. You'll get your rail warrant and pay. Ten days FS leave from midnight tonight. You've missed the boat train but there's another up to London sixteen-thirty. Report back here 0-eight-hundred on the twenty-sixth. Welcome home and have a good leave. Staff Sergeant!'

Time suddenly speeded into top gear until Alice found herself squeezing into a corner seat of a Southern Railways third-class carriage with her luggage stashed above her head on the rack, having been whisked there by several eagerly willing pairs of male hands, their owners also in military dress. The nearest was, like her, in thick khaki; a bit too near for her liking, as she felt his hip and the side of his thigh pressing companionably against hers. But then she was prepared to concede that it wasn't entirely his fault, as the banquette they were sharing was also occupied by four others, and the seat opposite was similarly jammed, the dozen booted feet and jutting knees equally intimate in their proximity. She had searched in vain for a compartment reserved for females only. In her haste to secure a seat, for the milling horde of uniformed figures resembled a small-scale Dunkirk, she had given up searching even for another woman, and wriggled, humped and squirmed herself and her kit into the nearest compartment, where she had been received with literally open arms as they divested her of her baggage like a pack of caravan robbers. They even bunched up to allow her a corner seat by the corridor.

She sank back, hot and sweaty, in spite of the January cold, which was already converting to foggy gloom. She was half-grateful, half-irritated at the way her fellow travellers responded to her gender. The heavy serge of her skirt and battledress blouse was uncomfortable, and she cursed the fact that she was forced to dress thus, instead of the slacks or shorts she was used to. The skirt especially was the bugbear as she resisted the strong urge to wriggle some more and try to tug it down over the brown-stockinged knees it no longer hid. What the hell! Let them look. Her legs weren't all that bad, and what did it matter anyway? But all these clothes were certainly a torture after the little they had needed in the Egyptian sun. She found herself thinking nostalgically of the cooling desert evening, and of Lynne Manning wandering about in that striped Arab *thobe* of hers – and totally bare-arsed beneath it, the little minx!

'You look browned off, Sarge? Where you back from, then? Somewhere a bit more exotic than this dump, eh?' Her immediate neighbour, the RAOC lance-corporal, now seemed to be joined to her from shoulder to knee. His expression and the tone of his voice had that condescension that could sometimes rouse her to a ready-to-spit fury. She could see, feel and hear it, too, in the other occupants of the compartment as they all looked smilingly towards her, and she struggled to push her anger away, down out of sight.

'Desert,' she answered, deepening her tone a little, making her words sound clipped. 'Just came in today on the *Indus*. Been quite a while. Since forty-two.' Yeah, Christmas Eve, forty-two, to be precise, she mocked herself. But so what? Who did these cocky buggers think they were, sneering at her and her three stripes? 'You been overseas yourself?' she asked, gambling on his pallid appearance and the pristine state of his uniform. She was rewarded by the immediate flood of colour up into his neck.

'Not yet. I've been lucky so far.'

He seemed to hint that it would not remain the case for much longer. Ooh, you bloody little hero! First on to the beach for the second front, eh? She contented herself with a cool nod, and hoped he would feel the reciprocal condescension in the movement and her silence. She dug into her bag and drew out the paperback novel. She had marked her place by folding back the corner of the page, and she felt an inward smile tugging at her as she recalled Elsbeth's shocked disapproval of such tactics. 'I was given a terrible ticking off by my English teacher at the grammar school for doing that! Sacrilege, she called it.'

Alice wasn't into reading at all in those days. But Davy had bought her a book for Christmas. A *real* book, not the *Film Funs* and *Radio Funs* she had occasionally received as a child. It was a novel by someone called Greene, *The Confidential Agent*, and to be honest she had struggled with it, so much so that Elsbeth had taken it from her and read it first, finishing it in a few nights. 'It's good,' was her verdict. 'Exciting. He's a good writer.' So Alice had dutifully struggled on, partly for Davy's sake but mostly for Elsbeth's.

Elsbeth would be proud of her now. Since joining the ATS Alice had become a regular reader, using the forces' library service at the camps where she had been stationed in England, and even in Burg-el-Arab, where a carton of books had been deposited from the FL, with some additions from the British Council office in Cairo. She had become quite a fan of Graham Greene; she'd actually purloined the present copy, *The Power and the Glory*, before she'd left. All in the cause of education, she'd told herself in excuse, though her conscience troubled her little. It would have lain neglected in the box until its pages turned damp and stained with mould. He was quite a deep one, was Greene, in spite of turning out thrillers that kept you page turning. Lots of stuff about conscience and right and wrong. Didn't think much of the church, judging by this story, yet it seemed to be on his mind a hell of a lot. She wished she knew a bit more about him, apart from the fact that he had been to Oxford. No doubt he was doing some sort of hush-hush job at present. Still found time to write, though. This one had only been written three or four years ago.

Her mind had snagged on Beth, as it so often did, so that the open book remained on her lap, the pages in this instance unturned. Usually she would give herself a good shake-up, a mental 'bollocking', when Beth started to take over her mind, but now, in her present state of inertia and exhaustion – it had been a long day and she had hardly managed to sleep at all as they had swung at anchor in Southampton Water last night – she was too tired to fight against it. She let it wash over her, all the joy, and tenderness, and love, and sadness she had known through Beth. She remembered until she felt the longing enfolding her like a familiar blanket.

Even the relatively short journey up to London would take hours. They had warned her to be ready for long periods of standing idle, shunted off to let some essential military traffic come through. 'It could be eight o' clock by the time you get into Waterloo. You'll not pick up a train from King's Cross tonight. Your best bet is to check in at the Union Jack Club or the United Services Club for the night – they're both handy from Waterloo. Or there's the Royal Empire in Northumberland Avenue, if you want a ladies only.' The sergeant in the Regulating Office had winked at her, impervious to her fiercest freezing look.

If it wasn't too late when she got in she could check in somewhere, then . . . she had the address of Beth's Bermondsey flat with her. She felt her heart beat faster. Dared she take a trip out there? She was loaded down with unexpected wealth. The pay she had picked up seemed like a fortune, it was making her wallet bulge. She could even take a taxi. Surely, Beth would be pleased to see her, after all this time? It was more than a year and a half since their last, wretched meeting, in the park at Margrove. No more than half an hour, which Al had forced, knowing all the while she had already lost her, until she was forced to tell her to 'bugger off', and Beth had fled in tears, but no doubt glad to escape, and left Alice slumped there, among the bright flowers and the sunshine, engulfed by her misery, her own face streaming.

What on earth would be the point of seeing her again? Why stir up all that pain and misery, for both of them, when it could achieve no good whatsoever? Except to see her again. The reply slammed into Alice's consciousness like a tree across the road. There was no getting round it. She smacked right into it, that deep, gut feeling, the helplessness of wanting to see her again. Whatever happened, however it turned out, if Beth's loving husband took her by the scruff of the neck and flung her on to the pavement, she had to try to see her darling just once more.

Elaine just wouldn't stop grizzling. Mother and daughter both had colds. Elsbeth wasn't sure who had given it to whom, but both of them were sniffing and snuffling, with noses cherry-red and runny. The interminable freezing journey back down south hadn't helped. You had to allow all the short hours of winter daylight and more these days to travel down from Margrove to London. Elsbeth no longer felt even a morsel of shame in cashing in on her femininity to help her, exploiting the pathos of pretty young mother and infant, to make the most of male gallantry to assist her with luggage, finding seats, stowing her baggage and fetching and carrying for her during those tedious hours. She'd even used it on her own family, persuading her father and Rob to run her through to Darlington to avoid the awkward train-hopping which would have been involved in getting from Margrove to the main-line connection with the capital.

The truth was, she hadn't even wanted to leave her parents' home at all. She'd used every excuse she could think of to extend her Christmas stay at Elton Grove, even lying to her mother about Arty's prolonged absence on duty, until his plaintive, querulous telephone call had rather given the game away. 'It's just so miserable in that awful flat when he's away so much,' she'd pleaded. But eventually, on the wet Tuesday of 11 January, she had given in. The head-cold was making itself felt, with the sniffles and the beginnings of a tickly throat – she thought seriously of using it as a last desperate card in her hand to avoid departure – but conscience had shakily won in the end.

And for what? She'd been back in the flat four days now, this would be her fifth night, and she had been alone for all but a few hours of that time. Well, perhaps more than 'a few', but not much more. Cold and shivering, move six feet away from the electric fire in the ironically dubbed little box of a 'living-room' and you froze, in spite of the ugly layers of clothing. She'd felt terrible, tried to summon up remorse and love at the tell-tale sight of Arty's relief at seeing them again, the love that shone plainly in his still boyish scrubbed face. But it only added to her guilt, for she still felt sick and chill inside at the thought of more days and nights trapped inside this gloomy box in this awful, cratered, ruined city, with no one but this mewling, all-demanding baby, sicking and pooing and demanding all of her time. The rinsing and washing of the nappies and baby clothes, the constant steaming damp of trying to dry them inside, strung up like banners all over the place, with scarcely room for anything else.

Arty had actually managed to meet them at King's Cross, had

commandeered a taxi cab to whisk them home through the busy black-out. He'd tidied the flat up after a fashion, and warmed it for them. So! He could manage to get some time off then, when he needed it? She tried to push those sniping, bitter thoughts away from her. They had gone to bed late. It had taken ages to settle Elaine down back in her own cot, in the corner of their bedroom. Elsbeth had resisted with indignant righteousness Arty's suggestion that they should move the baby into the tiny boxroom, on which the landlord had grandly bestowed the label of 'guest'. 'What about when she wakes up? She still doesn't sleep through, usually. She might choke. We'd never hear her. Or smother herself in her blanket.' She had built herself up into a matronly outrage which had squashed his shameful protests. Another reason which made her so determined to keep Elaine in their room, a reason she tried not to acknowledge because it made her so uncomfortable, was that the baby's presence was a powerful inhibiting factor on any sexual activity; any 'hanky-panky', as Alice had comically dubbed such things.

Elsbeth was ashamed of her continued reluctance. Kissing, cuddling; yes, she still liked those well enough, but anything beyond that . . . even the gentle, intimate touches, which had so roused her and had made their love so astonishingly easy, she no longer welcomed. She would get over it, she tried to tell herself. Meanwhile there was that tension of strung-out nerves between her and her husband, the sense of brooding, unspoken undercurrents, and sullenness. Arty was away for longer than ever now. Like tonight, for instance. He had left this morning before she was dressed, telling her that he would not be back until late tomorrow, probably. She felt neglected and wounded, yet traitorously a deep part of her was relieved that she would have the big old bed to herself tonight, at least until she brought Elaine to share it with her if the baby woke at some point.

The bell rang, and she jumped, her heart racing. Who on earth. . . ? No one ever called on them, certainly not at this time of night, after nine o'clock. Arty? Could something have happened, something wrong? Seared by guilt she raced along the dark passage, dragged back the curtain and scrabbled at the lock to open the front door, to find the muffled, uniformed figure of Alice Glass staring apprehensively up at her.

CHAPTER TEN

The pause was so long, the strange, strained look frozen so long on the face staring down at her, that Alice's heart thumped in choking dismay. Elsbeth's mouth hung gaping, and her eyes filled with tears. A fearful Alice had time to notice the shiny red nose, the poor condition of the reddening skin, and that disturbing stricken quality on the remembered features. She could only interpret that expression as one of stunned horror. There was a touch of panic in her opening remark; she began to gabble in her own fear of the effect she had caused. 'I'm sorry, Beth – Elsbeth. I didn't mean to give you a fright like this . . .' Then why the hell did you turn up on the doorstep after all these months without any warning? she savaged herself, even as her voice ran stammering on. 'I should've written or summat. I just got off the boat this morning, at Southampton. I'm home again . . .' She ran out, ran down into silence, felt the strength drain away to a hulk of misery. Her throat closed. 'I'm sorry, love,' she whispered huskily.

'Oh God! Al! I can't believe it! It's you!' Elsbeth launched herself at the dim bulk of the figure a step below, her arms outstretched, and Alice caught her. She felt the face buried in the turned-up collar of her greatcoat, felt the arms encircling her, then the spasms of the body clinging desperately to her. Elsbeth was sobbing, her sobs tearing through her, and Alice was swamped in a rush of violently confused pain, and shock, and huge, deep gratitude at the feel of the convulsing embrace, and love that overwhelmed her.

Somehow, they managed to get inside, Elsbeth still hanging round Alice's neck. In all her shock and confusion, Alice had taken in the joyful fact that the girl had called her 'Al'. She felt the wisps of that remembered golden hair across her nose, the feel of the little ear, the sweetness of the neck, then they were kissing, mouths locked, tears mingling, faces scraping together in cancellation of all the long cruelty of denial they had known. Then fear swelled up once more at Alice's realization of just how abandoned Beth's grief was. She released her embrace, gently, and adjusted her hold, leading the trembling figure along the gloom of the unfamiliar passageway, into the tiny room where the electric fire glowed, and the rows of nappies hung in the dim light like banners in a misty cathedral.

They sat together on the small sofa, while Elsbeth continued to weep, more quietly now, and Alice, all gentleness, held the shaking form. At last, with loud, crackling sniffs, and gulping sighs, Elsbeth got control of herself, so that she could draw back, dab at her ruined face and gasp out some words of apology. 'I'm so sorry. I – it was just such a shock, seeing you standing there, when I'd just – been thinking about you so much today. It's – I couldn't believe it. It's like a dream. Still is.' The watery, washed out blue eyes stared at her, still with a hint of disbelief, and a cold hand came up to lay itself softly against Alice's own wet cheek. The tangled blonde head shook. 'I've been so low. I'm not too good – things aren't too good, at the moment.'

'Everything's all right, though, isn't it? The baby – and Arty, I mean?' Even as she spoke, Alice scornfully acknowledged the stupidity of her own words. Everything's all right! Her poor girl looked heart-broken.

'Oh yes! Yes! Of course! I'm sorry.' Helplessly Elsbeth glanced about, then reached out for a clean nappy and used it to wipe at her face and to blow her nose noisily. 'You always said what a useless drip I was.' She managed a pleading little smile, which prompted Alice to grab at her and crush her to her chest again with a penitent cry.

'I just didn't know whether you'd want to see me. I guess that's really why I just turned up at your door. I was frightened you wouldn't want to . . . if I let you know.' She glanced around the tiny room, cluttered with all the paraphernalia of a baby. 'You're on your own?'

'Yes. Just me and Elaine. We usually are these days.' She blushed, the untidy fair head went down a little. 'I shouldn't – it's not Arty's fault. He's so busy these days. Run off his feet.' There was a short pause before she added penitently, 'I don't help much, I'm afraid. I'm not strong enough, left on my own with the baby.' She gazed at Alice, her blue eyes filling with fresh tears, the cool fingers reaching out to rest on Alice's wrist. 'I've thought so much about you lately. You won't believe me, but I've wanted so much to write.' The head dipped fractionally again, the hold tightened. 'I thought you'd never want to have anything to do with me ever again, after the way I . . . behaved to you. I'm sorry.'

Alice gave a kind of moan, of love, of pain, of forgiveness, and they clung again, wrapped up in each other, and Alice rocked her back and forth, never letting go until another fit of crying had worn itself out.

'Oh God!' Elsbeth said at last as they disentangled from each other again. 'You haven't even got your coat off.' She sniffed, managed a little laugh. 'You can see I haven't changed much, eh? I'm still as hopeless as ever. Come on. Get out of those clothes. There should be enough water for a bath. You'll stay with me, won't you?' The plea was so plain to see, and to hear, that Alice was weak with gratitude. It still felt unreal.

'If that's all right? I can book in somewhere, the Union Jack or somewhere if it would be easier . . .'

'Don't you dare! I'm scared to let you out of my sight for a minute, I'm so frightened I'll wake up and find I've been dreaming!'

'That's how *I* feel!'

There was a flicker of hesitancy, a suggestion of shame as Elsbeth said, 'Elaine. She's asleep. She probably won't stay that way but we can creep in. You've never seen her.'

'I know. I'm dying to have a look at her.' Alice had a strange sensation that they shared some kind of complicit guilt about the baby. Almost as if they were both acting an eagerness of shared delight that was somehow dishonest. They both stared down at the sleeping, snuffling, red face above the blankets of the cot, in the flickering light of the nightlight. 'She's full of cold. Like me,' Elsbeth whispered.

'She's lovely.' The words came awkwardly from Alice. She stared down at the swelling brow, the cap of fine dark hair, the puffed-out red cheeks and snotty button nose. Alice was confused, and guilty at her failure to register the appropriate emotion, and what to her was her lie. Again came that strong sense that Elsbeth was somehow linked with her in this guilt, shared in it. They turned and crept out again.

'Tell you what. Why don't you have a wash in here? A strip-wash, in front of the fire. It'll be just like the old days.' Elsbeth's voice faded on the last words, and she blushed crimson, but her gaze stayed fixed on Alice for a long second. She gave a small whimper. 'I am so sorry, my love – for everything!'

Elsbeth brought in Elaine's little bath, and Alice helped her carry in the pans of hot water from the tiny space which had been converted into a bathroom and lavatory. 'I feel . . . shy.' Alice could feel the heat in her face as she stood in her underwear.

It was such a strange reversal of their roles, especially when Elsbeth made a brave effort and said, in a fair imitation of Alice's old brusqueness and accent, 'Don't be so daft, lass!' She added swiftly, 'Hurry up, before we both wake up and find we've been dreaming again!' And Alice quickly peeled off the rest of her clothing, while Elsbeth exclaimed at the brownness of her shoulders and limbs, and the contrasting paleness of breasts and flanks.

Afterwards, Elsbeth bathed, too, then they both lay, Alice in her striped pyjamas, Elsbeth in her thick floral nightgown, on the settee. 'Where'd you get these?' Al fondled a bare breast hanging from the gaping bosom of Elsbeth's gown. She had meant her remark to fit with the old teasing, tender dominance of her relationship with the blonde girl, but she was suddenly uncomfortably aware of the reality which lay behind it. The breast was much fuller, the blue tracery of veins standing out on its whiteness, the nipple darker, and larger, rough with its miniature surface cracks. 'You're not still feeding the baby?' she ploughed on hastily, to crash through the blundering awkwardness following her flippant comment, just managing to avoid calling Elaine 'it'. All at once they were in the middle of a minefield of emotion.

'No. I did, until . . . my milk was no good for her. We had to go on to the bottle. National Milk. You can get it from the town hall. I've dried up now. They're still a bit tender.' She moved, and Alice felt its warm heaviness in her palm, her embarrassment eased by the way Beth placed her hand over Alice's, kept it to her. 'The doctor gave me something. It was awful for a while.' She gave a kind of nervous giggle, her voice catchy with confession. 'I had a pump. A kind of suction thing. Arty had to milk me – like a cow.'

The mention of his name, in such an intimate context, caused another hidden danger to be suddenly exposed. Alice felt a little shiver of distaste and fear. She tried to push her thoughts away from all that had happened to her lovely girl since they had parted, the gulf of their vastly differing experiences, the irony of it all. She had always felt she was the worldly one, the protector, and Beth the beautiful young innocent. It was she who had led, always, who had brought her to that wonderful, shocking knowledge of their love for each other, and the

81

physical expression of it. But now folk would say Beth was the more knowledgeable one, the more widely experienced – wife, and mother, while Al was the virgin.

Even Beth's body unambiguously declared it: the full, heavy swell of breasts, the fuller, fleshy curve of hip and buttock and thigh, the rounded belly. Alice buried her face in the golden hair, hugged her close, as though to forget the wave of longing and regret for the slight, pink tipped bosom, the slim-hipped, thin-thighed, pale maidenly lust and love she had enjoyed and hungered for in their stable flat in Howbeck.

Perhaps Beth was still attuned to her thoughts and mood, for she held Alice's hand more firmly, guided it to her pliant body, offering herself. 'I'm sorry for hurting you the way I did. I don't care any more – about all the rights and wrongs of it. Except to tell you it was *me* who was wrong. I've tried to hide from it, to push it away, for so long now.' She stirred against Alice's embrace, her head gave a little shake. 'With Arty – I was . . . he was so good, and kind, and he loved me. I suppose I do love him, in a way. And certainly I love Elaine—' her voice suddenly took on an intensity, almost fierce as she mentioned the baby, as though someone had challenged her. 'But nothing's ever felt like this. Like it does with you. As soon as I saw you standing there tonight, it was like a revelation. All at once, I just knew I'd been trying to lie to myself. And I'm so sorry, my darling. Love me, I want you so much.'

Lieutenant Arty Clark, jammed between two of his colleagues in the back of the canvas-covered jeep, prayed that their driver, a black shape in front of him, did not feel as exhausted as he did. These Yankee vehicles were everywhere these days. You were lucky even to catch a glimpse of a good old solid staff car any more. And they were so light they seemed to send you shooting skyward every time they ran over a pebble. He began to wonder if he should have stayed back at the camp outside Salisbury for the night, even if it meant sleeping under canvas on a sagging camp-bed wearing every article of clothing you possessed in the freezing temperature.

When he heard there was a place going spare in the jeep, he had impetuously jumped at the idea, thinking only that it would get him back home to Elsbeth and Elaine much earlier than anticipated, and that was what counted. But for what? he began to question himself morosely as the long drive through the darkness began. Assuming he survived this wild drive – and the odds on that were even, considering the amount of night traffic moving on the roads these days; the whole countryside south of London would be choked soon if the build-up of men and materials continued in this vein – would Elsbeth really appreciate the effort he was putting in to get home to spend a few precious extra hours with her? Even with the corporal's maniacal driving, it would be well into the early hours before they reached London. He would have to wake her, unless he dossed down on the sofa until Elaine stirred or yelled for her early-morning feed. But perhaps he could steal into the bed, slide quietly in beside her. He thought with longing of the feel of her warm, abandoned flesh, of cuddling up close to her, and felt his body stir now at the voluptuous pitch of his imagination, picturing her stirring, coming slowly half-awake to his contact, his slow caresses, turning, welcoming him in. More likely, she would groan, then shove and flounce away with a bitter hissing reprimand for his selfishness. *His* sefishness!

He pulled his mind away to another delicate area of their private life, and another problem. He felt bad about keeping it secret, but he could see it might well be yet another thorny barrier between them. He had just learned details of what he had known vaguely for some time now. Elsbeth's brother, Bill, who had been his closest pal since they had first begun their training together in the Signals Corps as newly commissioned second lieutenants, was involved, and had been for some time, in highly dangerous work, out on the Burmese border, where he had been posted immediately on completion of their training.

Arty had been deeply disappointed at not being given a Far Eastern posting himself, not least because it meant being separated from his friend. Arty was an only child. His mother died while he was still at boarding school, and his father, a captain in the Merchant Marine, spent months at sea, on the Atlantic convoys. Arty had been moved at the way Bill Hobbs had taken him under his wing, inviting him to his home to spend Christmas with his family. Where, of course, he had met Elsbeth. It was the chance to be near her that was his chief consolation after losing Bill.

Arty had never been what might be called a dominant personality. He was content to remain in others' shadow, even to look to them for support and strength. When Elsbeth had determinedly shown her love for him, he had been overjoyed – and overwhelmed. The diffidence he had seen and recognized in her was magically overcome and their romance had blossomed with dizzy swiftness, until they were sharing everything, including their bodies, in a series of illicit rendezvous, and he had dazedly found himself a father-to-be. He was afraid of what their families might say, but again Elsbeth had shown him the way, and their marriage was arranged. He found the courage to face her aggrieved parents with the truth – at her side – soon after the ceremony, in plenty of time to prepare for the baby's arrival. He had told his absent father of the first happy event without mentioning the anticipated second. When Elaine had arrived six months later, Captain Clark had sent a generous cheque and made no comment beyond wishing the couple well and expressing his hope of meeting his daughter-in-law and granddaughter soon.

Bill clearly had not wanted his family to be worried, and warned Arty not to let Elsbeth know. *She was always a bit of a blabbermouth*, he wrote. But now Bill was working with Major-General Orde Wingate, and had made several trips behind Japanese lines, his job to organize the signals for the airdrops and pick-ups in the jungle that were so vital to the guerrilla force. He made it sound like some jolly wheeze, in the stiff upper lip tradition of the British hero, but Arty was deeply anxious for him – and wretched about keeping his secret from Elsbeth. She should be the one to decide whether her parents should learn the truth. What if, God forbid, the worst should happen? Besides, he did not want to have secrets of any kind between him and his wife. That was the whole point of marriage, sharing everything, good and bad. On the other hand, they were having a rough enough time as it was at the moment. He kept hoping things would get better, but it saddened him to admit that there seemed precious little sign of it so far. What would telling her about Bill and the perils he faced do to the precarious balance of their relationship?

The Jeep dropped him off at the end of the long row of terraced properties. It was after three o'clock. He should have waited after all. He could have been back by teatime at the latest. The place really was quiet. There hadn't been an air-raid for months. The numbing cold seemed to settle like a blanket over the city, deadening the sounds further. He turned the key in the door. Elsbeth hadn't slid the long bolt home, thank goodness. She never did these days, with his irregular comings and goings. He placed his bag down carefully at the foot of the stairs, and climbed them as stealthily as a burglar, avoiding all but the softest of creaks. He'd undress before he used the lavatory – he only needed a pee and wouldn't pull the chain – and risk slipping in beside her. He had removed his boots inside the front door.

He could hear Elaine snuffling in her sleep, and Elsbeth, too. Driving them home, by the sound of her. He moved towards the bed, unbuttoning his shirt as he did so, tugging at his collar, and stopped, frozen. There were two heads: a dark mop of curls on his pillow, Elsbeth's fine gold hair spread out across her own, her face turned away from the stranger. A visitor? But who? An ex-colleague from her service days, maybe, a fellow Wren? Yes, that must be it.

He made to turn away, and just then his wife moved, with a vague sigh, turning away from her companion. The sheet slid down, and Arty saw the pale exposed shoulder, the bare arm. With a jolt, he realized that that was all he could see, bare flesh, with no sign of a nightdress. Then he saw it, draped carelessly across the bottom of the bed. There was a further stirring, under the bedclothes, and the arm groped across, feeling towards the bedfellow, and the strange girl gave a restless little moan, surfaced to consciousness and sat up, half-turning towards Elsbeth as she did so. Arty saw the high, naked breasts. At the same instant the girl let out a sharp yelp of alarm as she saw him standing there, and clutched the sheet to her bosom.

CHAPTER ELEVEN

'Another cup of tea?' Arty asked, with weary politeness. His eyes itched with tiredness, and his exhausted brain spun with an awareness of the ludicrous charade of good manners. It had existed all the way through his stumbling, garbled apologies as he backed out of the bedroom, then the fiasco of the two girls appearing in their night things, clutching a vociferously disgruntled Elaine, her bawling urgency a convenient shield against that brief flash upstairs, which his mind had struggled and was still struggling with.

In the harsh light of the living-room, containing a ghostly reminder of its earlier heat, and with the electric fire newly aglow, a flustered Elsbeth had dumped his daughter on his lap. 'You said you wouldn't be home until tomorrow. Today!' she amended, sounding perilously close to tears. She made it sound like an accusation, as though he had deliberately deceived her. 'This is Alice, by the way. Remember? You've heard about her often enough. The girl I shared the flat with in Howbeck. The one I was at junior school with back home.'

'Of course, yes! It's nice to meet you.' Ridiculously he half-rose, supporting the smelly baby on one hip as he reached out to shake hands with the pyjama-clad figure, who was hastily scrambling into her army greatcoat as a dressing-gown.

Elsbeth's voice, high and strained, came from the annexe that was the kitchen, where she was clattering pots and pans. 'She just got back this morning – hell, yesterday morning! From Egypt. Docked at Southampton. I nearly passed out when I saw her on the doorstep. I thought I was seeing things!' Arty and Alice smiled at each other in painful embarrassment. Her stuff was all over the floor. Kitbag, haversack, holdall. The squat kitbag had been stood on end, its top unlaced.

86

A pair of stockings was draped like snakes across its top. The shiny buckle and narrow white strip of a suspender strap peeped coyly from beneath them.

And so it had gone on, through the long process of changing and feeding Elaine, making tea and toast, the polite conventions of hospitality, the pleasure of such an unexpected reunion, all the unconvention of what he had briefly witnessed swept aside as though it had never happened. The grey light of Sunday morning had dawned well before Elsbeth rose with her newly wrapped and sweetened, replete infant and announced she was going back up to put Elaine in her cot. 'We can all catch another couple of hours.'

Alice had already nobly offered to abstract herself from the domestic scene. 'I can be off. I'm on my way home—'

She was cut off by Elsbeth's cry. 'No! You said – you said you'd stay today! Arty! Tell her – I haven't seen you for two years and you want to go running off!'

And she had looked at Arty, her face pleading, alight, and he had found himself saying, 'Oh, please do stay if you can. I've got to go back to work later. I may not get back again.' He felt himself colouring up as he ploughed on. 'In fact, I know I won't be home tonight at all, so you can have the place to yourselves. Make up for lost time.' He laughed, a too-hearty guffaw that sounded shockingly like a *double entendre*, and blushed even more.

'I'll just settle baby down. Give me five minutes then come on back to bed. She'll sleep till after nine now.' She was not looking at either of them as she clutched the docile infant to her chest and hurried out.

'No thanks,' Alice answered to Arty's offer of another cup. 'Listen. I'll be fine on the couch here. I can kip down anywhere. You must be shattered.' She just corrected herself in time. You can't say 'knackered' to an officer, you clot! But of course, he was not only an officer but a gentleman, and firmly refused her offer.

'Nonsense! If you could see some of the places I have to sleep in these days! The old sofa will be a luxury.' He made a gallant show of talking small talk and she played along admirably, too. She had raised one leg, the striped pyjama-ed knee jutting up out of the divide of her army coat, and he stared distractedly at her ankle and the bare foot resting on the sofa's edge. Her foot was broad, almost stubby, but her toes were even, and unfussy, the nails neatly trimmed and palely free from paint. He thought of his wife's red toenails, the funny little irregularities of the shape of the smallest toes, the often chipped varnish. And all at once he thought hotly of this stranger's small, high breasts, the sight of both her and Elsbeth, naked side by side in the bed.

'Good night – or rather, good morning!' he hawed-hawed to the retreating figure leaving the room. She looked very young and diminutive, swamped by the military coat which enveloped her. When she had gone, he slipped off his trousers but kept the rest of his clothing on, including the thick grey socks, and settled down on the restricted lumpy space of the settee. It was only a two-seater, so he had to fold his knees under the makeshift arrangement of baby-rug, shawl and blanket. Either that, or let his feet stick out over the arm of the sofa, and it was too cold for that at the moment. He had toyed unpatriotically with the idea of leaving the fire on, but conscience had won the day and he had switched it off. It had been on since before dawn, and probably late into the night, before the girls went up to bed. Before . . . the visions rose again of their naked bodies together, and his shocking and shocked imagination rioted once more. He thought of their nightclothes tossed carelessly across the bed and the floor.

The blackout was an effective barrier to the grey light trying to seep around its edges at the window, so the stuffy room was almost in darkness, but his fevered thoughts would not allow his exhausted body rest. Why had they taken their things off? Elsbeth and he never slept naked, not even after making love. At least, not since their earliest days, before they had had to get married. His conscience balked at that 'had to'. It was what they both had wanted, more than anything. But since they had become man and wife they always dressed again afterwards. Anyway, it was such a rare occasion nowadays he had forgotten what it was like, almost. Only once since Elaine was born, and Elsbeth hadn't taken her nightdress off, only hitched it up over her hips and spread herself, martyr-like, for his brief pleasure. Duty done. It had been almost a year since the time before that, and he had endured the celibacy nobly, he thought.

He deserved a medal. Almost with relief he diverted his thoughts to the other matter which had been disturbing him earlier. Elsbeth's brother, and his best pal, Bill. Arty had learnt a good deal more about the Chindits' activity, and the strange character who led them, General Wingate. Bill must have met him, must know him quite well now. Their strikes into the north Burmese jungle were becoming something of a sensation, helping to disperse the myth of the Japanese superiority in jungle warfare, following their shamefully swift, comprehensive success, which had brought them to the very gate of the Empire in India. Wingate's force went deep behind enemy lines and more important, came out again, with astounding success.

Bill was playing a considerable part in achieving this. They had developed a new type of aircraft, an American design, which could land and take off in an amazingly short distance. Rough airstrips could be hacked out quickly in the dense bush, and the planes could ferry in supplies and take out the sick or wounded at very short notice. It was much more successful than the parachute drops on which the troops had had to rely in the early days. A well-organized and maintained signals technique was vital, and Bill was playing an essential role in the transmitting and receiving of the coded messages. He didn't spend the entire time of an operation with one Chindit unit, but moved around, surveying locations, organizing the communications, flying out with the aircraft then back in days later to a new location.

Bill's own letters were naturally guarded, and necessarily vague, though he was able to give Arty quite a flavour of the adventurous life he was leading. And Arty had learned more from various well-informed sources up at the Big House, the War Office itself. It all sounded very high-risk stuff. Arty was ashamed of his envy. How could he wish himself across the other side of the world, facing such perils, when he had a wife and beautiful little daughter to look after now? Yet Elsbeth's recent insinuations about his safe existence compared with her brother's distant posting had cut his pride deeply. She had even tossed the name of Alice Glass at him – the girl who was now occupying his place in the marital bed. And that brought him again, in a very swift circle, back to the point of his chief disturbance. Worse than, or at least as bad as, his improper speculation as to what had happened in that bed, was the shameful knowledge that he lacked the courage to resolve it; to face his wife with a direct question. But then how could he? It was beyond him, it was too ungentlemanly; it was not the right thing to do, damn it! It was, literally, unspeakable.

So why not unthinkable? Why should his mind race along such sordid lines, fling up such loathsome images? Could it be his brain that was wrong, was conjuring up ideas that were simply a condemnation of his own sick personality? Perhaps it was something girls did, a female thing, still innocent in its own right, lying naked together?

All at once, entirely unbidden, came a memory of his childhood, and his time at his prep school on the south coast, when his mother had first become ill. He was eleven. The boys were all into making dens in the wooded grounds around the school: bunkers, really, they were obsessed with war games, brought up on hero worship of military might, tales of the Great War. He had palled up with Thompson – he couldn't be sure of his first name now, they never used them. Sometimes nicknames, or altered forms of the surnames, were used. That was the case with 'Tommo'. Tommo was a charismatic figure, at least to Arty. He had dark, thick hair, standing up in tight curls at his brow. He was quite short in stature, an inch or two less than Arty, and his complexion was swarthy, like a gypsy's. His eyes were very bright, black-looking, and shining. Arty thought he was very handsome, and admirable in both physique and in manner. He was flattered that Tommo had chosen him to be his pal, and the blond boy was content to let him dominate.

In their den one warm afternoon, well hidden in the dug-out hollow covered with branches and leafdrifts, a fight started. Arty couldn't recall the reason for it; it was probably half-joking, a 'rag' started by Tommo. But somehow it had become serious, Tommo urging him to put up a proper fight, to stop being a 'mummy's boy', a 'Nancy boy'. He had tried, for a while. They had threshed and squirmed about, wrestling, bucking, the branches hissing and leaves cascading about them, until Arty was breathless and choking with dust, blinded by it, along with the sweat dripping and stinging in his eyes. He sank back, with a soft sob of capitulation, and felt his thin wrists seized, his arms pinned out beside his head. He was weeping softly.

'You're beaten, Clark. I've got you, haven't I?'

'Yes.' The sobs grew suddenly, welling up, filling Arty's chest, and tears ran through the dust and sweat, made channels on his cheeks.

'You stink!' Tommo thrust his face into Arty's. Arty felt the nose pressing into his neck, and suddenly he felt a strange, confusing lassitude, a weakness that was physically and sensuously thrilling as he yielded, his whole frame slackening. And as he did so, Tommo's pinning weight began to thrust into him, battering him, in regular rhythm, while the boy grunted in time with his thrusts. Arty exhaled, in softer grunts, but in timing with this weird assault. His loins began to respond, they thrust their bellies together, through all the thickness of shirts and the thick grey uniform shorts. The weakness became a kind of melting feeling, centred about his genitals, but without any of the reactions their sniggering peers had talked and whispered and hinted at. It was oddly unfocused, grew like an electric current passing through his insides to a crisis point and he cried out and suddenly Tommo's pounding rut stopped and the dark boy lay heavily on him, gasping, his face at Arty's neck and shoulder, their sweat running and mingling.

Thinking of it now, forgotten for so many years, Arty felt his body react swellingly under the blankets. He turned, his forehead pressed against the musty back of the settee, fondling himself as his mind filled again with images of the girls up in bed.

Alice could see the curving shape of Elsbeth in the bed, facing away from her. Elaine was sleeping, her breathing audible in the gloom. Alice let her coat slip quietly to the floor and eased herself in carefully. She fitted herself gently around the curve of Elsbeth's back, felt the warm material of the nightie, then realized with a great sinking of dismay that the body was shaking, she felt it against her. Elsbeth was weeping, silently, in shuddering sobs, and Alice gave a small moan and fitted herself closely to the spasming figure, hugging her, her lips soft at the temple, nuzzling the wisps of gold hair.

'Oh my love!' she crooned. 'Don't! Please! I'm so sorry. I can't—' Elsbeth's movements grew even more pronounced, and she began to make snorting sounds through her nose and her mouth. 'Don't—'

Elsbeth turned swiftly, heaved herself round, the noises through mouth and nose spluttering, louder, and all at once Alice realized she was convulsed with laughter, trying to keep it stifled, shaking and weeping with it, as she flung herself into Alice's embrace, buried her face in her chest to muffle her hysterics. 'Oh God! His face . . . when he came in . . .' she moaned in agony, thrusting her face into Alice's breast to smother her helpless mirth.

It was immediately infectious. It came bubbling up from Alice, too, a great welling of dizzy relief, and they hugged each other. 'Sh! Sh!' Alice gasped, their faces touching, their mouths kissing. 'Don't wake the baby.' The bed trembled with their laughter. 'Stop it, Beth! Right now! Shut up, for God's sake! He'll hear us.'

Beth could hardly speak, she had to fight to get her words out, her cheeks glistening with tears. 'When he came in – his face! Did you see his face? Oh!' She collapsed anew, buried herself against Alice once more.

'See it? You should have . . . did you see. . . ? I sat right up, he looked straight at my tits!'

This time the explosion was mutual and they clawed at each other like drowning souls and dived under the bedclothes, dragging them up to form a tent to shut out the world from their view.

CHAPTER TWELVE

Arty tapped on the closed door of the bedroom. He could hear the girls laughing and talking to Elaine. 'Can I come in? Are you decent?' Why did everything he said sound like a *faux pas*? No doubt to their sensitive ears it bristled with accusation. They called out for him to enter and he came in, carefully balancing the two cups of tea on the little tray. He was wearing a dark sweater over his uniform trousers. 'Here. This is fresh.'

The baby was lying contentedly between Alice and Elsbeth. Arty's gaze took in the striped pyjamas, the sprigged nightgown, before darting away again. At least they were wearing them rather than scattering them about the floor in wild abandon. 'I'll just grab a few clean clothes. I've had a bath. The heater's on. It might take a while—'

'We'll share a bath, won't we, Al?' Beth said pertly. 'Just like old times.'

'I'll take Elaine while you have your tea. I have to go about eleven. It'll be late tomorrow probably before I get back. Have to be down in Kent, near Dover.' He delved in the chest of drawers, taking out a small bundle of garments. 'I promise I won't come barging in on you tonight, frightening the life out of you. Ha-ha!' His jollity sounded terribly false, he could feel the heat in the tips of his ears as he made his escape. It felt like escaping an hour later, too, when he bade a bright goodbye to their guest. 'Will I see you again? Will you still. . . ?'

'I'll *have* to head up north in the morning,' Alice answered. 'I haven't seen my folks yet. They're expecting me any day,' she went on over Elsbeth's childish wail of dismay.

'You *will* see her again, though!' Elsbeth's tone sounded almost snappish. 'She's being posted to Southampton, so she'll be able to get away

93

whenever she's free.' Beth slipped her arm round Alice's like a police-man making an arrest. 'I'll make sure she does!'

Arty coloured a little as he laughed. 'That'll be great! I'll look forward to it. Well, enjoy your day, you two. Don't sit up nattering all night.' He bent his head quickly, aimed a kiss at his wife, whose yellow head turned just enough to take his kiss on her cheek. ' 'Bye, darling. See you tomorrow night some time.'

Beth blew out a noisy sigh, which sounded suspiciously like relief as she closed the front door on him. 'You run the bath. I'll settle her nibs down. Don't start without me, mind!'

'Yes, ma'am. Bossyboots as ever, eh? I'm surprised they didn't make you an admiral in the Wrens.'

The day was as magical as they had hoped it would be. And the long winter evening, and night, too. Even Elaine seemed to have joined in the conspiracy of insulated happiness, being 'as good as gold', settling down after her six o' clock evening feed, having to be woken for a half-hearted somnambulistic effort to take more milk at 10.30, and drifting quickly back to a sleep that lasted through until dawn, which was considerably more than the girls managed to achieve. They lay together in front of the fire after supper, until well after midnight.

'I don't want you to go tomorrow. Can't you just stay here with me, for ever?' Beth wriggled closer, her face half-buried in Alice's warm breast.

Alice, too, was reluctant to face the thought of departure, now only a few hours away. 'I wish! Just think, though. Yesterday I never thought this could ever happen, not in a million years! I never thought we'd be together again – like this.' She felt Beth's nod, the shudder of relief that transmitted itself through her.

'Can't you get a transfer nearer? In London somewhere? There's thousands of ATS about.'

'Listen, a month ago I was three thousand miles away. Let's count our blessings, eh? Southampton's a damn sight nearer than Egypt. I'll be able to get up here regular, just try and stop me!' She hugged her closer. After a lengthy pause, she went on, her voice softer with her reluctance. 'What about Arty? Will he mind. . . ? He's a real nice bloke, Beth—'

'Don't talk about him! Don't spoil our time together. Please. We've just—'

'We've got to!' Alice felt sickened at letting the outside world in on them, into the exclusivity of their own world that they had so wonderfully discovered, but there it was, all at once pressing in on them. 'He's your husband. Elaine's his baby, too.' It struck Alice with considerable shock that that was just what they had been doing, the two of them, closing out that real world, in the joy of finding each other again, even incorporating elements of that other world to fit in with theirs. The baby for instance. Elaine had become part of them, an extension of her mother, for Al to share in. As though Alice were replacing Arty in the trinity. Beth had placed Alice in the father-figure role, tenderly, teasingly making Al hold Elaine, struggle with changing a nappy, bathing her, until Beth had stepped in with that loving, gentle, mocking superiority: 'Here! Not like that – give her here – don't be frightened. Get hold of her, she's not made of china!'

Alice felt cruel at the way she was pricking the balloon which had held them throughout this miracle of reunion they had found, but she felt driven, by a fear of what might be worse if she didn't. And she could hear, and feel, the sudden tension, in Beth's voice and body, and in the atmosphere suddenly, like a chilly draught. 'He must wonder . . . already. He saw us in bed together—'

'So what? We've only got the one bloody bed, for God's sake! Why shouldn't we sleep together?' Beth's voice was high, shrill with aggression, but still not disguising the evasion.

'Come off it, Beth! You know what I mean! We had nowt on!' She found herself resorting to the broad, accented bluntness of old that she had used when confronted with Beth's 'airy-fairyness'.

'What are you getting at? You're saying it's wrong now? We shouldn't have?' She gave a harsh laugh at the irony of it, yet another role-reversal of their former situation. Back in the minefield again. She gave a long moan of pleading and frustration, squirming up in Alice's embrace until she lay on top of her, pushing her face close, planting soft kisses. 'Oh please don't, Al! I know we have to face things, but not now, not right now. We've just found each other again, let's leave it. All right, I have to let you go tomorrow, I accept that, even though I'll probably weep all day after you've gone. I'll sort Arty out, I swear. He's a good boy, really. I just have to tell him you're very dear to me. I'll even be discreet – I *can* be, you know!' She kissed her on the mouth again. 'But let's just be you and me for tonight. That's all I want – and to know that

95

I won't lose you again. I admit – I was so wrong about everything, but we're together again now. That's all that matters, isn't it?'

The parting, when it came the following morning, *was* tearful, and desperate enough, with Beth hanging on to her, clinging round her neck in the gloomy passage, her face smeared with tears, to tug at Alice's heartstrings, in spite of her brave reassuring words. 'Don't take on, lass. I'll be in touch. I'll write as soon as I get back to Southampton, let you know my address, and I'll be up the line first forty-eight I can get. A week or two, that's all, love, I swear. Shush now. You'll upset the baby.'

It was when she was squeezed at last into a third-class compartment on the King's Cross-Edinburgh train that the unwelcome thoughts returned to take away from the euphoria she tried to cling on to at the miraculous events of the weekend. There was more than an element of desperation in Beth's attitude. It was in keeping with her dear girl's character, she had to admit, this inclination to be extreme in her emotions – 'to tear the arse out of something,' to use the old Alice's more homely phrase. She remembered the downright hysterical flavour of the break-up; Elsbeth's complete renunciation of their love, when the news came of Luke Denby's death, her utterly illogical conviction that she had caused it, by her passionate attachment to Alice. And the extremity of her reaction: not only ending their relationship but rushing off to join the Wrens, followed by her equally wild decision to give herself to Arty, her pregnancy and subsequent marriage.

Alice felt dazed yet again as she reflected on the events of the past forty-eight hours. What if she had not found the temerity or foolhardiness to present herself at the Bermondsey address on Saturday night? She was dismayed at the disloyal thought that edged into her mind that it might have been better if she had not done so. You've been sick to your guts at the loss of her for the past two years! And now you've found her again. You're lovers again, what on earth more could you want? Yes! Lovers! And her a married woman with a baby, not to mention a husband who was very much on the scene and who had just about caught them at it in his bed to boot!

She shifted in her seat at the uncomfortable nature of her thoughts, and caught the flicker of the aircraftsman's eyes opposite, flashing over her stockinged knees. Another of them, by God! The sooner she could get home and get into some decent, warm slacks the better! Never mind, erk! I can appreciate a pair of pretty knees just as well as you can, sonny, and I did, too, and a helluva lot more last night! The images of Beth that flickered across her mental vision were disturbing, too, though in a very different way from her previous reflections, and highly successful as a diversion.

Alice's guilt soared at the warmth of welcome when she climbed grandly from the taxi cab at No 19 Maudsley Street. The afternoon was already a grey twilight, with a few large, wet snowflakes falling, which quickly gathered in intensity until the air was filled with them, their soft, fluttering, silent descent muffling sound, even the excited cries of the knot of spectators which inevitably gathered at such an event. 'Hiyer, Alice, luv! Smashin' to see yer, honey! By, isn't she brown? Like a darkie, you are!'

Maggie Glass was blubbering, her wet face mashed into Alice's, her arms locked about the neck. 'Eeh, lass! Thank God yer 'ere! Ah've not been able to rest since we got yer letter! Come on in!'

Alice was glad that there was no one in the house except her mam. 'Your dad's on two till ten. He'd've swopped shifts if he'd known when you were coming, luv. Ethel won't get in till after nine tonight, neither! There's only our Algy. He'll be in any minute from school. He's dying to see you. God! I can't believe it! Get your things off, let's get a look at you. Kettle's on, get sat in front of the fire. You must be frozen after where you've come from. Our George was home a couple of weeks ago. Just after New Year. He's been moved again, further away, down south. I don't know where. I've got the address of his camp – Bodmin summat, I think.'

It was right that the two members of the family Alice cared most about should be the first she was reunited with. Algy was eight now, taller and quieter than she remembered him, but he gazed at her with tongue-tied devotion that indicated he still valued the closeness they had shared when they had lived together with the Aygarths in Howbeck. It contrasted sharply with Ethel's cool greeting when she arrived later that evening, and her self-centred complaints about the hardship of her life at The Groves. 'I wish to hell they'd call me up, I can tell you!' she affirmed. 'I can't wait!'

But it was her father's attitude which made Alice's hackles rise highest, as she had anticipated, in spite of her best efforts not to let him upset her homecoming. He was jealous, she knew that, of the glamour of her return, the aura of her travels, her rise to staff-sergeant, but whereas Ethel's selfishness and envy only mildly irritated her, her father's sullen boorishness made her inwardly furious. It was as if she was somehow threatening his status as 'king of the midden', his jealously guarded power as head of the household. There was that old sneering challenge behind every snide remark in answer to all her talk about her experiences. She soon shut up, despite her mother's encouragement for her to take centre stage.

It upset her a little to realize how much of a sexist clash it was between them. He saw it as a challenge to his masculine authority, his male dominance. He even mocked at her rank in the ATS, in the guise of 'joshing' her, just 'a bit of fun, you know'. But she knew better. Born at the beginning of the century, he had been just too young to be caught up in the Great War (though, as his 'mouthy' daughter had once pointed out, there were plenty of lads who did manage to get into the forces before their eighteenth birthday) and, at thirty-nine when the present conflict had broken out, had avoided conscription because of his occupation at the steel works. But lack of military experience did not prevent him from loud proclamation of the incompetence of soldiers and statesmen, from the deployment of the BEF to the débacle of Dunkirk and other worldwide failures from North Africa to Burma.

But then, was the real reason behind her ancient rivalry with her da not so much a detestation of all his bigoted intransigence but a declaration of war between the sexes, which she had unconsciously been waging since her earliest infancy? As much a fault of her abnormal personality as his entrenched prejudices? Was it her fault, her refusal to accept the way the world was? Well, if it was, what the hell could she do about it? And what the hell did she *want* to do about it? This just less than twenty-four-hour reminder of the pathos of her mother's life here, the total suppression of any aspiration on her own part in her slavish submission to her husband and his demands, made the answer undeniably clear to Alice.

To assuage her uncertain guilt, Alice lavished a great deal of her inflated pay on her mother, urging her to 'treat' herself, with the emphasis on the reflexive pronoun, then announced, 'I have to be back by Friday, Mam. I thought I'd go through to Howbeck on Thursday and stay with the Aygarths. So I can see our Doreen and a few folk. I can get the train through to Scarborough and then to York. Be back in London for Friday night. But listen, I'll be posted down south some-where. Won't be going abroad. I'll be able to get up for weekends nearly every month, I expect. That'll be good, eh?'

You're becoming bloody good at lying! she reprimanded herself. And cheating, too. She thought of the youthful face of Arty Clark, and his utter astonishment at seeing her sitting up bare breasted in his bed, his naked wife at her side. Could that still be called cheating, when you'd been caught on the job, as it were? Poor Arty! He was a nice fellow, really, and Beth had him twisted round her little finger. She was right. He'd probably never even mention it, because, as far the toffs were concerned, such matters were absolutely unmentionable.

He couldn't very well knock her block off, or challenge her to pistols at dawn, as he would if she were another chappie. She almost wished she were. It would make her feel a hell of a lot better if she could fight him for Beth. But no! That was one thing she definitely did not want to be, a man! However sick or twisted the world might consider her, she would stay just as she was, thank you very much! Not that she had much choice, mind you. She might not understand the ins and outs, the reasons, for her deviance, but she knew the incon-trovertible fact of it. She was what she was, and nobody could do a damned thing about it; not even poor old good old sweet old Davy, her one and only pal, man or not. She was determined to see him. She would leave Howbeck on Friday, head for York, and land up in Dubry Street, on his doorstep, just as she had turned up on Beth's. And look how that had turned out!

Back to 'tangled webs' once more. Davy had told her about some Scotch poet who had written something about the mess you got into when you told a lie. Well, at the last minute she hadn't lied to Davy, but she knew he wouldn't turn his back on her, in spite of his dismay. Mind you, what would he say if she had the guts to be honest yet again, and tell him it was all on again, full steam ahead, with her and Beth? Which it was, she was certain, no matter how uneasy and sick she might feel about it.

Poor Arty. He was the innocent party, the sinned against, certainly not the sinner. She had a sudden feeling of helplessness. She was play-ing the male role in so many ways: the seducer, leading the virtuous wife astray. *Virtuous?* Just who had led whom astray in front of the fire in

Bermondsey? Never mind, Arty, old son, she reflected, turning to savage humour to ease her troubled mind, at least you got an eyeful of my tits, ould lad, and there's not many males can say that.

CHAPTER THIRTEEN

The snow had not really taken hold at the coast, and the streets of Margrove soon shed the cleansing white for their usual wet black grit, but inland it lay four or five inches deep, transforming an already attractive scene to one of almost fairytale beauty. Once the train had left the pall of smoke and grime behind in Middlesbrough, the further it progressed along the winding foot of the Esk Valley the more breathtaking the views from the steamed-up windows became. Alice's heart beat faster with pleasant anticipation as the train chugged into the familiar little station and she heard the shout of, 'Howbeck! Howbeck!' She even recognized the voice as Mr Lonsdale's. He had been porter here during her stay in the village, and here he was, ruddy-cheeked and portly as ever, hurrying forward with a polite little touch to his cap, to help the smart young lady soldier with all her gear. 'Mornin', ma'am! Let me give you a hand with that lot. Not billeted round here, are you?'

Alice laughed. 'Do you not know me, Mr Lonsdale? Alice Glass. Remember?'

'Well, I'll be blowed! What a turn-up, eh?' By which time Malcolm Aygarth had come forward and gathered her into his arms, lifting her off her feet as he delivered a smacking kiss to her cheek, and the guard leaned out from his van at the rear to see what this unseemly huddle was about. Mr Lonsdale belatedly remembered his duty, and fumbled for his whistle. 'Mind the doors, please! Mind the doors.' The guard's piercing blast came in return. Not to be outdone, the locomotive added its hoarse little toot, a blast of sooty smoke clouding into the clear morning air, and the carriages rattled away down the dale towards the sea at Whitby.

'Eileen's been up baking since crack of dawn,' Malcolm told Alice, when he had released her from his enthusiastic greeting. 'She's never stopped since we got your message. She insisted you had to be back in your old room, yours and Algy's. How is he these days? A big lad now, I bet?'

She arranged with Mr Lonsdale to leave her kitbag and cases in the office at the station. All she needed for her overnight stay was her canvas grip. 'You can bring it all up if you want, lass,' Malcolm offered. 'I've brought tractor down, like. Don't trust owt else to get up and down t' 'ill, wi' all this snow on it.'

It was good to hear the Dales speech again. She was a little taken aback at the depth of emotion she felt at being back here. After all, she had not spent that long in Howbeck – only a year and a half. But then, of course, most of it had been the happiest time of her life, and to hell with the pyramids and the sands of the desert and her sergeant's stripes. It was here she had really got to know Elsbeth, in the wonderful, shabby little flat in the stable yard of Howe Manor.

There was a touch of the prodigal's triumphal return about the welcome awaiting her at Beck Side Farm. The whole clan had turned out, including Malcolm's brother, and his father, now seventy-two and as capable as ever of putting in a long, hard-grafting day. Only the children were missing, and they would be racing up the snowy slope as fast as they could as soon as they were released from the village school. Little Malcolm had stolen a march on them. His fifth birthday was still several months away, and so he was at home when Alice made her appearance. He had been a two-year-old when she had seen him last. He would hurl himself enthusiastically into her arms on sight, and delight in the rough and tumbles on the high old bed she shared with Algy, and would snuggle in sleepy contentment on her knee in the warmth of the kitchen of an evening while she went through his beloved and well-worn picture books. Now he hung back, a tubby figure with thumb seeking out mouth as he gazed in awe at the lady soldier.

'Why don't you bring Doreen back with you for tea? She can stop over with you, if you like. She won't mind sharing a bed, I'm sure.' Alice was aware of a slight hesitancy in Eileen's voice, and the touch of heightened colour in the pink cheeks. 'It's ages since we've seen her. I know she's busy with her schoolwork now. I hear she's doing ever so well at the grammar school. She'll go far, will that sister of yours.' The homely face lit up again. 'Like her big sister, eh? Eeh, it's grand to see you again, lass. Sergeant Glass, eh?'

'*Staff*-sergeant now!' Alice laughed, making it clear she was poking fun at herself. 'They'll be making me an officer if I don't watch out!'

'And why not? You'd be as good as any of them lot, that's for sure.'

'Oh, I don't think so, don'cher know!' Alice guyed, in a mincing imitation of an upper-class drawl. 'They wouldn't have a tyke like me in the officers' mess. Not that I'd want it, mind! Some of them haven't got the sense they were born with!' She grinned, tapped the stripes on the sleeve of her shirt. 'It's us that keeps them going anyway.'

But Alice was still thinking about her young sister. She was hardly surprised to hear that Doreen had not bothered with the Aygarths. The selfish madam had got way above herself, settling far too well into the elevated background of her ward and fairy godmother, Miss Elizabeth Ramsay and her genteel kind. She couldn't even be bothered with her own family, let alone the Aygarths. She'd never go back to Margrove at all if it were up to her, Alice knew well enough. Uncomfortably, she had to admit to a certain reservation about condemning Doreen for that. If it wasn't for mam, Alice would find it difficult to find any solid reason to draw her back to Maudsley Street. It might be painful but honesty compelled her to acknowledge the lack of feeling for any of her siblings, except for little Algy, even though she was the first born, and had played a major role in helping to care for them during her childhood.

Mam had dropped them regularly, at three-yearly intervals, starting with Alice herself in 1921. There had been a birth between George and Ethel, in 1926 – a boy who had lived no more than two weeks. Mam called him Harold. Alice never knew if he had been baptized. She wondered just how many miscarriages there had been, possibly induced. It had been common enough in places like Maudsley Street; no doubt it still was. Still, five survivors was more than enough to be going on with. Alice remembered when mam had fallen with little Algy. It had been five years since Doreen's birth, and mam at thirty-three was already old-looking, and hoping she was done with all that. Alice had been thirteen then, and had just started her periods. 'You just be careful, lass,' Maggie had told her bitterly. 'Don't you let any lad near you to get you into trouble, you hear?'

She'd heard all right. No need to worry, Ma. No fears on *that* score! No lad had ever got *that* near, not in twenty-two years, and never would.

She supposed she was lucky to be here herself. When Alice was grown up, mam had told her how she'd 'got caught', at nineteen, and how dad had done the right thing, stuck by her and married her. Otherwise, Alice might have begun and ended as a foetus hidden under a paper draped over a chamber pot and carried through to the yard to be tossed out with the night soil. Yes, indeed, who could really condemn Doreen for seizing the opportunity for escape from that kind of harsh reality? And she even sounded uncannily like the gentlefolk she was aping and hoping to join. Alice had rung Northend Cottage from the phone box in Lister Road, and it was the youngster herself who answered. 'Hello. This is Howbeck 215. Who's calling please?'

She'd sounded pleased enough to hear her. But there were no breathless squeals, or yelps of startled delight. The clear voice sounded so cool, so poised and contained, even when caught in such surprise. 'Alice! How lovely to hear you. Where are you calling from? Is everything all right?' The note of caution there, even then. What's happening, how will it affect me? Keeping her distance. Oh yes, she was learning well, she would make it all right, this cool, cocky young madam. And Alice, somewhat ashamedly, could not suppress a grudging admiration.

She was waiting to meet Doreen from the train, which pulled in soon after four. It seemed almost all the passengers which it disgorged at Howbeck were schoolboys and girls, all from secondary school. In spite of the prohibition about the mingling of the sexes, there seemed to be a deal of interplay between males and females. Doreen was on the look-out for Alice and disengaged from a group of chattering companions. 'Hiya, our kid!' Alice sensed the slight restraint from her sister, in contrast with the abandoned quality of her own enveloping embrace.

'Hullo, Alice. It's good to see you. You look so brown!'

'And you're so tall! You're nearly as big as me already.' Alice's kiss had landed on Doreen's cheek, and not as she had aimed, on her lips. She relinquished her hug, and instead linked an arm with demonstrative enthusiasm. Doreen answered a few calls from her school-friends, aware of their curious glances. 'Hope you're not ashamed of me, me not being a captain, or at least a lieutenant.'

'Don't be silly!'

'Only joking!' Alice answered, squeezing the captive arm tightly. When had 'daft' been replaced by 'silly'? she wondered. She tugged

Alice towards the left at the end of the short lane, to head uphill. 'Come on. We're having tea up at Beck Side. Eileen's doing a special spread.' She felt the resistance as Doreen stopped.

'Oh? Hang on. That's a bit awkward. I told Aunt Elizabeth you'd call in. She'd like to see you.'

Bloody liar! Alice thought, but she nodded quickly. 'Righty-ho. Best be quick, though. You can change if you like. Get into something a bit more comfortable.'

'You don't think the uniform suits me?' Doreen wriggled her arm free and gave an elegant little dancing swirl, sending the heavy grey skirt swirling round above her black-stockinged knees.

'No, it looks very smart. I just thought you'd be glad to get out of it. Into summat warmer, a pair of slacks.'

They were heading down the slope to the stone bridge over the beck, which Alice could hear flowing noisily in the dusk. As they crossed, they could see the white of the broken water rushing over the stones. It was still quite shallow, but when the snows melted it would be swollen and roaring. The chinks of light showing through the curtains of the Oddfellows' windows reminded Alice of the free and easy attitude towards wartime regulations in the Dales. She thought of the brassily blonde landlady, Vera Rhodes and her 'foreign aid', Gus Rielke. 'How is Vera these days?' Alice grinned, nodding towards the pub as they passed. 'Has she replaced the Big Swede yet?'

Doreen giggled. 'Not permanently, I think. But there've been quite a few applicants!'

'Eh! You sound like you're growing up fast.' Alice was glad of the gathering darkness as she added with careful casualness, 'Have you started your monthlies yet?'

'Of course I have!' Doreen answered, with scorn and with no sign of embarrassment. 'Ages ago!'

'Ay, well.' Alice was half-amused at her acknowledgement that she was probably the more embarrassed of the two. 'Just remember, you be careful around lads. I saw some of them back there giving you the once-over. You're a bonny lass, so you'd better get used to it. Still, I suppose a right little smart arse like you knows all about such things, eh?'

'Yes, thank you,' Doreen said, lightly mocking. 'I know all about the birds and the bees, and the stork, and what you have to do under the gooseberry bush to get a baby.'

'Cheeky monkey! Well just don't forget it, that's all I'm saying.' Then she changed, gave a suggestive chuckle and grabbed Doreen's arm once more, her head bent close as they approached Northend Cottage. 'One thing's for sure. I bet you never learnt nowt from your Aunty Elizabeth on that score! P'raps you could give her a few tips, eh?' She was rewarded by the unaffected nature of the laugh that rippled from her sister as she pushed at the gate opening on to the long front-garden path.

Although Alice had visited Northend Cottage many times during her twenty-month residence in Howbeck this was the first time she had been offered a seat in the living-room and a cup of tea. She had opted to change her skirt for khaki trousers, otherwise she was still in uniform, including battledress blouse, shirt and tie, and Miss Ramsay commented on how smart she looked. 'You're looking very well yourself, miss,' Alice replied awkwardly. The spinster's dress was almost a uniform itself: the restrained heathery pattern of the heavy, stylish skirt, the pastel-coloured twin set and the double row of pearls, and the neatly regimented hairstyle of tight waves carved into aligned submission, perhaps just a little frostier in its colouring since they had last met.

Doreen sat primly at Miss Ramsay's side, black knees pressed in lady-like symmetry together. 'Would you like to be mother?' Miss Ramsay asked. Alice felt a sudden irreverent urge to giggle, in view of the exchange which had just taken place between the sisters at the gate. She glanced at Doreen to see if she was experiencing the same reaction, but the long, dark eyelashes were demurely low, the delicate face perfectly composed as she concentrated on the ceremonial task of dispensing the tea in the flowered china cups. 'We're very proud of you,' the older woman declared patriotically. 'Aren't we, Doreen? And we've so much enjoyed hearing all about your adventures. Doreen's looked forward so much to receiving your letters.'

'Yes, all three of them,' Doreen said, her tone as neutral as the deadpan expression on her face.

'Same as I got from you!' Alice shot back, with a wide grin. So! The old biddy had read her letters to her sister, had she? Just as well Alice had been careful not to say anything that might have caused offence. She'd had a feeling the old girl would get to read them, one way or another! 'Afraid I can't stay long, Miss Ramsay. We're invited up to Beck Side for a meal. They've said Doreen can stay the night up there.'

106

It was clear that the spinster was not in favour of the idea. 'Oh! Has it been arranged? She *does* have school in the morning. And what about prep, darling?'

'I made sure I got it done at lunchtime. I thought I could take my school things and go straight from the Aygarths' to the station, if that's all right?'

Alice beamed a bright smile at the woman opposite. 'Two years since I've seen my little sister. Lots to catch up on. Family news and all that.' She noted the flash of irritation and distaste on the well-bred features, and took a mean satisfaction from the fact that the word 'family' had done the most damage. 'I've got to be off myself again in the morning. Back to the war. Duty calls, eh?' And she held the beam of the bright smile directly on her target, in assurance of victory.

Alice lay back on the pillows, watching her sister as she came huddling back into the bedroom, swamped by Alice's greatcoat, which was draped round her shoulders as a dressing-gown. The crisp chill of the clean sheets had been well thawed by the earthenware hot-water bottles that Eileen had placed in the bed earlier. Alice was amused at the way Doreen turned her back, and kept the coat hanging round her while she stepped out of her navy-blue knickers and into her pyjama bottoms. 'Leave your vest on if you're *that* cold.'

'I don't sleep in my undies!' the girl answered disapprovingly. She kept her back ostentatiously turned towards the bed as she hastily wriggled the woollen vest over her head and drew on the jacket.

'Good God! There's no need to be so bashful. You've got nowt to hide anyway. You'll have a tough time if you ever have to go in the forces. No good being shy in a barrack room.'

'It didn't bother you, I bet!' Doreen fired back. She slipped beneath the bedclothes, squirming with her feet to seek out the bottle, lying on her side, facing Alice. 'Is that why you like it so much?'

Alice felt the colour mounting, and she strove to keep her tone casual. 'What do you mean by that? What are you trying to say?'

'I'm not *trying* to say anything. Just stating the blindingly obvious – that you enjoy being with a load of girls.'

'And what the hell's wrong with that?' In spite of all her effort, Alice could not keep the sharp, defensive challenge from her tone.

'Absolutely nothing, if you're that way inclined.' Alice felt the scald of shame sweep through her frame, her toes stiffened with it, as she made a growl of protest, over which Doreen coolly continued. 'You don't have to pretend any more with me. You and Elsbeth Hobbs. You were completely soppy over each other. Anyone could see. You should have heard what some of the kids at school used to say about you.'

For a second or two Alice was speechless, consumed by the blaze of shame, which was heightened as she heard herself trying to deny or disguise the truth. 'Dirty little tykes! You're too big for your boots, you are! You don't know what you're on about. You wait till you get some-one – a special mate, that you really click with.'

It won't be a *girl*!' Doreen said, with withering contempt. 'I'm thir-teen, not three. I know all about crushes – and lesbians!'

'Sh!' Alice's eyes were wide with involuntary alarm at the bald utter-ance of the word, its sibilant, hissing obscenity. 'It's not – like – the way people make out.' She felt bruised, shockingly exposed, and close to tears.

'As I said, it doesn't bother me at all. As long as you don't start trying any of your weird ideas on *me*. I'll scream the bloody place down, and we'll see how your friends like that!'

Alice was outraged. 'For God's sake! You're my little sister! You don't think—'

'It didn't stop our George with Ethel! They thought I was too little then to know what was going on. What he used to ask her to do for the sixpences he gave her!' Alice stared at her helplessly, and the elfin features were transformed with a wide and knowing grin. 'You said you're off to York in the morning. On your way back to Southampton. You going to see Davy Brown?'

The youthful face was staring at her with a far too penetrating look. Alice felt lost as she nodded. 'Don't let our mam know, will you? I never let on. I didn't want to upset her. To let her know I was leaving early.'

Doreen gave a satisfied nod, the grin still in place. 'See? You don't want to be at home a minute longer than you have to. You're no differ-ent from me, really. Are you, big sister?'

Alice studied her almost as though she were seeing her for the first time, and with a new and grudging respect. 'Oh no! I think you're very different. I think you'll leave us all way behind, my lady.'

PART II

THE OVERFLOW OF HEART

CHAPTER FOURTEEN

During the opening days of 1944 Davy Brown was riding a violently plunging emotional switchback. He soared to dizzying heights, but the plummeting dive to stomach-churning depths was waiting, as inevitable as the early icy dark which followed the grey daylight. And he was sick at times, disgusted with himself at his infatuation for Reeny Lumley. His feeling for her had him trapped like some hormone-enraged adolescent.

He had always found his landlady attractive. Her quiet, understated beauty had moved him from the start. The surroundings were far from romantic in their cosy domestic setting: mealtimes at the kitchen table, the steaming copper and washtub in the scullery, the ironing-board and clothes' horse. And Reeny in her drab work-clothes: pinny and head-scarf, curlers and slippers, or, in the early morn when she was always up to serve him breakfast before the early shift, the large checked dressing-gown that was almost identical to his own. But there were always those slim and palely pretty ankles peeping between the gown and her floppy slippers, to spark the little flame of guilt at his surreptitious, sneaking glances. How innocent those snatched glimpses seemed now, and the whole quixotic nature of his admiration of her during those long gone days.

The change had been sudden, and he could pin-point not only the day but the minute, even the second, that it had taken place, on the day near Christmas when the departing Bob Noone had made his dramatic revelation of Davy's secret history. Since then, everything had changed between them. Everything was a confusion of extreme opposites, of heaven and hell. He was ashamed of the fierce, elemental joy he felt in knowing she was physically attracted to him. He could not forget the passion of their embrace on New Year's Eve, and how they were both caught up in it for those snatched moments. Followed, of course, by their equal shame, and their inability to acknowledge it. He went along with her fiction of being 'too squiffy' to remember what had really happened. But since then she had made it plain, on more than one occasion, that she was very much aware of what had taken place. There had been other kisses, not quite so blatantly abandoned, but far from innocent. And yet Reeny insisted on keeping up a façade of artlessness, as though it were some kind of innocent affection they shared. 'I'd never do anything bad!' she'd whispered, while they were still holding each other, breathless from an embrace that could not be interpreted as anything other than a lovers' kiss. She meant it. But couldn't she see that what they were continuing to do, under the guise of her definition of harmless, was perversely worse than the sin she insisted on avoiding? It was like sharing all the little intimacies of lovers, without the consummation such a state demanded. And it was driving him wild.

He was by turns both infuriated and relieved by her conviction that they were doing nothing 'bad'. When his conscience was plaguing him, as it so often did, he was tempted to fling the words of the Good Book at her, from the Sermon on the Mount:

Ye have heard that it was said by them of old time, Thou shalt not commit adultery: But I say unto you, That whosoever looketh on a woman to lust after her hath committed adultery with her already in his heart.

Well, he certainly 'lusted after her'. Was she really being honest with herself when she could kiss him like that, with parted lips and searching tongue and bared teeth, and still claim that she wanted nothing beyond that? That those wonderfully intimate looks, the soft fleeting caress of hands, the brush of bodies and limbs, was enough? Maybe, he conceded, for all his scepticism, it was, for her. Maybe women were different in that way. Ignobly, another thought wormed its way into his brain. She had already tasted the thrills and comforts of a comprehensive relationship, still enjoyed them. She had her husband, she had a child. He couldn't steer his helpless tormenting thoughts away from the marital bed and his visions of all that passion that he knew lay within her.

Or did he? He scarcely knew anything much any more, except for this boil of raging desire for her. And let's face it, even the Good Book had been officially overruled these days, for hadn't Christ also said, *Love your enemies, bless them that curse you, do good to them that hate you*? He knew from bitter experience what happened if you tried to put that precept into practice.

He was ashamed of the way he began to look upon his work as a welcome diversion from his private situation, but it was true. He was grateful therefore when DI Holden called in at Tower Street and sought him out. 'Got a job for you, Davy. Thought you'd be interested. We need you to go a little bit further afield, lad. Same thing we've been working on in the city, but it goes a bit beyond that bunch of iffy market traders supping in the Punchbowl. Be a bit of undercover work involved, and you'll be working with another force. The North Tyne lot. You'll liaise with their detective force, under a DI Daniels. Seems all right, I've had quite a few meet-ups with him. It could well lead us to some of our old sparring mates, the gang that got you mixed up with us in the first place. You and that gutsy little lass of yours. What was her name again? Alison?'

'Alice Glass, sir.' And she was never my lass, he wanted to add, but he didn't.

'That's right. You still hear from her? She left and joined up, didn't she?'

'Yes. The ATS. She's out in Egypt now. Been there over a year.'

Holden grinned. 'I reckon you were a bit slow there, old son, letting her get away like that. Has she been snapped up by some Desert Rat yet?'

'Not as far as I know, sir.' And never will, an observation he again kept to himself.

He seized on the file that Inspector Holden passed to him. 'Find a quiet spot to go through it, but keep it in the station, and don't let anybody else get a look at it. It's only a temporary secondment,' Holden told him. 'Stay up there a few days, get to know the lads up there, and the lie of the land. It'll all be hush-hush. We don't want anybody knowing you're a bobby. That's the big advantage. You're a new face. You know yourself how quick the local villains are to twig on who's in the plain-clothes branch. Where are we now?' He looked at the wall calendar. 'Today's the seventeenth. We've got some papers for you. ID, the lot. Bit of a dodgy character, you are.' He nodded at the buff folder. 'It's in there. Mixture of fiction and fact. Ex-jailbird, call-up dodger.' Davy tried not to show the sensitivity he felt at Holden's words, and to meet the direct look his superior levelled at him. 'You'll go up to Newcastle

tomorrow afternoon. Daniels will meet you, have a word. You'll meet
the lads you'll be working with. They've fixed some digs for you, and
they'll show you which pubs to hang about. Come back here Friday,
have the weekend off. Unless anything's kicked off before then, but it'll
take a while. Just keep your wits about you, there's some ugly customers
involved. Remember your old mate, that Norwegian feller? More of his
sort.' He smiled. 'Might even bump into him again, you never know.
We heard he'd gone back to sea.' He nodded again at the file. 'And as
you'll see, we think most of the stuff is coming in by boat, as contra-
band. Especially the fags, from across the water. Mind you, there's so
much Yankee stuff about nowadays, with half their bloody forces over
here. Including no doubt some right fly boys of their own – and I don't
mean the Air Force!'

Dick Lumley was at home, stretched out in his favourite chair before
the kitchen fire, in collarless shirt and braces, with the seven-year-old
Micky sprawled on the rug at his feet, playing with his homemade
wooden Spitfire and Lancaster bomber, their roundels and markings
still pristine since Father Christmas had left them three weeks ago.

'How do, lad!' Dick greeted Davy, stirring himself to move his chair
a little to the side. 'Come in and get yourself warm. Still bitter out
there, eh? It'll freeze over again tonight. Shift up, Micky. Let your Uncle
Davy get himself warmed. Why don't you play with them on the table?'

Davy heard the pattering run of Reeny's slippered feet down the
stairs, and the door swung open. 'You're early!' she said, a little breathless. Her cheeks were pink, her eyes bright. 'They've not changed your
shift, have they? Supper's not even on yet.'

For a wild instant, he thought she was going to maintain the hurry of
her entrance and come across to embrace him. 'Not exactly. You're
going to get me out of your hair for a while,' he answered brightly. 'Got
to go off up to Tyneside for a few days.'

'Eh?' She was still now, staring at him. 'Why? What's up?' Her tone
was sharp, and edgy, he thought, and he was deeply embarrassed,
afraid that Dick might notice.

'Oh, nothing very exciting. Just some job we're tied in with. I should
be back Friday.'

'Eh, come on, luv.' Dick chuckled comfortably. 'You should know
better than that. You can't ask a copper what's to do! You know what

they say. Careless talk, eh, lad?'

Davy laughed dutifully in return. 'That's right, Dick. I've got to go up and meet the King and Winnie, but don't say anything, will you?'

'Oh! You men! Think you're so clever, don't you?' She flounced her shoulders, and pulled a pouting face, and Davy felt himself stir at her movement, as she advanced and grabbed him by the waist, thrusting him vigorously towards the fire. 'Go on then! Sit yourself down there, and keep your daft secrets if you don't trust me! I'll put the kettle on – again! That's all I'm good for, to skivvy after you two!'

'Nay, not me, lass. I'm hardly ever here, you're always telling me.' Dick picked up the kettle and passed it to her, winking at Davy as he did so. 'You see far more of your lodger than you do me.'

'That's true enough.' She let her hand fall on Davy's arm. Her skirt brushed against his leg as she eased past him.

His skin was tingling, he felt as though there were an electric charge crackling in the air between them, that her husband must feel it, too. He was beginning to hate these times when the three, or four when Micky was present, were together, the easy familiarity of man and wife and their child, and then the hidden intricacy of his relationship with her. He thought of her in the chilly darkness of his bedroom that morning, the weight of her sitting on the creaking bed, the sweet morning smell of her, and the heat of her kiss, searching out his mouth, his awareness of her body so close, pressing to him, and his own, hot under the blankets, his fierce and helpless, unfulfilled hardness, as he yearned for her – until he wanted to seize her, pull her down, under him, or thrust her bodily from the room. And she knew, despite her talk of 'innocence', for she drew back after the kiss, breathing heavily, saying nothing, and leaving swiftly, of her own volition.

What Dick had jokingly said held more than an element of truth. The moments when all of them were together were rare enough. That was the trouble. If Dick had a job which brought him to hearth and home every night, this whole situation would never have arisen. Perhaps Providence had intervened after all, with this new involvement requiring Davy to be away for a while. And who knew how long it might go on? It could be weeks, if his part in the investigations bore fruit. It was certainly easier to avoid the sin of temptation from a distance of ninety miles than with no more than the width of a sheet and two blankets and an eiderdown intervening.

Reeny gaped at the tanned figure in khaki standing on the slushy pavement with her baggage bundled about her, then at the black taxicab, which was just pulling away from the kerb.

Alice grinned. 'Hello, Mrs L. Doesn't anybody recognize me any more? I haven't changed that much, have I?'

'Alice! My goodness! What a shock! When did you get back? Davy never mentioned . . . did you let him know?'

'No, I'm afraid not. I should have done. But everything's been happening so fast. We only docked at Southampton last Saturday. I've hardly had time to sort myself out.' She glanced over Reeny's shoulder, into the passage. 'Sorry if I gave you a fright. Is he in? Or is he still at work?'

'He's not here. I'm sorry, love. He's away. Been up in Newcastle all week. But come in. Look at me, keeping you stood on the doorstep like a brush salesman!'

There was something odd about her manner, something more than just the surprise at seeing Alice turn up out of the blue. An awkwardness, a kind of embarrassment, she wasn't sure what it was, but it was something. All at once the disturbing thought came that Mrs Lumley knew the truth about her. It hit her like a blow. But how could Davy have betrayed her to his landlady, however friendly they were? Surely he would never disclose something as shameful as that? Why *shameful?* she upbraided herself. Stop thinking like everybody else. What did they know about the truth of it?

Belatedly, Reeny reached forward, picked up the haversack and the grip. 'Here, let me help you with that lot.' Alice expertly seized the kitbag, swung up her knee to assist its hefting up to her shoulder, and followed Reeny into the dark, narrow passage. 'Have you been home yet? Seen your folks?' She led Alice into the fuggy warmth of the kitchen. 'Just dump your stuff down here. You've caught me on my own. Dick's away – of course!' She laughed heavily. 'And Micky's at school. He'll be back in an hour. Time for us to have a quiet cup of tea. We've been hearing all about you from Davy. He always tells us what you've been up to, when he gets your letters. But come on, get your things off and sit yourself down. We'll make the most of it while we've got the place to ourselves.'

Alice removed her cap, and the greatcoat, and the battledress blouse. She rolled her shirtsleeves up above her elbows, and Reeny complimented her on her tan. 'I should have let you all know I was coming. It's my own fault, I thought I'd surprise him.'

'You've certainly done that, young lady.'

Alice watched her surreptitiously as she busied about making the tea. She was an attractive figure even in her drab working garb. She was friendly enough, but still there was an indefinable air of reservation about her. It was quite a while before she said, 'Actually, he *did* say he might be back some time today, but he wasn't sure.' She glanced at Alice's kit, piled in the corner of the room. 'Where are you off to? Are you still on leave or what?'

'I've still got a couple of days. It's a shame . . . *my* fault,' she repeated. 'I don't suppose you could put me up tonight?' She felt herself blushing. 'I'll pay of course.' She laughed self-consciously. 'I've never been so well off!'

'Nay, it's just . . . a bit difficult. Micky's bigger now.'

Alice sensed her reluctance, and was both hurt and embarrassed by it. What on earth was it that was disturbing the woman? Surely Davy couldn't have told her?

All at once, Reeny seemed to draw herself up, as though she had made a snap decision. Her face was still a little flushed. 'Oh, look, I can put him in with Davy for tonight. That's if Davy comes back. And you can get in Micky's bed. I'll change the sheets.'

'I don't want to put you to any bother, Mrs L. I'm sorry for turning up like a bad penny—'

'Don't be daft, lass!' She came over impulsively and put her hand on Alice's brown arm. 'Davy would never forgive me, turning you away, after you've come halfway round the world to see us. It's no bother at all, don't fret.'

'What about Davy's roommate? Bob, isn't it?'

'Oh, he's gone, love. Before Christmas. Transfer to Leeds. He's courting a lass over there.'

'He was a bit of a character, wasn't he?'

Reeny's face became serious. She gazed at Alice for a second, as though she were debating how to go on. 'He found out about Davy. About what happened at the beginning of the war. Thought he'd make trouble. Davy told me everything,' she ended quietly, and again touched

Alice's arm. 'I know all about it, him being in gaol and everything. And what a brick you were when he came to Howbeck. He thinks ever such a lot of you.'

She spoke with a kind of reluctance, which, this time, Alice did not pick up on, in her erroneous belief that she had discovered the secret of that initial reserve in Mrs L's attitude towards her arrival.

CHAPTER FIFTEEN

If Davy had thought his latest assignment would occupy his mind to the exclusion of all else he was so far sadly disappointed. On the contrary, he seemed to have even more brooding time to spend upon his personal problems, for a large part of his working week had consisted of long spells of inactivity, nursing half-pints of bitter in various dingy pubs along City Road or in the vicinity of the shipyards of Walker and Wallsend, or lying on his lumpy little bed staring up at the flaking and suspiciously stained ceiling of his bare room in the tenement block lodging just off Broad Chare. 'Broad', as a description of the narrow street leading down to the east end of the long series of river berths that made up the Quayside, was something of a misnomer, since it was permanently shadowed by the tall, soot-encrusted buildings on either side. It had been so named, DI Daniels, who fancied himself as a bit of a local historian and keeper of Geordie folklore, had informed him, because the lane, unlike many of the alleys that ran through the maze of buildings around the docks, was wide enough to allow a 'chare', or cart, to pass along it.

Inspector Joe Daniels was tall. So were all the regulars in the City of Newcastle force, for they had long insisted that all their recruits should be at least five foot ten and a half inches. His height helped to make his rotundity less conspicuous than it would otherwise have been. His girth he owed to his seemingly inexhaustible capacity to sink pints of Exhibition ale, which also gave his open, fleshy features a permanent ruddy glow, and contributed to a largely false impression of outdoor healthiness. He smoked Capstan Full Strength – one was scarcely ever more than an arm's length away from his lips – and he wheezed and coughed alarmingly, especially when he was convulsed by one of his own pearls of incisive wit. But he was, as DI Holden had intimated, affable, and probably good at his job to have reached the rank of inspector.

Davy was surprised at his friendliness towards a lowly special constable like himself, especially given Joe Daniels's amiable scorn for anyone unfortunate enough to be born south of the River Tyne, or, as he put it, 'the wrong end of the bridges', which included all the inhabitants of neighbouring Gateshead. He was also honest. 'I can't afford to put one of my lads on such a long shot as this. Can't have good men idling about at a time like this. But your gaffer's not bad – for a Tyke – so I don't mind taking you on board for a bit. Be good experience for you, if you don't end up with your head caved in and floating in the coaly Tyne.' He paused while he began the heaving eruption of splutters and coughs which were all part of his expression of merriment. When he had recovered he rather took the shine off the light-hearted atmosphere by adding, 'And I'm not joking, hinny. There's some very nasty buggers out there mixed up in this lot. It's not just a couple of pairs of them Yankee stockings and such. It's a big operation they've got going and they play rough. We'll try to keep an eye on you, but you'll be on your own a lot of the time. There's numbers here to ring if you want to get something through to me. Don't try any other ways.' He gave Davy a very old-fashioned and direct look. 'Don't think any of the uniforms'll do. Don't pass on anything over the front desk of any of the stations. You understand what I'm saying?' He nodded back at Davy's nod.

For the first couple of days, Davy had felt that mixture of excitement and fear tightening his stomach. He was tensed up, watching everything and everyone around him. It was bad enough trying to deal with the local accent, whose fast, singsong flow was baffling to say the least. He felt hopelessly inadequate, a square peg in what needed to be a very smoothly rounded off hole. He was all too aware of his lack of experience in this kind of covert activity. It was like being a spy, and here he was, being dumped in the heart of enemy territory with no training – unless you could count the few hours of surveillance he had clocked up in the Punchbowl and one or two other inns around York; or indeed the operation which had led to his joining the police force in the first place. He had felt very much the amateur he was then. All it had involved, really, was hanging about the bar of the Oddfellows and letting the Big Swede know how anxious he was to make a few extra bob and how little he cared about the ethics of how it was done. The rest had been easy. Pass on the information about the intended movement of the black market stuff, go to his post as appointed lookout, then be taken home by police car. The only slip-up had been the wriggling through the net of Rielke himself. His dim-witted accomplice, Bob Symmonds, had not been so lucky. There was little doubt that Rielke had been ruthless about sacrificing him in order to effect his own escape, and the hill farmer had suffered a beating from his fellow villagers severe enough to put him in hospital for several weeks, before serving a sentence of almost two years. In fact, Davy had only recently learnt of his discharge from prison.

But it would be, as Daniels had said it would, a waiting game, with the possibility that nothing would come of it in the end, the dangling bait would not be taken. Meanwhile, uncomfortable as it was on the end of a hook, he had to drift in all the right places and hope eventually to be snapped up. 'We'll give it two or three weeks,' Daniels observed. 'Your lot are convinced the stuff floating about down your way is coming in through the Tyne. And I don't think they're wrong, either. So, as long as your gaffer's prepared to let you swan about the bars and brothels of God's own country, we're happy to have you around.'

As DI Holden had said, Davy's cover was a meld of fact and fiction, and not that much of it came simply from vivid imagination. Even his name didn't change. He was Davy Brown, and he had served time, though in this version it was for 'contravening the National Registration Act 1939', without any mention of his being a registered conscientious objector. He was simply a petty thief and call-up dodger who had been caught. Just the sort of rootless drifter who would be up for any chance to make some dishonest money in the burgeoning undercurrent of lawlessness in these unstable times.

As far as roughing it was concerned, he had certainly gained some experience in what he looked back on, from the wisdom of his twenty-six years, as his misspent youth, in pre-war London, and then as a participant for a year in the brutally savage conflict of the Spanish Civil War. He had seen bloodshed and cruelty to last him a lifetime, and it made him determined never at any price to be involved in war again. A fond hope. It seemed no one could avoid being tainted in some degree by this worldwide battle.

121

So he sat, unshaven and unwashed, in his shabby, smelly clothes, in the corners of bars like the Eagle, and the Ship Inn, and chatted with the barmen and barmaids and the working-class customers when the opportunity arose, without giving too much away or being 'pushy', always remembering DI Daniels's warning – 'They've got to make the first move.' So far, in four days, no one had.

So here he was, on Friday afternoon, staring at the ceiling, while the gloomy daylight faded and the chilly corners grew dimmer, waiting for six o'clock and his rendezvous with one of his contacts, DS Paul Kelly. The meeting wouldn't take long, unless Sergeant Kelly had something for him, for he had nothing at all to report, not even the faintest sniff. There was an eight o'clock London express – unless it was delayed (likely) or cancelled (possible) – which should have him back in York by ten o'clock. He thought, with considerable eagerness considering he was heading right back to the centre of all his personal disquiet, of the pleasures of being 'home' once more; the comfort of a hot bath, an escape from these odorous clothes, and the prospect of seeing once more, and hearing, and even – he groaned aloud – touching his lovely Reeny again. Not *his*, no, definitely not his, but he had a heady, clandestine share in her.

It was after eleven when the train arrived at York. Davy ached with weariness, after standing among all the kitbags and the uniforms in the crowded corridor for the whole of the three-hour journey. He had endured, too, the curious, then disgusted glances of his nearest neighbours as they caught a whiff of him, and plainly drew back, to put what distance they could between them and him. He had only an old haversack, and despite his tiredness he stepped out in lively enough fashion through the freezing night, all too aware of the inadequacy of his unsavoury garments and longing even more for the embracing heat and fragrance of the bath now that it was so near. His breath formed clouds of steam round his face. He knew it wasn't just the imminence of the hot bath awaiting that spurred him on, quickening his step and his thoughts, but the delight of seeing her again. Would she be waiting up for him at this late hour? He had told her when he had left on Monday that he might be home on Friday. But nothing had been definite, and he had not been in touch since. It was bad enough having her occupy such a large space in his thoughts, without actually trying to communicate with her. Besides, what on earth could he say? *I don't know if I'll get back on Friday but I do hope so. By the way, I love you, I'm mad about you, and can't stop thinking of you. PS. If you're reading this, Dick, I'm only joking ha-ha.*

The pavements on the main roads had been largely cleared of snow, but when he got to the narrower streets of Clementhorpe the slush had hardened into frozen little corrugations, which made it dangerous as well as noisy to walk on. He was glad of his filthy but stout workman's boots. His gloveless fingers were clumsy and numb as he fumbled with the key of No 25, and thrust his way through the heavy blackout curtain. There was a light on at the head of the stairs and he could hear water draining from the bath. She was up! But then she appeared in the doorway of the kitchen, in her checked dressing-gown, and the scarf round her curlers. 'In here. I didn't think you were coming.'

He glanced quickly up the stairs. Curses! Dick was home. He was ashamed of the sinking feeling the knowledge gave him. 'You shouldn't have stayed up so late.' He had an almost overwhelming desire to step over to her and enfold her in his arms. It would be perfectly safe, Dick wouldn't be down for a minute or two, maybe not at all. He might be going straight to bed. Then he experienced an absurd disappointment that she had not taken the chance to come to him and kiss him. But she was standing, over beside the glowing range, not moving, looking at him . . . how? As though he had done something, had unintentionally upset her. What was wrong?

She cleared her throat, as if she had been waiting to make some kind of announcement. Everything seemed still, suddenly. She smiled, a bright, beaming grin, which looked as though it was costing her a great deal of effort. 'Look who's come – to see you!'

He heard the quick rush of feet down the stairs and a fragrant waft came ahead of the pyjama-clad figure, who appeared, barefoot. The bronzed curls looked burnished, lightened at the brow by a strong foreign sun, the face beneath exotically tanned. 'Davy!'

His jaw dropped, he blinked in disbelief, before he croaked out her name and she launched herself with a rapturous, tear-tinged cry into his arms, driving him backwards with the force of the embrace, and then his face was half buried in those tight unruly curls, and her mouth was lifting, searching out his. He felt her body straining against his, her arms crushing his neck. Over her head and the sound of her sniffling laughing and crying, he could see the frozen grimace of Reeny's fixed bright smile.

Reeny stirred up the embers in the high grate, then spoke without looking at either Davy or Alice directly. 'You can put another shovelful of coal on if you're going to sit up half the night nattering. I'll leave you to it. An old body like me needs me sleep.' She turned to Davy, still managing to avoid meeting his gaze. 'I've put Micky in your room, to accommodate your young lady here.' Her light laugh served only to highlight the awkwardness of the phrase. 'I suppose I could have left young Micky where he was, but I have to watch my good name. I keep a respectable house.' She had got as far as the doorway, and the false little laugh trilled again. 'You can stop down here as long as you like. Nobody'll disturb you. Dick's not due back till tomorrow night some time. 'Night, God bless.'

The awkwardness hung on in the silence that followed in the kitchen, as they listened to her footsteps, then the closing of the bathroom door. 'I don't think Mrs L is best pleased to see me turning up again like a bad penny.' Alice grimaced and nodded towards the ceiling. 'I think she feels I did the dirty on you, ran out on you.' As Davy started to protest, the fair curls shook again. 'I was beginning to wonder just how much you'd told her about me.' Both of them felt the heat rise to their faces.

'She knows how I felt about you. Feel,' he amended, and she noted the change of tense.

She had had enough of small talk during the long hours she had spent with Reeny and her little boy, and the short spell of uneasy conviviality through the last half-hour when Davy came down from his bath, before Reeny had made her escape. 'You're not still carrying a torch for me, are you?' She was immediately stung by the tawdry, cheap Hollywood touch of the metaphor. 'You haven't still got any hopes? You know what I mean.'

He gave a grimace of a smile, but his eyes were sad. 'Why? Should I have? Have you changed your mind while you've been away? Are you ready to say yes?'

Suddenly her throat closed, she felt the threat of tears, and a deep sadness for the way things used to be between them, back in Howbeck, when they were 'good mates', with none of the complications that twisted their threads about them now. She had to speak. 'I called in to see Elsbeth in London. Before I came up north.'

'Oh yes? How was she? Was everything all right?'

Alice nodded. She sank back in the easy chair, her bare heels resting on the fireguard, the warmth almost too much on the backs of her ankles and calves. Although she despised herself for a coward, she was glad she didn't have to meet his gaze. 'Aye. She didn't throw me out. I stopped there, a couple of nights.'

The phrase, and all its unspoken implications, hung for a second between them. She felt as though they were standing either side of a deep chasm.

'Oh yes?' he repeated. He was not going to be the first to attempt the leap. 'And how's she enjoying married life? You saw the baby? And met her husband? He's still stationed in London, is he?'

'Yes. He's a nice chap. He was only home for a few hours while I was there. And little Elaine's lovely. Beth's a lovely mum. She's put on a bit of weight, but it suits her. She looks fine.'

Another dragging second of a pause, before he spoke. 'That's good. I'm glad you've made it up with her. I know she meant a lot to you.'

Alice couldn't stand any more of this circling round the issue. 'Nothing's changed! I mean between her and me. It's just like it was – before!' She realized all at once that he was kneeling beside her; she could feel his body pressing against her leg.

'You can't!' She saw the blazing intensity of his expression. Now his hand was on her forearm as it rested on the wooden arm of the chair, his fingers clasping tightly about her. 'Not now! You have to leave her alone. She's married! A mother!'

His shock and anger, and her own confusions about the morality of what had happened with Beth, caused her to twist round to face him, to tear her arm free of his hold. 'So what? She made a mistake. She admitted – she still feels the same – we both do.'

'And will she leave her husband? Her baby? Just walk out on them? And what about you! The army? Your duty?'

'I don't know!' They were both struggling to keep their voices low, their words humming with the intensity of their feeling. 'She wouldn't leave Elaine. She wouldn't have to. We've just found each other again. We'll have to wait, work things out. But at least we can see each other! Love each other!'

'You'd break up her marriage, wreck all four lives? Her husband and the baby – and her? And yours? You can't do that, not for . . . for . . .'

his voice faded, and she was choked with her helpless fury, so that she wanted to hurl herself at him, to batter at him with her fists, gouge at his face with her nails. How could he make it all sound so dirty and disgusting and perverted?

The tears came, she couldn't hold them back any longer, they rolled down her cheeks, and that bolt of rage subsided into hopelessness. Why had she come back to see him? Why had she hoped he would understand, when she had known all along how he would react?

He reached forward, pressing even closer, trapping the front of her knees and her feet, pinning her into the chair, while both his hands seized her arms tightly, lifted her upper body forward, pulling her close to him. His mouth covered hers, she felt the pressure of his lips painfully against hers, then the heat of his breath as he whispered against her wet cheek. 'You've never made love properly, have you? Never been with a man. *I'm* not some bloody sexless cold fish. *I* want you, too! You know I do! You know how I feel. I'll show you about making love! If it's sin you want you can have it, now!'

His right hand moved, tore at her jacket, a button popped, and his hand was inside, on her warm body, clawing at a breast, hurting, brutally cupping and clutching at her, sliding down, over her stomach, pressing against the tightness of the cord of her pyjamas, thrusting down, invading, searching out the moist folds of her between her thighs, savage and unyielding. She bucked, arched beneath him, felt amidst the great wave of shock an even more shocking response of arousal, along with her disbelief and a sense of outrage, of revulsion with everything: his hitherto unknown animal brutality, the raw unthinkingness of it and her excitement, and finally the weakness of her desire simply to give up resistance, to absolve her traitorous flesh from any blame.

CHAPTER SIXTEEN

The deed was done! In block capitals of fiery red! Part of Alice's mind screamed with a mocking devilish laughter. So that was what all the fuss was about? Full of sound and fury and signifying next to nothing. But mostly she was still in a state of shock, that it had happened at all, and that it had been so brief and bereft of anything meaningful. It hadn't even hurt anywhere near as much as she had always feared it would. Not that she had ever had any plans to discover it for herself. It hurt more now. She felt sore and tender and bruised now, afterwards, after all the shameful mess of it was done: the buffeting of her shoulders on the coir matting of the rug in front of the kitchen range, the weeping scrabble for her pyjama pants, which were hanging over the edge of the table, the crouched shuffle of her with them clutched to her loins (she was still wearing the jacket even though it gaped open) as she made for the scullery over the freezing stone floor, to the lavatory which was out there. It was only as she fled that she registered the fact that he had put a cushion under her spine when he attacked her.

And it *was* an attack, though she found it almost impossible to believe Davy, *her* Davy, could have done such a thing. But everything was stood on its head now, his frenzied madness, and her own submission to it. She could have screamed, fought with all her clawing strength, kicked him from her, but she had done none of these things. She had scarcely put up any kind of resistance, apart from a weak, squirming, girlish kind of reluctance, an initial stiffening of limbs, a feeble pushing against his shoulders with the heels of her palms, soon yielded. It was an assault in which she had somehow been complicit. She had allowed it to happen.

The grotesque farce of it continued humiliatingly to haunt her. They were even dressed – or undressed – alike. He had on his gaping jacket, she hers, not that she had looked when he had finished battering into her, subsided, slithered and torn himself apart from her, before she had fled in that ridiculous, bare-bummed way. He was tightly wrapped up in his dressing-gown when she eventually came back to the red kitchen glow. She wasn't sure whether she was sorry or glad that he had not slunk away upstairs in her absence, which must have been a lengthy one, certainly a lot longer than the brief *grotesquerie* of their copulation.

She could not see it as anything else. It was so far apart from the loving she had known with her own sex: the splendour she had shared with Beth, and even the passion and fulfilment she had known with Lynne, and with little Mary Douglas. She was bemused by it, the witless, grunting rut of it, and its conclusion. She knew when she came back that Davy had been crying. It was evident in his voice, the catch of his breath, and she felt vaguely sorry for him. But really she was too bemused by what had happened to be sure of any strong emotion beyond a kind of disbelief.

'I'm sorry. Alice, I'm so sorry.' He couldn't look at her as he took a tentative step towards her, but then, bravely she supposed, he did lift his eyes and gaze tragically at her and drag himself close enough to reach for her, to put his hands lightly on her shoulders. She accepted his embrace, moved in to him, even let her head dip briefly against the broad woollen lapel of his dressing-gown.

'Let's just go to bed.' Her voice sounded dead, even to herself. 'Don't say anything now. We'll talk in the morning.'

'But – will you – is it . . . all right?'

Somewhere in the back of her brain, the savage laughter screamed out, and she imagined herself flinging words at him. All right? What do you think? That I'm bleeding, torn apart, the shattered virgin? The innocent victim? The last word echoed in her mind. She felt she was, indeed, somehow a victim, but of what, and how, she did not know. She just knew she could not stay in the same room with him a moment longer. Her bare toes dug into the hardness of the floor with her urge to flee. 'I'm going up. Give me five minutes.'

She shivered, in spite of the blankets and the bottle Reeny had placed in Micky's narrow bed. She began to weep silently, until the pillow was wet, her hair stuck wetly to her temples. She couldn't stop. She lay on her side, with her knees drawn up to her chest, her hands between her thighs, holding herself, feeling the soreness, the tenderness. Only now, with a flash of real fear, did she understand what he had meant when he said, *Will you be all right?*

She almost gave way to the panicky urge to jump up once more, to hurry to the bathroom and behind the locked door bathe herself in water as hot as she could stand it. She cursed herself for her ignorance, and Davy for his manhood. Could he have planted his seed in her? The mocking inner voice screeched at her again. Could? There's no 'could' about it, love. He *did*! Did you, good and proper and it'll serve you right if you're carrying his baby already.

She had cleaned herself as comprehensively as she could, at the coldwwater sink of the scullery, though the thought of preventing conception had not even entered her mind at that point. She thought back over the smutty sniggered and whispered folklore of school and barrack hut. You can't get knocked up over one lousy go! You've got to do it loads of times before you get caught!

And what about Davy? What would he be thinking, right now? Did he think this would mean she would have to marry him now? That he had saved her from her own ungodly perversion by his desperate act? Back in Howbeck, when Beth had left her, and he had asked her to marry him, then departed, too, she had thought about him, about what marriage would be like. She had even, ashamedly, thought about *it*, having sex with him, what that would be like. Her thoughts, her imaginings, had even excited her. But they had been nothing like the howling reality, the emptiness of that buffeting coupling. And that it had taken place with Davy, the only one she had ever tried to picture being with, had turned the world upside down for her. It left nothing for her to cling to, to believe in. Except Beth.

She had no idea how long she had lain in the blackness before she had fallen asleep. That had been five minutes ago, she would have guessed, but the beginnings of a grey day were seeping in when the blackout curtains were drawn aside, and Davy was sitting there on the edge of her bed with a cup of tea. We'll never be able to face each other, she had told herself in the dark night. He'll probably leave early, claiming he had to be at work, and that would be best, for she didn't know how she could face him, either. But now here they were, she was in bed and he was beside her, and she didn't know how she felt, except weary and still with that sensation that what had happened hadn't. It was still dreamlike and utterly implausible.

He was brave, she had to admit that, and very contrite. He bent forward and very gently kissed her tousled hair. 'I'm sorry,' he said again, and that infinitely sad look in his eyes stirred her more deeply than any part of the whole bizarre episode so far. Her own grey eyes filled, she bent and kissed his hand.

'Don't. I could have stopped you. Should have.' She didn't know whether he really believed her. She knew she spoke out of compassion, a desire to make him feel better, and realized then, with something of relief, that the deep affection she had for him was still there in her heart, even if it had taken something of a knock. 'And if you say sorry one more time I'll clock you one!' She managed a smile, and the ghost of the old Alice and their former warm relationship flickered briefly about the dim room.

'But we can't just . . . pretend it never happened.' At least he could look at her again now. 'I didn't want . . . didn't mean for it . . .' he shrugged hopelessly. 'But it did,' he went on flatly. 'Please hear me out.' He drew a deep, shuddering breath. He waited, while she quickly drank off the remainder of the cooling tea and gave him the cup, which he placed on the floor. He took her silence for consent, which it was. She even let him take her hand, even though it remained unresponsive in his grip.

'I did a terrible thing—' He saw her look, felt the resistance and hastened on. 'I know it, can't explain it, even to myself.' He thought of Reeny Lumley, of all the boiling frustration of his passion, his sexual urgings for her, and thrust them away from his consciousness. 'But it doesn't alter the way I feel about you, the way I have since Howbeck.' How *did* he feel? his spinning mind had time to prod him before he plunged desperately on. 'I love you. Please believe that, in spite . . . even after what I've done. I don't suppose . . . I *know* you don't feel the same for me. You couldn't right now, after . . . I couldn't ask you to. But I'd still like . . . I'm asking you again, in spite of everything, to marry me. I'm not asking you to change, or be different in any way. I'd never ask you to do anything . . .' his voice faltered, but his eyes clung to hers, he didn't look away. 'If you didn't know before, you certainly do now, how far from good *I* can be. But we're still friends, aren't we? In spite of that . . . we can still care for each other. Take care of each other. I swear I'll never again ask you – make you do anything you don't want to do.'

She moved, wriggled up in the creaking bed, put her hand around his shoulders and her face against his. 'You're a good man, Davy. I know that about you. I'm even glad that if it had to happen, it had to happen with you.' She was glad that she could hide her face in his shoulder while she spoke. 'I *do* love you, as my best friend, and I always will. But it wouldn't be right to marry. You know it as well as I do. I love Beth. She's the one I want to share my life with, like that. In that way. And I know that shocks you. I understand that. It shocks everybody – it would if they knew. But that's how I am. I can't tell anybody else, but at least I can be honest with you, Davy. Nobody else.'

She felt him stir, he moved his head back a little, to look at her, and now she found she was able to meet and hold his gaze. 'But what about. . . ? What we did, what if it isn't all right? If I've made you . . .'

'I don't think it'll happen,' she said, with more confidence than she felt. She clung to him more tightly again, to stop him from going on, and put her lips close to his ear. 'It's one of those complicated women's things. To do with timing and all that.'

He made an indeterminate sort of grunt, and she felt a sudden urge to smile, thinking about those female barrack-room chats that would probably cause the hardiest male to blush like a beetroot at their frankness. Her next period was due within a week, so she could only hope those founts of worldly, profane wisdom were right. She extricated herself from the loose embrace, and winced as she did so. Again came that swift sense of disbelief at what had happened to her only a few hours ago. The unreality of it helped her now to move on. This was Davy, *her* Davy, sitting on the edge of the bed, so gentle, and looking thoroughly wretched. They must dismiss from their minds what their bodies had done in that plunging madness.

'What time is it? I'll have to be making a move. I have to get down south before the morning. It might be tricky getting back to London, with it being a Saturday.'

The dismay was plain on his face, to which the colour mounted, as he said, 'Oh! Do you *have* to? I mean – I'd like to spend more time with you. We need to talk.'

'I have to be back,' she lied. '0-eight-thirty tomorrow. You don't want me put on a charge, do you? Not when I've just been made up to staff-sergeant!' She gave a bright grin, and felt a lurch of sadness at the stricken look he returned. 'Look! What we really need is some time, to get over what's happened. I'll write. As soon as I get back. It might be easier to put down all we want to say on paper.' She smiled. 'As long as you don't tick me off for my spelling!' His face crumpled at her brave effort at humour, and she saw that he was close to tears again. 'Come on! Out you go! I want to get dressed.' She swung her feet vigorously out from under the covers, and he fled. When he'd gone, she gave a stifled moan, and she moved much more gingerly as she went to gather her washbag and towel and make for the bathroom across the little landing.

'We've been here before.' He glanced about him at the platform and the sooty vault of the station curving away towards the brighter daylight along the glistening tracks. She was leaning out of the opened window. He noticed again the burnished effect of her curls, and the brownness of her face. He *did* love her, and he *did* want to marry her, he assured himself, weighed down by a tremendous feeling of guilt, made worse by his uncertainty about his own assertion. He didn't know anything any more, not even about himself. Except the present restirring of his body and his sudden fierce longing to be wrapped up in a warm bed with her. *Nothing else would matter in the world today, We would go on loving in the same old way.* The words of the song heard so much on the wireless these days echoed in his tired brain, the strong bass voices of men singing in unison. Their simplicity no longer seemed tawdrily sentimental, but carried a genuine ache of longing, and he swallowed hard.

She was nodding, remembering their last goodbye in these very circumstances. Her eyes shone, she was smiling bravely, but he knew that the shine was due to the tears filling them, and he wished they could both just hold each other tightly and weep for their lost . . . innocence? Neither of them could claim that quality for themselves, but what they had, in the old days, had been good, and free from sin. And he had spoilt all that, last night, and he hardly knew why . . . or didn't want to face that unpalatable truth.

The whistles shrilled, and doors slammed. She was thinking: she felt as though she'd spent half her life on trains. 'I'll write, I promise!' she called clearly, praying that she would hold back the tears until the train had moved off. 'Soon as I get back. We'll fix up properly – to meet.

When I can get some leave.'

He moved closer, seized her hand urgently, squeezing it painfully. 'I meant what I said. Please think about it. Marrying me. I want – so much . . . I wouldn't . . . I don't want to change things – you don't have to change, for me . . .' His broken words ran down, and she couldn't bear his suffering a second more. She nodded, stabbed her face at him, her mouth open, they kissed clumsily as the loud reverberating skids of the great wheels on the rails thundered, and the train took her away from his dwindling figure, still and stricken, through the blur of her tears.

Outside the station, he waited to cross the busy roadway, over to the blackened ramparts of the medieval city walls. He turned to his left and followed them down towards the river, seeing ahead of him the rawness of the repairs carried out on the guildhall, and further over to his right the jagged ruins of St Martin's. It was nearly two years since the night of the air raid, in which he and Alice had been caught as they came out of the picture house. He remembered the feel of her body, trembling as he pressed himself over her, lying in the lee of the churchyard wall of Holy Trinity, the roar of engines and the clatter of machinegun fire. He had loved her then all right. He had been ready to die for her.

It was too late to get a drink now. The pubs would be chucking them out for the three-and-a-half-hour spell before the evening session began. The city centre would be lively again tonight. Betty's, alias The Dive, and the other popular watering holes, would be packed with the wild Air Force lads, the bomber crews letting their hair down, shooting their tall yarns, probably Canadians and Yanks, Poles and Britishers the best of beery buddies until closing time, or unless the flocking girls weren't enough to go round. Then fists and glasses and even boots would fly. Who needs a world war to spill blood? He felt a wave of sympathy for the poor beat bobbies on tonight. He'd done some of it himself in the past.

He quickened his pace, angry at the abundance and variety of the uniforms on the crowded pavements, despite the late January gloom, most of them with at least one girl hanging on their arm. They all looked happy enough, despite the dangers of the time. Perhaps that was why. Eat, drink, and be merry – some of these girls looked as though they certainly knew how to enjoy themselves and pleasure their partners, too. And who the hell was he to condemn them? The arch-hypocrite, crying out at the sinners, when he had practically raped Alice last night and lusted after another, a married woman, morning, noon, *and* night?

He used the walk through the city to exorcise his demons and exercise his body. He needed to keep himself fit, and he had spent the past week sitting in various drinking dens, supping beer. By the time he reached Dubry Street once more he was sweating inside his winter clothing and dusk was already falling. It was a time he used to love as a kid, this winter darkness seeping in, making haloes round the gas lamps, seeing the lighted, curtained windows, and anticipating the sealed-in warmth of his own glowing hearth, and the love waiting to enfold him within its safety and its sureness.

Reeny was wearing one of her smart costume skirts and a pretty dove-grey jumper. She had on a pair of her precious fine, dark stockings and high-heeled shoes. Her dark hair was combed and softly waved, and she was wearing make-up. He could smell her fragrance. 'You look nice,' he said, and saw her face pink a little.

'She get off all right? I wasn't sure whether you were coming back or not. I thought you might be staying in town. Meeting someone.'

'Naw.' He shook his head, sat on one of the hard chairs at the table, staring into the fire.

'Listen. Dick should be in soon. We're going down to the Institute. Why don't you come? I can get Mildred Raine to come round to sit with Micky.' She paused. 'You look down in the dumps. Missing her already?' She tried to make her voice light. 'Well, I'm sure you'll be seeing her again soon, now that she's stationed back in England. She'll be up here every chance she gets.'

There was something in her tone, almost a kind of disapproval. Did she suspect something, something of what he had done last night? His own wretchedness made his answer carry an edge of sharpness. 'I doubt it. It wouldn't make any difference, anyway. I've told you. There's nothing on between us. Nothing like that at all.' He stared at her, almost groaned as he looked at her pretty feet, and thought of what he had been doing on that spot where she was standing, less than twenty-four hours ago.

CHAPTER SEVENTEEN

It was Arty Clark who answered to Alice's ring. 'Sorry to turn up like a bad penny again, so soon. I hope you don't mind . . .'

'Oh, hello! It's you! No, of course not, come in! It's freezing again out there.'

Despite the fact that she could not see his face in the blackout, she was perfectly aware of the dismay in that instant of hesitation before his gushing answer. In the dimness of the bare hallway his eyes darted and his polite smile seemed as fixed and as false as her own, even though, to her surprise, he ducked his face quickly under the peak of her cap to place a fleeting kiss on her cold cheek. By which time there was a highpitched cry of wild delight, followed by the bawl of an enraged infant as Elaine was thrust back into her pram, which served as cradle, and then Alice was treated to an embrace very different, much more unrestrained, as Elsbeth threw herself into her arms and clung to her with smothering tightness. Alice was both thrilled and embarrassed at the display, very conscious of the husband, fussing with her bags beside them as they hugged. Alice found herself responding physically to the feel of Beth's waist, its soft, desirable new plumpness, vividly recapturing the memory of its spareness, the prominence of the rib cage, in their former happy days at Howbeck.

Beth clearly didn't want to let her go, and Alice, recalled to a sense of propriety and Arty's proximity, had to resist the urge to reach up and detach the wrists locked at the back of her neck. When at last they did release her it was only to capture her right arm and link it firmly in order to lead her into the living-room into which Arty had preceded them. He gathered up his crimson-faced, noisily indignant daughter, holding her with familiar ease over his shoulder and patting her into

135

snuffly quietude. Alice again poured out profuse apologies for once more descending without warning, which were quashed by Beth's enthusiastic counterpoint. 'Don't be so *daft*!'

('Daft', Al noted rapturously, not 'silly'. Her girl was even speaking their own language again, which Al had insisted on as often as she could in their time together.)

'It's the nicest surprise we could have had. Isn't it, Arty?' There was a hint of challenge in her question to him, like a mother's warning to her child to remember its manners.

'Yes, absolutely! First class!' His effusiveness was charming. 'You're staying the night, of course?'

He made his question sound rhetorical. Through the undercurrent of embarrassment she could not help, Alice felt sympathy for him. At 7.30 at night, and with that accoutrement of baggage she had dragged with her, it was hardly likely she would be merely popping in for a quick chat and cuppa. But she must make the effort, to match his. 'Well, if that's all right,' she began tentatively. Any doubt was knocked on the head, as she knew it would be, by Beth's ringing affirmation.

'We've got a camp-bed. We dug it out after last weekend. It's already rigged up in the boxroom. Arty won't mind sleeping on it, will you, sweetheart? You've got to be out early, anyway. Crack of dawn job, isn't it?'

He laughed bravely. 'That's right. No rest for the wicked, not even on the sabbath. Car's coming at seven.'

'No! Look!' Alice's protest was genuine, she felt perturbed and anxious, quite convinced of his awareness of the significance of the girls sharing a bed. 'I can't put you out of your bed tonight! I wouldn't dream of it! I'll be fine in the spare room. I'm used to—'

'Don't be silly, Al!'

Beth's tone was shrill, an edge to it. Back to 'silly', are we? Alice observed. Speaking hubby's language now, eh?

Beth was going on. 'You're our guest. Arty's used to roughing it, too. Besides, he has to be up so early tomorrow. It'll give him a chance to get some undisturbed sleep. Elaine still doesn't always go through the night, does she, darling?'

'That's true.' He smiled, that grin manfully plastered across his youthful face. 'Really, I'll be fine. And I know how Elsbeth loves chatting to you. Old times and all that!' He was quite good-looking, in that sensitive way. Perhaps a bit too pretty for a bloke, Alice thought. She was a little ashamed at her acknowledgement of a kind of weakness in him, probably a result of his background, his class. But then she *and* Beth should be glad of it. She could feel herself blushing a little at her selfishness, and her determination to ignore the moral implications of what she had done – and was about to do again, even if it meant waiting for his early-morning departure before they could enjoy in full their rediscovered love for one another.

With hindsight, when Alice lay blearily abed next day, after Arty had left, and she watched Beth's splendid advance on her after settling a replete Elaine into her pram in the adjacent living-room, she had to admit that it had been worth waiting until they were truly alone except for the blissfully ignorantly slumbering baby before satisfying their need to the 'full'. But she understood *full* well the meaning of the new word Beth taught her, which was 'surfeit', and even grudgingly acknowledged the power of the old-bard himself, Willy Shakespeare, and his verse: 'My salad days, when I was green in judgement,' Beth quoted, when talking of their early days at Howe Manor, and how much more forthright her outlook was now. She proved it, too, by the eagerness she brought and gave to their loving. 'And damned be him that first cries, "Hold, enough!" ' she added, mixing her plays and her metaphors, but Al got the picture.

It was Beth's new determination to give as well as receive that made her notice the small bruises on Alice's upper arms, two small, dark discs, a matching pair on each of her biceps, like thumbprints, which, indeed, they were; and other, fainter smudges, but equally symmetrical, on her upper thighs. Those, and a certain instinctive, flinching tenderness from her lover, made Beth stop suddenly, kneeling very tense and still, over her. 'What's this?' She touched and pointed. Her face, already flushed, gazed at Alice, her lips parted, already assuming a wounded look.

For just a fleeting second, Alice's mind fluttered about in panic and a lie came readily to her. Why, that's you, you daft sod! That's from *last* Saturday night. A joke even spun round in her disordered thoughts: *I don't know what's happened to my sweet little gentle Beth, her old never-say-boo-to-a-goose!* But she didn't voice her thought, or make her excuses. Instead, she found herself confessing, in a low, husky murmur, all that had happened to her at Dubry Street. It startled her to recall that it had been scarcely more than twenty-four hours ago, for, as she told her low-voiced, sorry tale, it felt as though she were describing something already long past and dimmed by time.

But its effect on her listener was profound enough. 'He forced you?' Elsbeth whispered, in revulsion, and Alice felt an even stronger urge to assent, to reach out and hide in all the compassion and sympathy she saw in the horrified gaze. After all, it would only be a half-lie, wouldn't it? But no. Some part of her, she did not understand it herself, had been a collaborator in the act.

'Not really,' she answered. 'I could have stopped him.' And she winced inwardly at the stricken look she saw on Beth's face.

'Oh, Al!'

The pain was evident, the wound of it, in Beth's voice and her look, the tears forming in those wonderful eyes, which were reproach enough for Al to feel wretched, and guilty, as though she had indeed somehow betrayed Beth and their love for each other. Perhaps she had. Why *hadn't* she fought against him, thrown him off with the strength she could so easily have mustered against his assault? Again, that stab of guilt at the very word she had chosen to describe the episode. But Beth was reaching for her again, murmuring contrite and loving phrases, offering soothing kisses, and closing the wonderful curtains of their love securely about them, to shut out all the rest of that world out there that had no part in their union.

Alice might have been comforted if she had known how close Beth's thoughts were to her predicament, for the golden-haired girl was reflecting on her own dilemma and the sacrificial discomfort she had undergone silently, possibly within an hour or two of Alice's initiation, while she lay and endured in this very bed her husband's fevered, fervent and mercifully rare coition.

If anyone had a right to feel aggrieved with the world it was himself. It was a thought and a feeling which rarely left the troubled mind of hill farmer, Bob Symmonds, these days. It was enough almost to make him wish he was back in the prison at Leeds, where the dreary harshness of each virtually identical day made it possible to slip through your life in an unthinking daze of repetition. Once they'd got used to him they left him alone, except for occasional outbursts of sadistic violence, to shuffle about on his crippled leg, feeding him, locking him up at night, watching while he performed his menial tasks, but leaving him shut up inside himself to get on with things. They thought he was half-daft, and he was sometimes surprised to find himself mumbling away to himself, but nobody took any notice of him really, and time slipped by without his noticing it.

Since he'd come out, it was all terribly different. The beating those bastards round here had given him before the police had picked him up had permanently disabled him. His left knee was smashed so badly it had never mended. He still couldn't straighten his leg, so he walked with a dipping limp. It made him drop his left shoulder, lurch along like some effin' humpback. The doctors had been on at him to use a stick, or even a crutch, but only when it came near the time for his release. Before that they'd let him hobble round the cellblock and the prison yard and gardens without anything, so sod them! He'd manage without and to hell with what people thought when they saw him lurching along!

People! That's what really got to him now. Banged up inside, he'd been able to keep himself to himself, even if he was never actually alone day or night. Nobody had bothered with him, except for the odd sadistic bastard, who'd soon tired of tormenting him when they saw how little response they got. Head down, say nowt, and take it all. That's how he'd got by, and it had worked. But it was different back here. He made people uncomfortable. Pricked their conscience, likely, as everyone knew damned well who had beaten him half to death and trussed him up like a fowl at the side of the road for the cops to find. He couldn't even set foot in the Oddfellows now, without halting all conversation and drawing curses down on his head, until in the end that slack tart, Vera Rhodes, had actually said to him, 'We don't want your kind in here!' The cheek of it! When he'd been part of the set-up that had helped to keep her doing so well with the booze and all the other stuff they had supplied when he was partners with the Big Swede.

If he was to feel bitter about anyone, it should be Gus Rielke, he supposed. The cops had mocked him, told him it was the Big Swede who had done the dirty on him, left him to take the blame and made sure he got away himself. There might be something in it. But you couldn't expect the Big Swede to stand by and get himself caught as well. He'd seen his chance to get away and taken it. There was probably nothing he could have done to save his partner anyway, thanks to that jumped-up conchy copper's nark and that curly-headed bitch of his! She'd had it in for him and his family all along, that one, her and her snooty friends at the school.

Besides, there were others, much closer to home and still about, to feel aggrieved over; his own kith and kin! He was no bloody use as far as the farming went, with this gammy leg, but even if he hadn't been lamed they'd have kept him out. His own flesh and blood had as good as stolen it from under him, running the place like it was theirs, which it was now, he'd discovered. Tenancy made over to his missus by Mr high-and-bloody-mighty Barr, the Denby estates agent, and run by his two oldest lads, neither of them hardly out of britches and yet lording it over him, making him feel as though he was one of the old collies, past its working days and sidling in to steal a place on the edge of the hearth and grovel for the few scraps of food tossed its way.

But it was the treachery of Edie, his wife, which cut deepest. It choked him to think about it, thickened his blood until he could hardly breathe for his sense of injustice and shame. Five kids he'd given her, though now even that was something she blamed him for rather than counting it a blessing. And the youngest, Peggy, was still just a toddler – he'd bought Edie a spanking new pram when Peggy was a babby, cost him a mint of money, but he hadn't begrudged her, even if she *had* nagged him day and night for it. He'd been making good money then all right, working with the Big Swede and them townsfellers. And a lot of it he'd handed over to his wife, to keep in the sock under the mattress, for all them rainy days that might lie ahead. Not all of it, of course. He'd made a bit more than he'd let on, but he was the one taking the risks; he deserved a few jars and a bet or two for his pains. And by God he'd paid for it! He'd had the rainy days all right, and all the while his missus had been making hay in her sunshine while he'd been banged up inside. No sign of the wad of money he'd left her, but the house full of brand-new things and her with new clothes on her back and a new personality to match. She was someone he didn't recognize any more, a bitch with a tongue like a razor who treat him like he was shit from the yard stuck on her new shoe and wouldn't let him anywhere near her. Acting like her word was law, and them two treacherous whelps of theirs ready to back her up with their fists if he tried to stand up for what was his by rights.

That was the whole trouble. He couldn't stand up any more, not for himself nor anybody else. He was use to neither man nor beast, and the fact was driven home to him every day. It festered inside him, like a smouldering fire that would never go out. If only he could get in touch with Gus again, or any of them fellers they'd worked with! Surely they'd find something for him to do, lookout or summat, anything to get him out of this hell-hole he was stuck in!

He made his slow, brooding way down through the woods alongside Barker's field and on to the lane that led into the village past the long brick wall of Howe Manor. Most of the snow had gone now, except for a few drifts on the upper north-facing slopes. There was nothing but the odd remnant of the blackened shovelled piles where it had been cleared to mark paths and to free the lane itself, full of puddles now, reflecting the dull metal-grey of the louring sky. It was still bitter cold, though. He thought of the warm inglenook in the Oddfellows, and how he would love to be sitting there, tucked out of the way, to listen to the crack and to join in – something, he acknowledged painfully, he had never done, even in the old days. Resentment flared again. He'd a damned good mind to walk in there, bold as brass and sit himself down – except that it was shut of course at this time of afternoon, and wouldn't open again until six, when darkness had long fallen and the place would be even cosier, with lights on and curtains drawn against the cold night.

He heard very faintly on the grey air the high, thin cries of young voices, the shrill of a whistle, and a wavering cheer. Them posh girls from the school at t' Big 'Ouse. He'd seen them, talking down their noses, showing their long, black-stockinged legs and them navy bloomers under the tiny black gymslips. Brazen hussies! Any ordinary lass showing what she'd got under her skirt like that would be given a bloody good hiding for being a tart. But not them nobs, oh no!

He had a sudden wild desire to shin up the wall, to take a peep over. See if he could see them running about in the little hockey skirts, the long-legged sluts! His lecherous imagination warmed him, sent him groping in his old overcoat pocket for the half-bottle he had there. He took a long pull of whisky, savouring the bite and burn of it in his throat, down into his gut, even though it made his eyes water and scalded down through his chest. He couldn't climb that ruddy great wall anyway, not even if he had two good legs. Sod them all!

Now that the bottle was out, he found himself reluctant to put it back in the deep pocket, and he took another long pull instead. No point in hoarding it like a miser. There was only a few inches left, might as well enjoy it, make himself feel better about things instead of sipping away like a tight-arse. Get it down, lad. Who cares if anybody sees you! He took a long pull, doubled up, coughing, and spat at his feet, then took another deep draught, and felt his head respond, and he grunted, gave a wheezing little chuckle, as much of defiance as anything.

He passed over the stone bridge, soothed by the angry rush of water from the beck below, the white swirls of it. With a bit of luck it might flood old Ma Lloyd's cellar, miserable old cow. Another one who never had a good word to say, even when he was spending money in her shop. He found his suddenly unsteady steps staggering between her shop and the garage, up the slippy, muddy little path that came out near the station lane. As he did so he heard the pant and puff of a locomotive, the teatime train from Whitby. He was surprised at the sudden liveliness when it hissed and farted to a cloudy halt, doors rattling, voices crying out. Shrill again, full of uncaring youth. Kids, filling the platform; more schoolkids, back from Whitby. They streamed out in bunches, through the wide-open gateway, some turning in his direction. A group approached, laughing. Ribboned hats, long legs, black stockings again.

' 'Bye, see you in the morning!' Then he saw her, as she broke away, headed straight for him and the muddy path back down to the bridge, on her way home, and he recognized her at once, the leggy, cocky little bitch, young sister of the bitch and her young feller who had spied on him and Gus, who had been responsible for bringing it all to an end, all the good times, and leaving him crippled and with a long stretch of gaol, and the present no-hope he had come out to.

CHAPTER EIGHTEEN

Doreen's first registered thought was of distaste rather than alarm when she saw the bent figure at the edge of the path. Some old tramp, it looked like, with that shabby, loose overcoat and filthy boots. Not that you saw many such figures these days. She edged past him, turning her head away from the unsavoury odour, not quite holding the skirts of her navy school mac away, but indicating plainly by her fastidious withdrawal her desire to put as much distance as possible between them. She had no idea who he was, and probably would still have failed to recognize him if she had glanced at the face, covered with a week's growth of beard, beneath the ragged cap. It was still not quite dark, she was close to the clean comfort of home, and in these familiar surroundings it did not occur to her to be afraid.

His attack came with complete surprise, perhaps almost as much for him as for her, as something snapped, an explosion like a light in his brain. Doreen felt herself swept up, lifted with ease and carried aside from the path, through the black wet branches of bushes and long soaking tufts of grass. They cushioned the violence with which she was slammed down on the steep slope above the rushing stream, whose roar would drown any muffled squeal which might escape through the clamping, stinking roughness of the calloused hand sealing her mouth and chin. In any case, the breath was knocked from her body by the brutal weight of her attacker thrust down upon her. She arched her neck, felt the wetness of the grass catching at her hair, crushing the brim of her hat into her neck. She fought to breathe, rather than consciously striving to escape, against the smothering hand, her nostrils dilating, her eyes wild with shock. There was a soft whimper in her throat. A great wave of whisky-drenched breath engulfed her, along with the horror of his scratchy beard and slobbering wet lips moving over her cheek. She felt them move on her skin when he whispered a string of obscenities at her, sullying her with his touch, and with the words themselves, shocking words, which she knew from another early life.

The hand that was not clamped over her jaw scrabbled and she felt it sliding under her clothes, ripping at them, up her leg, clawing at her stocking, her underclothes, scratching at her sensitive skin. She knew that he was going to rape her, at the same instant that she realized who he was and the import of his obscenely hissed litany in her ear. She felt bile in her throat, was afraid she might choke on her own vomit. She let herself go limp, waited until she felt that hand below reach up into her hidden softness, buried under her clothing, and then she gave a mighty heave, thrusting up her lean body against him, drawing up her knees, writhing like a snake. Her suddenness and force dislodged him sufficiently to allow her to squirm from under him. She felt his hand dragging across her, trapped within her clothing, and she gave another great heave. She tried to scream. Nothing came except a gasping sob, but she was free, her knees were drawn up and she flung out her feet and caught him in the chest. He slid down the slope, cursing, so that she was able to twist away and scrabble further up, clawing at the tufts of grass. She felt the claws of his hands, both of them now, at her left leg, digging in, trying to drag her back, and she felt the thick woollen stocking slipping with his hands down her limb. Still sobbing softly, she turned on her back again, facing him, saw his dark bearded face in the dimness and kicked out with her right foot, smashing the heel of her stout school shoe squarely into his jaw, and magically he was gone, his hands free of her as he hurtled backwards with a snapping of undergrowth and a last foul curse, strangely muted in the last of the daylight.

Her heels dug into the slipperiness of the grass, she slithered on her bottom and her elbows, further still up the bank. She was shivering violently, her teeth chattering, her weeping almost like hysterical laughter, and she did, even in her fright, experience a rush of triumph. Take that, you dirty old bugger! But she had to get to her feet, before he came back at her, and her sobs turned to frustration at her own clumsiness. She rolled on to hands and knees, saw the gaping hole, the mud and blood of her flesh through her stocking, found it impossible to stand upright, to get back on the path and flee.

144

Then she realized he wasn't coming after her, that he had slid all the way down to the edge of the beck; she could see his sprawled, twisted shape, feet splayed grotesquely, head hanging down to the torrent as though he were drinking. She stared, kept her eyes on him, then she did manage to scream as her heels went from under her on the wet, flattened patch of grass and she slipped, too, in a plunge that almost brought her right back into his lap once more.

She saw his head was turned at an unnatural angle. His cap had slipped comically askew, its ragged peak sticking up in the air, above his left ear, and the other side of his face was covered with blood. She thought he was dead, but then that sickeningly lolling head moved, and his eyes, too. They flickered, opened a little, and looked at her. His jaw dropped, she saw his badly discoloured teeth and the black gaps. He made a gargling sound. His body shivered very slightly, then moved again. That grotesque head slid further, the face disappearing, and the head and the shoulders went under the water, its whiteness flowing over them. She thought he would plunge into the river, be swept away under the bridge only a few yards away, but he stuck there, above the stream. She could see his muddy boot, and a ridiculously thin ankle in a black sock, and a hint of pale flesh in the gap between it and his muddy trousers.

'You silly stupid *dirty* old man!' she whimpered aloud through her tears. She had a hard time climbing back up the bank, reaching the path. She was crying quietly and muttering all the while as she searched the area where they had fallen and rolled together, gathering up her school bag, bending and peering in the almost-darkness to make sure there was nothing else left of hers.

Why are you doing this? she asked herself as she searched, but at least not aloud now. He attacked you, he wanted to *do* you! She was shocked that she had reverted to the crude vocabulary of her other, earlier self and life, which she had sworn she was done with for ever. There were worse words for it, that even then, in those former years, only the most wicked and foul-mouthed girls would use, certainly not the old Doreen. But then there were nothing *but* low, filthy words for what he had tried to do to her, the stinking beast! He'd have a terrible, sore head in the morning, and serve him right.

She started to cry again then, moaning and murmuring, 'It's not my fault!' She was covered in mud. All the back of her mackintosh was smeared with it, and her legs. One stocking hung down below her skirt. Her pale knee, soiled with mud and drying blood, showed through the gaping hole. Her skirt was dirtied, too, and was dragged round, the buttons of the fastening gaping. 'Serve him right!' She said it out loud, through her shivering tears, and walked stiffly over the bridge, and past the pub, with not a soul in sight. She started to run, painfully. She knew in her heart she was lying when she thought of Bob Symmonds being steeped in remorse on the morrow.

'It's a difficult age for girls,' Dr Ryder said diplomatically, when he came downstairs after leaving Doreen sniffling quietly and sitting up in bed looking like an illustration for *Orphans of the Storm*, with those great big tragic heroine's eyes of hers in that delicate pale face. 'Give her another dose of the mixture, with a glass of warm milk before she settles down for the night. It should help her sleep. She'll probably be a bit drowsy this evening. She's a bit calmer already, I think.' He took the cup of tea Miss Ramsay gave him. 'Thank you. It was just a fall, you say? Nothing else?'

Miss Ramsay sat on the edge of her chair. The anxiety showed in the set of the fleshy face, the tension in her stance and her voice. 'She came in in floods of tears. I thought something dreadful had happened. She was absolutely covered in mud, her stockings all torn. But that's all she said. She'd just said goodbye to her chums. She was running to get home, she said, because she thought it was going to rain again. She said she tripped and fell just as she came over the bridge. But I was so alarmed. She was almost hysterical, and shaking like a leaf. I got her undressed and into a hot bath. I was afraid she might have broken something, but really all there was were those cuts and bruises. I was so worried – she seemed so distressed. I hope you don't think I've wasted your time calling you out, Dr Ryder. But really, I was very concerned.'

'No, no!' he assured her. 'Better to be safe than sorry. She certainly does seem upset over something. Like I said, girls can be very temperamental at this age. It's difficult.'

He noted the slight rise of colour in Miss Ramsay's face, the hurried way in which she reached for her cup to hide behind the mechanics of sipping her tea, and he knew she understood. He backed away from pursuing the matter, though he wondered just how skilfully a sixty-year-old spinster would prepare a child for the onset of puberty and deal with the problems of adolescence that would follow. 'Has she been moody, or distressed about anything in particular, lately?' he asked, partly as a sop to his conscience. 'She hasn't had a falling out, a quarrel with one of her chums?' Did genteel little girls resort to physical violence? he speculated. The skinned knee and bruises on her leg could well have been caused by a violent shove, and Doreen was definitely agitated far more than you would expect from someone who had slipped over in a puddle. But maybe she was just one of those emotionally charged youngsters. Drama queen, or at least princess, maybe. He was aware of her background, which had been very different from the privileged lifestyle of Northend Cottage when she had first come to Howbeck as an evacuee from Margrove. He was also well aware of the malicious gossip at how the comfortably off spinster had virtually bought the rights to assume parentage over Doreen. Perhaps the poor child was emotionally disturbed about being taken away from her family and recreated as a middle-class schoolgirl in such an alien environment.

'I'm sure she'll be fine after a good night's sleep,' he said, as Miss Ramsay showed him out into the blackness. 'There's a very small dose of sedative in the mixture. Should ensure she calms down. In fact, it seems to have started working already. But don't hesitate to give me a ring if you're concerned for her.'

'Goodnight. Thank you so much, Dr Ryder.'

Elizabeth Ramsay went straight upstairs after she had shut the door on the doctor. Doreen was lying back on her pillows. There were dark smudges under those great eyes, which were still brilliant with threatening tears. She really was such a beautiful child! Elizabeth thought, and felt her own eyes dampen with love. She sat on the edge of the bed, and took hold of the thin hand. How thankful she was to God for sending her this gift to cherish, for such this child was, she was convinced. She thanked Him in her prayers each night.

She wondered if Doreen really knew how much love her benefactor felt for her. It was true the girl was affectionate and grateful, and certainly, thank the Lord, had no regrets or qualms about being taken in by her. Just sometimes, Elizabeth felt the slightest bit uncomfortable at the mercenary quality of the way she had acquired her guardianship over Doreen, from those dreadful parents of hers: that dreadful, grasping man with his animal-like beady look, his foxy cunning, and that vacant, half-simple shadow of a wife. Small wonder that Doreen was so reluctant even to return there for a visit. It was only because of Elizabeth's Christian charity that she continued to allow her girl to keep up the link. And Doreen had certainly repaid all the love and attention Elizabeth had lavished on her and would gladly continue to do until the end of her life – and beyond, for she had already made provision to ensure that her girl would be well provided for. But did the child truly understand the measure of Elizabeth's feeling for her, the depth of it?

There were still some in the village who regarded Elizabeth Ramsay as an incomer, even after thirty years. She had come to Howbeck as a personable and well-set-up thirty-year-old single lady within weeks of the outbreak of the Great War. Both by breeding and by nature she gave little of herself away. She was not outgoing, and she had found in the dales village the sequestered peace she had long sought. No doubt there had been plenty of speculative gossip as to why such a handsome and comfortably off spinster had settled herself in a place like Howbeck, but she had not fed that gossip. Nor had she shown herself eager to take any precedence or even part in village and district activities and had thus slowly, over time, been absorbed into the fabric of village life and its hierarchy.

Her perfectly polite reticence did not encourage any attempt at getting close. They knew her father was widowed, that he lived somewhere near Pickering, and that he visited once in a blue moon and never stayed more than two or three days. It was known, too, that there was a brother, Gordon, a year or two younger than herself, who lived down south somewhere, and came with his family to her, and that she went to him for longer periods, in the summer, or at Christmas. But as the years had passed they had come to know little more of her than when she had first arrived. They had simply got used to her.

As the years of the war progressed, even a village such as Howbeck was affected. There were eight names to be carved on the roll of honour in the churchyard after the Armistice, but in towns up and down the country the names were inscribed in hundreds and in thousands, and added up to stunning millions: death on an incomprehensible scale. Elizabeth had to struggle hard to repudiate a sense of bitter satisfaction when she saw the growing numbers of widows' weeds, the black armbands, and the black drapes of mourning in the windows throughout the conflict. She found it hard to stomach these public

displays of grief, and the welling tide of corporate sorrow which culmi-
nated in the grand ceremony of the unveiling of the new Cenotaph in
Whitehall and the consecration of the Tomb of the Unknown Soldier
at Westminster.

For she knew just how private and painful such loss should be. Her
most closely guarded secret had been that, at the age of only eighteen
years, in her youthful bloom if not downright beauty, she had lost the
love of her life, in an earlier and already little-regarded conflict, the
South African War. Arthur Glethyn had been twenty-two, a subaltern
in a county regiment, from a minor titled family. She had met the young
officer at one of the first balls she had attended. Metaphorically swept
off her feet, the heady, stolen embraces they had shared became the
only things she felt really mattered to her. She was deeply shocked at
the staggering response of her body and its secret longings in the
courtship, for that was what their relationship had become. Their feelings for each other had been made known to their families. A formal
engagement was talked of, and agreed, between their parents, but
Arthur's father had persuaded him to wait until his return from active
service overseas. The century had just turned, and the second Boer War
had begun. But British supremacy had been established, and his spell
of duty in South Africa would amount to nothing more than garrison
service. 'And Elizabeth will have celebrated her eighteenth birthday
when you come on leave. Better all round if we announce the engagement then.'

Arthur acquiesced. Not many people argued with Sir Roderick. The
nearly eighteen-year-old was disappointed, but all the older and wiser
heads agreed, and she stifled her dismay and made the most of the last
fleeting days before his embarkation for the dark continent. She was
frightened anew at the depth of passion she felt for Arthur during their
final hours together, and the abandon of their kisses, his arms around
her. And she was unprepared for the desolation which swept over her at
his departure. 'You must pull yourself together, Elizabeth,' her father
told her, his sternness kindly meant, and she made a great effort to do
so.

Arthur's leave did not come as quickly as they had hoped. 1900, and
her eighteenth birthday, passed. They exchanged long and loving
letters, fit only for their eyes, and Elizabeth kept all of Arthur's tied in
ribboned bundles hidden in the back of her cabinet. The war had taken

a new turn. No more pitched battles and outright victories. The new commander, Kitchener, found the vastness of the country impossible to police, and the enemy fought a guerrilla war, with mobile commando units striking at communication lines and isolated garrisons. It was on one such raid, near Colenso, that Lieutenant Arthur Glethyn and a large number of his detachment were cut off and shot down. Arthur was fatally wounded, survived no more than a few hours after the engagement. His commanding officer, and the staff, paid glowing tribute to his bravery and sacrifice, and eighteen-year-old Elizabeth Ramsay's life was blighted for ever.

She never loved again, not in those all-encompassing terms. She seemed strong enough, withdrew from family, from friends, from the company of the young. She saved her love for creatures, like the succession of small animals, the terriers she became vehemently attached to. And much, much later on, at the time when most folk would have been astounded to learn that Miss Ramsay had ever in her somewhat reclusive and proper life suffered 'a broken heart', for the large eyed, grubby little waif she saw standing so forlornly and so exquisitely out of place, in the village hall on that autumn morning more than three years ago.

She gazed at that face now, comforted by the dawning beauty, its fragrant setting amidst the cleanliness and comfort of these familiar surroundings. 'You're all right now, sweetheart. Nothing to be afraid of. You'd tell me if there was anything troubling you, wouldn't you? Anything at all? We must never have any secrets between us, must we?' She thought of the tied, sweet-scented, ancient letters lying in the back of her drawer, in the locked cupboard.

Doreen thought of that foul hand clamped over her mouth, the evil smell of that stubbly face, those slobbering lips pressed to her, the hand driven up beneath her clothes, touching her in such vile intimacy; the feel of her shoe slamming into those features, that strange flickering look as the broken head turned, then slid beneath the rush of water.

She seized the wrinkled hand that was caressing her cheek and put it to her lips. 'No, Aunt Elizabeth. I know I can talk to you, always. About anything. I love you.'

She closed her eyes and the twisted body, the splayed feet and that silly spindle of an ankle, all disappeared in the blessed warmth and security which was enclosed round her.

CHAPTER NINETEEN

Doreen slept remarkably well, thanks to the sedative the doctor had left. It was light when she woke. She felt fuzzy and strangely detached, but not enough to fail to remember, as soon as she was conscious, the frightening events of the previous day. First, she was glad that she had not suffered nightmares about them. In fact, she could not recall dreaming at all. Even now, when the memory of them did return, there was this odd mistiness clouding her mind, which filtered away a lot of their horror, made them less real; even though the second thing that registered in her waking consciousness was the stiffness and ache of almost every muscle, and the throbbing of her bandaged knee.

But her overwhelming feeling was one of relief, at being safely in her warm, pretty room, snug beneath the covers, and clearly being awarded the rare privilege of a day off school, for Aunt Elizabeth would otherwise have awakened her at least an hour before in the darkness, in time for breakfast and the hurried walk up to the station for the morning train at 7.45. A glance at her clock told her the train would already be pulling into Whitby. With a great sense of luxury, she stretched her aching limbs and wriggled down in the sealed in warmth of the blankets, savouring the decadence of the moment and its sense of freedom.

However, the sound of voices raised in animated conversation dispersed that aura of well being in an instant. She could hear Mrs Addis's louder, rougher tones dominating, interspersed with Aunt Elizabeth's more modulated speech, and her stomach churned with unease. She shivered, half-rose from her bed, strongly tempted to creep out on to the landing and listen, but reluctance won the day, and she sank back, biting at her lip, fear again clenching her insides, making her feel sick. She had that bad taste in her mouth once more, could feel the pressure of that hand at her jaw, could smell its disgusting odour. She lay back, drew the sheet and blankets up to her chin, shuddered. She was startled to hear herself praying frantically inside her head. Please, God, no! Don't let it be that! Don't let it be him! Please let him have woken up, the water would wake him, let him have gone staggering back up to that weird place on the moor, let him be waking up with a sore and bloody head. But she had a sickening suspicion that God didn't listen to wicked girls' prayers, especially when they were so belated.

She heard footsteps coming quietly upstairs, and closed her eyes, but opened them when she heard the door open. She gave a loud, theatrical yawn, stretched her arms out above her in the chilly air. 'Morning, Aunt. I feel sort of funny. Oh gosh! I've slept in, haven't I? Why . . . what happened?'

Miss Ramsay had drawn back the drapes, turned back to her. 'I let you sleep, sweetheart. After yesterday . . . I think you need a day off. Dr Ryder will probably call in after lunch, just to see how you are. It must have been quite a day for disasters. There's been another accident in the village.'

Doreen's heart thumped. She held her breath, waiting for Miss Ramsay to go on.

'You remember that fellow Bob Symmonds? The man who was sent to prison, from High Top? They found him last night, down by the beck. Drowned, apparently. He must have fallen. He was drunk. They found an empty whisky bottle on him.'

'Oh, the poor man!' Doreen's voice shook.

Elizabeth came quickly over to the bed, bent and gave the dark head a quick kiss. 'Yes, of course. But these people! They bring it on themselves, I'm afraid. He was never any good. All those things he had hidden away up on his place. The petrol. And sheep-stealing, from his own neighbours!'

Doreen felt a sudden contrary urge to defend him, to atone for her own sin, but also from a malicious pleasure in pricking her guardian's conscience. 'Yes, but it wasn't just *his* fault, was it? I mean Gus – the Big Swede – people said he was the real ringleader. And they never caught him, did they? He got away and left poor old Symmonds to take the blame.' She could feel the discomfort she had stirred, could detect it in the defensive answer.

'Yes, but Bob Symmonds was a local man. He was robbing his own kind. Gus Rielke was a foreigner. It wasn't the same for him.'

Doreen knew Elizabeth was thinking of all the favours the Big Swede had done for her in the past, the cheerful way he used to work in the garden, bring the 'little extras', the luxuries of jam and marmalade and extra sugar and such, that he brought in little wrapped-up parcels, and for which Miss Ramsay paid him generously. 'I liked Mr Rielke,' she said firmly, careful to disguise the sly taunting behind her remarks. 'He was funny. Always laughing. He used to give me a thruppeny-bit sometimes, to buy something at Mrs Lloyd's.' She almost sniggered as she visualized Miss Ramsay's reaction if she should disclose the real reason for his largesse.

But such a diversion was not enough to keep her anxiety at bay for long. Twenty minutes later, when Mrs Addis came upstairs with a tray bearing her breakfast of porridge, toast, and warm milk, the cook and housecleaner was more than ready to discuss the sensational talking point of the day in Howbeck. And Doreen was too worried to try to deny its reality any longer by pushing it from the forefront of her mind. 'What exactly happened?' she asked, wide-eyed with what she hoped indicated a very natural curiosity.

Mrs Addis plumped up the pillows, and perched her beam at the bottom corner of the single bed, while Doreen began spooning in the hot porridge. 'They reckon he must've slipped, fell all the way down the bank. Just t'other side of the bridge, near Station Lane. I thought he'd been in the water, like, and they'd fished him out, but no. Apparently he'd smacked his head on one of the stones. The' reckon he was hanging half over the bank, only his head was in the Beck. Must have knocked himself out, clean cold. But they reckon he'd supped a bottle of whisky. Dead drunk! Probably wouldn't have known a thing about it. Nobody else did.'

'How did they find him? Who was it . . . that found him?'

'Some lads were coming out of Oddfellows. I must admit, that's where I thought he'd been when I first heard. Come out staggering drunk and lost his way. But our Colin says Vera Rhodes wouldn't have him in the place. And none of the regulars would welcome him, neither. It was when they were leaving round closing time. One of them saw something from the bridge, down by the bank. Couldn't tell what it was at first, just a black thing. But they went down, by that path down from Station Lane, and there he was, half-in, half-out of t'water.'

She stopped, glanced swiftly at the open door, as though suddenly aware that perhaps she should not be filling the child's head with such unsavoury matters. She nodded. 'Come on, luv. Eat that porridge up afore it goes cold, and get a bit of that toast down.'

'So they don't really know *what* happened? Didn't anybody see him at all?'

Mrs Addis shook her turbanned head. 'Nay, lass. He might have been lying there hours. They sent for PC Rowe once they'd pulled him out of water, and the constable went round for Dr Ryder. It were pretty clear what had happened, the doc said. Apparently his family said that he'd been drinking all day. He'd wandered off before dinner-time, never showed up again. He's been funny ever since he come back from gaol, poor feller. You've got to feel sorry for him, but really he's never amounted to owt. To be honest, I don't think even his fam'ly'll miss him that much! Awful, really!'

Doreen was surprised suddenly at how hungry she felt, as she munched at the toast and washed it down with the warm milk. 'He must have tripped over in the dark,' she offered, her heart beating faster. 'Shows how dangerous the blackout is. It's bad enough even in daylight, this time of year. That's how I fell yesterday, on the way home. I slipped on something.'

'Ay, that's right! It was t'same place, weren't it?' Mrs Addis sounded quite animated. 'Funny that, eh? Might have been *you* lying there! Fancy!'

'No, no!' Doreen cut in quickly, her voice rising. 'It wasn't – I was on the other side of the beck. This side of the bridge!'

'Nowt but a few yards away, though, really. Bloomin' blackout! Just goes to show. It's not just in the big towns you get terrible accidents. Don't know why they can't put the lamps back on. There was always one outside the pub. Might have saved ould Symmonds's life. We haven't had a siren going in months.' She reached forward and took the tray from Doreen's lap. 'Go on! Can't you finish them crusts? You'll never have curly hair if you don't eat your crusts.'

'Thank goodness!' Doreen gave a shake of her long, tangled brown locks. 'Look at Alice! She's still got a mop of curls. She looks like a blonde gollywog.'

Doreen was up, sitting by the living-room fire, in her dressing-gown and slippers, when Dr Ryder called in the middle of the afternoon. 'Just a bit stiff,' she said gamely, as she hitched up her flannelette nightdress for him to examine her wounded knee.

'That's fine,' he pronounced. 'Put some more ointment on. Keep the lint and bandage on for another day or so, just to be on the safe side. Those bruises,' he continued casually, nodding at the marks at the back of her calf, and higher, on her thigh. 'Goodness knows how you managed to get those in a fall!'

'Oh, they're probably from games on Monday. We were messing about in the gym, some of us. Just fooling around.'

He laughed. 'My word! You play rough, you young ladies of the grammar school! You'll be putting up a soccer team next!'

Doreen quickly pushed the hem of her nightgown back over the exposed leg and pulled her dressing-gown about her. 'I don't think so, Doctor.'

'Oh, I don't know.' He turned to Miss Ramsay, with just the hint of a mischievous glint in his eye before he did so. 'Remember that ladies' team from Preston, Miss Ramsay? From that factory? The Dick Kerr Ladies, they were called. Just after the war.'

Miss Ramsay shook her head, with that genteel look of diffidence, and Doreen knew very well that Dr Ryder was doing a bit of gentle leg-pulling for her benefit. He turned back to his young patient. 'They were jolly good as well. They used to get crowds of twenty thousand or more, just like a proper match. The football authority tried to ban them, wouldn't allow any of the big grounds to let them play on their pitches. They kept going, though. I remember they played an international match against France, just a couple of years before this present lot started.'

'Really, *some* young women these days have no shame at all! And goodness knows what ideas they'll get now, with all the things they've been doing. The sooner we defeat Hitler and get things back to normal the better!'

Doreen could see from the twitch at the corner of Dr Ryder's mouth that he had succeeded in his intention. Partly to terminate what Miss Ramsay considered a rather unsavoury topic of conversation, the spinster said, 'I hear we had a rather tragic event in the village last night. You were called out, I believe?'

'Yes, that's right.' Professional reticence did not deter him from

155

discussing the matter which had caused such a stir in the close-knit community. 'Quite a day for accidents.' He smiled at Doreen, who fussed a little with her dressing-gown cord, and prayed she was not turning scarlet. 'Rather more serious, though, in this case. Poor Bob Symmonds, from High Top. He's not had much luck these past few years, God rest his soul.'

'Amen. Is everything clear? How it happened?' Miss Ramsay could not disguise her interest, as she leaned forward slightly, and Doreen felt her heart skipping about, and her fingers tightened about the silk tassels she held in her grasp.

'Oh yes, fairly obvious, I'd say. Fellow was staggering drunk. There was a bottle of whisky smashed in his coat. They gave me a knock about ten. The Oddfellows were just turning out when they saw him down at the beck. He must have slipped and fallen from the top of the bank. Gone headlong right down, hit his head on a stone by the edge of the water. There was a bad cut, must have laid him out. Not even the water brought him round. Just one of those unfortunate flukes, I'm afraid. He actually drowned. His head was under water, no more than a few inches.'

Miss Ramsay seemed somewhat belatedly to recognize that this was not perhaps a suitable topic to discuss in the presence of a thirteen-year-old. But Doreen could not keep herself from saying, 'How awful! When – when did it happen? Surely someone must have seen. . . .?' She let her voice fade, and Dr Ryder resumed his tale.

'Oh, some time after dark. Hard to say. Apparently he'd been seen staggering about half cut most of the day. He'd already been drinking when his family last saw him at home, before lunch. In fact . . . you didn't see him yourself?'

He was looking directly at her, and Doreen prayed, for the second time that day. Please God don't let my face turn like a tomato, don't let me give myself away. Her face was hot. Perhaps he would just think that she was shy, self-conscious as a young girl was inclined to be. She opened her dark eyes wider, seeking for an expression of innocent surprise. 'Me? No! Why on earth should I have seen him?'

'Oh, it's just that somebody said they'd seen him hanging around by the station. Just about the time when the school train got in.'

'No, I came straight home. I always do. Too cold to stand around talking. I was in too much of a hurry to get home. That's why I slipped myself, and that was *before* dark.'

'Just goes to show, eh? There wasn't anybody around to help poor little you, and as you say, it wasn't even dark then.' He placed his cup and saucer on the low table and stood. 'Well, I must be off. Glad you're on the mend, young Doreen. Poor old Symmonds. Death by misadventure, the coroner will record, I suppose. There'll be an inquest, but it all seems straightforward, in spite of our home-grown Sherlock Holmes!'

'Who's that?' Doreen asked, so sharply that her 'aunt' glanced at her in gentle reproach.

'PC Rowe, of course. He was back there this morning, searching about on the bank, as though he was looking for a murder weapon or something.' He laughed dismissively. 'He seemed to think there are plenty of folk who still hold a grudge against Symmonds. Maybe even enough to do him in. But I told him they'd already had their revenge on the chap. They *half*-killed him last time, before the police got him. No need to waste his time on this case.'

Doreen made to rise as he picked up his bag, but Dr Ryder reached out, patted her on the shoulder. 'No, don't get up. Stay there. Make the most of it, enjoy being pampered. I'm sure your . . . Miss Ramsay is spoiling you a little. And take care, eh? Don't forget your name. Remember, glass can be broken if you're not careful, ha-ha!'

CHAPTER TWENTY

On Tuesday, 25 January, the last day of Bob Symmonds's life, Alice was preparing at the Bermondsey flat for what she knew would be a tearful, wrenching parting from Beth. They had had three glorious nights and two wonderful days in the dingy little capsule of the apartment. It could have been anywhere – Ben Gunn's cave on Treasure Island – it wouldn't have made any difference to their happiness at finding each other again. Neither baby Elaine's nor Arty's presence had seriously intruded on their bliss. Arty had left before daylight on Sunday morning, returned late evening to another night on the camp-bed in the cupboard/boxroom, prior to an equally early departure on Monday morning, with the promise, expressed conventionally as polite regret, that he would not be able to get back home before Wednesday night, or, more probably, Thursday morning. As for the infant, Beth swore she had never known her daughter behave so impeccably. 'She must know who you are,' her mother declared, and, to be truthful, Alice got rather a kick out of being part of the insulated threesome, accepting the 'paternal' role Beth allotted to her.

On Sunday, the girls had forced themselves to get out of bed by eleven, bathed, and braved the cold to walk in the nearby park with Elaine tucked like a papoose in her shawl and blankets, the pram hood firmly raised against the cold damp. On Monday, they were decadent, the rattle of sleety rain on the windows easing their consciences, and they lazed about in their night things, sprawled in front of the fire, heading back to the unmade bed after Elaine had been settled for her afternoon sleep.

When tranquillity had eventually been restored, Beth lay with her head on Al's still tanned thigh, her golden hair spilling in a tangle, and gazed up to meet the loving gaze down on her. 'Stop all the clocks, cut off the telephone,' she intoned solemnly, and Alice smiled down at her.

'What the hell you on about, you daft Arab?'

'It's a poem. By W.H. Auden.'

'Who the hell is he when he's at home?'

'It means I don't want you to leave me tomorrow.'

Alice watched the sadness steal over the lovely face, the anticipated sadness in the blue eyes. 'I can't give you poetry,' she said. 'But I *have* got summat for you.' She scrambled up, and Beth yelped as the yellow hair flew and she was dumped back on the bed. Alice was delving in her holdall. 'I was waiting for the right time to give it to you. This will have to be it.'

She came back to the bed and held out her hand. 'I had this made, just for you.' She opened her palm and Beth saw a gold ring nestling there. 'I just never thought I'd ever get the chance to give it to you,' she added softly.

Beth gave a quiet cry of delight. What looked like three very small diamonds were set in the thin gold band. 'It's beautiful! But how can I – I can't take this.'

Alice smiled, reached out for her once more. 'Just try it. I know you can't wear it, but just see if it fits. For me.'

'No, I didn't mean – I'd *love* to wear it!'

It wasn't until Beth was tugging at the rings already on her finger that Alice saw how closely the engagement ring resembled the one she held in her own hand. 'No! You can't take off your rings – yours and Arty's.'

But the engagement ring had already slipped off easily, and with a little further twisting Beth slid off her wedding ring. 'I always take them off. When I'm bathing Elaine, or working. Here.' She held out her left hand, the ring finger extended. 'Put it on for me.'

Alice did so. 'It's a bit tight.'

Beth raised her hand to her mouth. Her tongue flickered out, licked about the ring, and she pushed it on down past the second knuckle. 'There!' She held her hand out once more, and the stones sparkled even in the dim light. Aware of the sudden tension which seemed to have gripped both of them, she said lightly, 'It's just like my engagement ring. He'd probably never know the difference.' She felt a stab of shame as she remembered the night he had given that ring to her, explaining that it was his mother's, which his sea-captain father had passed to him, for when he 'met the right girl'. She shied away from pursuing the thought, but Alice had caught something of the sudden shadow.

'Except mine aren't real diamonds. *Desert* diamonds, they're called. Just like bits of glass. Or sand, really. Ground-down rocks. You can find them sometimes in the desert. We used to go out at sunrise, first thing. That's when you spot them – if you're lucky. You see them sparkling away like mad, just on the ground. If they're good enough' – she nodded towards Beth's finger – 'they can be polished and made into jewellery. The gold's real,' she ended, with almost a hint of defiance.

Beth knelt up, put her arms round Alice's shoulders. 'It's lovely. And I swear I'll keep it always. I'll treasure it.'

'You can't let Arty see it,' Alice said sombrely, his shadow falling over both of them. 'He already knows about us.'

The defiance was from Beth now, despite the colour that swept up into her face. 'I'm going to wear it. Along with his rings. I don't care. I'll tell him you brought it for me.'

Alice left after lunch next day. She persuaded Beth it would not be wise to accompany her to Waterloo. 'I'd rather say goodbye here.' She glanced around at the drab room. 'It's like our place at t'Big 'Ouse. I love it!' She saw the tears already in the blue eyes, and swallowed hard. 'Listen, give my love to Arty. Take care of him.' She paused, her voice husky with the awkwardness of the moment. 'He's a good chap. He's . . . very understanding.' Beth said nothing. She gave a kind of moan, pressed herself against Alice, holding her as tightly as she could.

'I can't bear to let you go again. Not now, after . . . I need you so much, Al.'

'Hey! Come on now. Be a good girl for me, yes? I'll write soon as I've got an address. First chance I get I'll be up here again. Nothing'll stop me. Just be good for me, right? You know what I mean. Things are so messed up right now. But it'll all come right, some day. I promise.'

'I just don't want to lose you again. Not after everything that's happened. I won't let it happen again. I promise.'

Al had to force herself from Beth's clinging tearfulness, her own cheeks wet as she somehow got out into the suddenly ironically bright day and the waiting cab.

*

Thou must be true thyself
If thou the truth wouldst teach,
Thy soul must overflow if thou
Another soul wouldst reach.
It needs the overflow of heart
To give the lips full speech.

Alice stopped, shaken by how deeply she was moved by the singing. The words came absolutely clearly to her on the shining morning, in the deep-bass unison of male voices. She glanced over the wall, on whose coping the marks where the iron railings had been removed were plainly seen. The mellow brickwork and the simple classical lines of the windows looked dignified, in spite of the many diagonal crosses of the anti-blast tape on the small square panes of glass. There were several pupils of this boys' school, in their dark blazers and striped ties and the blue-and-black-quartered caps, being marshalled by the gate which led into the lawn and the gravelled paths outlining the quadrangle in front of the building. Two older boys – young men, they were, Alice amended to herself, whose tasselled caps, looking slightly incongruous, marked them as some kind of prefects, were marshalling them. Latecomers, probably, 'on a fizzer', which was army slang for a charge. Well, those monitors or whatever they were would soon be exchanging their school caps for something a lot more military, in light or dark blue, or khaki.

That must be some kind of hymn she could hear being sung inside. Morning assembly, she supposed. She felt pleased that this school was still functioning as it was meant to. It was of course well out of the town, at least three miles away from the centre, but she was nevertheless surprised, after seeing the flattened, devastated waste much of Southampton's heartland had been reduced to. It was land mines, they said, that had done most of the damage. Blown everything above the surface to small bits for yards and yards around. She had noticed nothing of it the day she had landed here, she'd been too involved in her own affairs. But then there had been so much to do after she had got ashore, and most of it had meant sitting about in that vast shed and the line of huts that served as offices behind it. By the time she was sorted out, and on the train that was to carry her to London and to Beth, it was dark anyway.

She'd had time to observe the effects of the war on the port since then. She'd been here six weeks now, almost to the day. And this was a day she was not likely to forget. Tuesday 7 March, Beth's twenty-second birthday. How she had hoped to be celebrating it with her. In the six weeks, they had met only once. Alice had got a lift up to the capital in a jeep, on a February Saturday afternoon that had seen the remnants of a gale blowing its rain-drenched tail out. Beth hadn't known when to expect her, for Alice had only been able to promise that all being well she would be able to get away sometime after lunch. And she had to catch a train back on Sunday afternoon.

It had not gone well. Arty had been at the flat when Alice arrived, and this time it was she who had greeted him with a kiss on the cheek; a Judas kiss, she felt, when Beth flung herself against her an instant later and held her so tightly she could hardly breathe. It was all too blatant, and challenging, and Alice felt uncomfortable all evening as Beth insisted on making physical displays of affection. Then there was the already familiar argument about the camp-bed, with Alice making a determined effort to stake her claim to it, and Arty's valiantly gentlemanly resistance to her pleas, until Beth became dangerously extreme and close to tears. 'What the hell's wrong with me? Do I snore or something? Are you sick of being with me already?' and Alice capitulated.

Later, in the enclosed darkness of the bed, the tears *did* come, and Beth whispered fiercely, 'I want to be with you! I need you so much – like this!' And they had made love, muffling their passion, and Alice was miserably aware of Arty's presence in the next room. She brought her guilt and her shame away with her. Beth had nothing else to think about, stuck in that dark little flat, day after lonely day, and many nights, too, with only her babe for company.

Alice felt even guiltier during the rare moments she had for such reflection. She had never found her work so hard or so challenging. The whole of Hampshire and its surrounding counties seemed like a vast military encampment, or rather a series of almost identical camps, a gigantic chessboard of army manoeuvres that never stopped. The unit she was helping to run, the transport maintenance and vehicle pool, was on the edge of the town, a few miles inland, in a large area of heath land known as the Common locally. The camp was fenced off, and consisted mainly of rows of Nissen huts for accommodation and larger structures, like hangars, for the work areas, which were always full of low-loaders, tank transporters, lorries, cars, and everything between, in various stages from stripped-down shells to newly washed, rejuvenated conveyances ready to hit the cluttered high- and byways again. It was Burg-el-Arab times at least ten, without the dust and heat and flies but with icy cold, snow, sleet and rain instead; and a vastly increased work load and pressure.

Alice thrived on it. Which meant more guilt for her to carry about in those rare moments when she had time to reflect on it. She thought how high she would have been in heaven to receive the letters she was getting from her darling almost every day now during those long, desolate months of their separation, in this country and then in Egypt. Not that she didn't love to receive them now, when she got back to her curtained-off, draughty little space in what laughingly passed for the Sergeants' Mess, at all hours of the day or night, to find sometimes two or three envelopes with the familiar writing lying on her bed. But often she was so weary the script wavered in front of her as she read; and she was ashamed of the scribbled, dreary notes she all too often penned in reply, in the precious, little time she could find for her own private world.

She was on the go most of each twenty-four hours that made up the day and night. She was out on the road more than she was in the depot. The camp was a transport pool as well as a repairs and maintenance centre, and Alice found herself leading convoys of several vehicles for miles around the neighbouring countryside. Apart from the unfamiliarity of the territory and routes that were planned to avoid as far as possible the arterial highways, there was the added hazard that these journeys were often scheduled to take place during the long winter hours of darkness. Lastly, nearly every lane and byway seemed to be filling with lines of stationary vehicles parked in hedgerows, on narrow verges, where soldiers bivouacked, living like gypsies. Their air of permanence soon made Alice think that if the much-anticipated great day of the invasion of France didn't come, the whole of the southern counties would grind to one hopeless, muddled halt.

There seemed to be more American troops than British. The towns and country pubs were crowded with them. Civilians and quite a number of British lads in uniform might grumble at their free spending brashness, but Alice found them refreshingly polite and anxious to be friendly. They were certainly popular with the girls, including her own, and she had to give several blunt warnings about over-fraternization. 'There's a difference between making them welcome and giving them all you've got, if you know what I mean!' Alice derived much private amusement at the way her rank seemed to have put an extra ten years on her age. A lot of the women under her charge were several years older than she was, but they accepted her authority with good grace on the whole. She was firm when she needed to be, but she didn't 'put on side', the way some of her contemporaries did. She made it clear that, in spite of her stripes and the responsibility they carried, she still thought of herself primarily as one of them, called up to 'do her bit', and she was good at getting them to pull together. Some of her officers were too fond of 'swank', the most junior 'one pippers' being the worst. One of the hardest and most valuable lessons Alice had learnt in her two years of service was the old army dictum of keeping counsel, the snappy salute and the 'yes, ma'am, no, ma'am, three bags full, ma'am'.

She felt bad that she had not been able to wangle at least a twenty-four-hour pass for Beth's birthday. Not that she'd have been in much state to celebrate. She had got back to camp with the dawn. They'd brought a breakdown with them on the back of a low-loader, and it had been light before she had seen her lasses watered (a cup of steaming char and a 'wad' for those that wanted it) and bedded, with a 'chit-wot-sez' for them to lie in until 11.00, before she went to her bed herself. But she'd woken after less than two hours, with the racket of another frantic day going on about her. She was off-duty until after lunch, but she couldn't get back to sleep. Her head was full of Beth, and how she would spend her birthday. She hoped fervently that Arty would have managed to get some time off, at least the evening and night. And that in turn disturbed her more. She was so confused about the complexities of their relationship. How could she reconcile the love she and Beth shared, had miraculously rediscovered together, with what surely must, *should*, take place between Arty and Beth as man and wife?

Her mind had been dwelling on it as she wandered away from the camp, and passed close by another sprawling tented encampment encircled by its trucks and bren-carriers and red-crossed ambulances, like the pioneers in some old time Western inside their laager of canvas wagons, awaiting a redskin attack. The sun was up and high, and actually warm on her shoulders through the thickness of her clothing. She came out of the wooded scrub on to the wide thoroughfare that led towards the town, and crossed it. This stretch, which ran into Southampton, was known as The Avenue.

She found the school along a quiet, leafy lane, just yards in from the main road. It looked so orderly, and so neatly enduring, especially in this novel, springlike mildness, of bright sunshine and blue sky and high white cloud, that, along with the strong, hopeful, youthful voices singing the hymn, it gave her a strange sense of security that was at odds with the chaos of her thoughts on her own private circumstances. 'God's in His Heaven, all's right with the world.'

Another of her Beth's sayings. She was full of such stuff. *And* nonsense, Alice used to tease her. Head full of poetry and you cannot boil an egg! But Alice knew fine well what a clever lass she was. If it hadn't been for the war, she would likely have gone off to college and really made summat of herself. *If only* . . . so many of them. She would never have met Beth again if the war hadn't come along, even though they lived within a couple of miles of each other. If only Luke Denby hadn't got himself shot down over Germany . . . if only her darling Beth hadn't rushed off and flung herself at Arty Clark, poor sod, and made herself pregnant with Elaine.

For someone who doesn't believe, I do a hell of a lot of praying! Alice ticked herself off mockingly as, nevertheless, she looked up squinting through her tired eyes at the cloud-racing sky, and thought: Please God! Let her have a happy day today, and let her know she's loved – by all three of us. Me, and Elaine, and Gentleman Arty, too, blast him!

165

CHAPTER TWENTY-ONE

Doreen acknowledged no doubts as to the existence of the Almighty such as those that her eldest sister struggled with. The thirteen-year-old was all too ready to accept the reality of a divine plan. Her vision however was a confusion of Biblical and classical mythology, as she waited day by day for the single hair to snap that held the Damoclean sword over her head. She began to fancy a certain speculative abstraction in Aunt Elizabeth's gaze when it was sent her way during the first days after Bob Symmonds's demise. 'That mac of yours is in a terrible state. Mrs Addis has spent ages getting it cleaned up. And those stockings were absolutely ruined. Not worth even trying to repair, she says. A button off your skirt! You must have taken an almighty tumble. It's a wonder you didn't break your neck, young lady!'

'I thought I had! I think I must have hit the edge of the wall, at the end of the bridge. It sent me flying into the grass outside the Oddfellows.' She busied herself searching for something among her schoolbooks, so that she would not have to meet that conjectural stare, and thought she did rather well with the bright dismissiveness of her tone. It was far from the way she felt. However many times she told herself that Bob Symmonds was, or rather had been, an evil old lecher (she had recently come across the word in Shakespeare studies and felt it suited him to a T), and that he had attacked her with brutal intent, she could not defend her own actions. True, she was the innocent victim of his bestial assault on her – she still shuddered with revulsion at her too-vivid recall of his hands seizing her, that hand which had so obscenely touched her flesh – and she had done nothing wrong at all in merely defending herself, even to that slamming kick right into his whiskery face. But afterwards, when that grotesquely twisted body had lain so still . . . and then there'd been that final twitching movement of the head, the flickering of his eyelids . . . she should not have scrambled away, back up the bank, should not have left him there, so still, in the growing dark.

You killed him! No, no! I left him. You let him die. No, no! How could I know? I thought he would wake up, I thought he would stagger up, maybe come after me. I didn't know, until they told me next day . . . Liar, little liar!

But then the next day turned into two, and the days followed, and gradually the tautness of her fear began to ease, and she was even defiantly proud of herself at the way she had behaved. Nobody had a clue. Not even the village bobby, for all his so-called investigation, and his stupid theories about murder. Nobody murdered him, Constable Rowe, not even me. He brought it on himself, through his wickedness. But she prayed for forgiveness for quite a number of nights afterwards, well into February. Maybe God knew after all that none of it had been her fault, and 'forgive us our trespasses' really worked. She was even prepared to accept also 'and them that trespass against us', though it was hard to imagine that smelly, shambling reprobate among the spotless mansions of God.

It came as a shock therefore when, coming down with a crowd of her fellow pupils into the station square to catch the train home one afternoon a young lad in rough working clothes came up to her and said, 'You Doreen Glass, miss?' and at her startled acknowledgement thrust an envelope at her. 'I was told to give yer this, miss,' and he turned away to leave her staring after him.

'Doreen Glass! You sly monkey! A billet-doux, eh? Your beau, is it?'

'Looks like one of the fisher lads off the trawlers!'

Her companions continued to tease her loudly as, with a quick glance at her name, written in a hand she did not recognize, she stuffed it into her pocket. In spite of her keen curiosity she was wary of satisfying it in such public surroundings. She was nothing if not quick-thinking. 'Oh, I know what it is. It must be the bill for some work my aunt had done. Something in the house. You tight Yorkshire tykes again, saving the money for a stamp!'

The generally good-humoured teasing was soon dropped. Doreen's puzzlement was tempered by an uneasy feeling, somehow linking the untoward event with what had happened to her on that afternoon a month ago. There was no reason for the two to be connected, she admonished herself, but her nervousness increased the nearer she got to home, and to the time when she could escape to her room to change and wash before supper.

Behind the safety of her closed door Doreen felt her fingers untypically clumsy as she tore open the envelope and took out the single sheet of paper. Still she did not recognize the writing, which had a look of painstaking neatness. But as she began to read, her eyes grew rounder and her heart beat faster, and her brain seemed to spin, as she realized there was indeed a connection, and a very strong one, with the terrible thing which had happened to her last month.

> *My dear little friend,*
> *You are not so little now I guess but you have not forgotten your old friend Gus I hope. I guess you are too old for doing the handstand for me now, yes? I sure you remember me and the times we had. I hear about my friend Bob, a very great pity and I am sorry for his wife and his kids. But listen now, I want you do me a favour, my old friend and tell no one you hear from me, yes? I know I trust you in this.*

For several seconds Doreen stared at the letter, the fear clutching at her throat. How could he know about Bob Symmonds? Then as her eyes darted in panic ahead, she realized that what Gus Rielke meant was that he had heard about Symmonds's death, not about her secret connection with it.

> *You meet me Saturday in Whitby outside Empire Café at noon and tell no one remember, or your old pal go to jail for long time. You know I do nothing bad, you know that we are friends yes and you help me. Some bad things happen if you do not come. Do not tell Miss Ramsay, come by your own. Is very important I need you do one little thing for me. It helps your sister and that boyfriend she have, Davy Brown. Nothing bad will happen to you, only me if you do not come. I know you not let me down little friend.*
> *Gus.*

Saturday! The day after tomorrow! She should show the letter to Aunt Elizabeth right now. Gus was a wanted criminal. He was the one who was truly responsible for Bob Symmonds's death. Symmonds would be alive now, up on that rundown farm with that brood of savage children and that witch of a wife, if it hadn't been for the Big Swede and his wickedness.

But Aunt Elizabeth would immediately send for Constable Rowe. The whole business of the drowning might be dragged up again. It would be better if she did as the Big Swede was asking, at least in the first instance, to see just what it was he wanted. She looked at the letter again. *It helps your sister and her boyfriend.* He wasn't quite up to date, then. Davy Brown was no longer Alice's boyfriend. In fact, he never had been, not really. Alice didn't have *boy*friends!

But how could the Big Swede help Davy Brown and Alice? Davy was still in the police, as far as she knew. Surely Gus Rielke would wish to keep as far away from the law as possible? Maybe he was suffering an attack of conscience, turning over a new leaf. It was not fear which made Doreen decide to keep the rendezvous Gus had suggested. She was more than a little nervous, it was true, but there was a kind of scary excitement involved in her decision, too. After all, strictly speaking, she had stepped outside the law herself, in not revealing what had happened to her by the beck last month, so, in a sense, she and Gus shared a complicity in the death of the unfortunate hill farmer.

It was not too difficult to get Miss Ramsay's permission for the trip into Whitby. She had made occasional visits with her friends to the seaport, for a trip to the matinée at the cinema, or simply to the beach and to wander about the old town. Her nervousness was not so great as to make her any less careful about her appearance. She chose her most elegant outfit from her growing wardrobe: a grey pleated skirt and striped blouse and a thick, knitted, pepper-and-salt cardigan to go over it, the least 'childish' of all her clothes.

'Oh! Aren't you wearing your uniform?' Aunt Elizabeth asked, with clear disapproval, for she had misgivings that the clothes were a little too grown-up. In spite of her slight figure, Doreen could well be mistaken for a fifteen- or even sixteen-year-old dressed like that.

But for all her youth, Doreen was a seasoned campaigner in the art of wheedling and cajoling, and her large-eyed winsomeness won the day. 'Oh, *please*, Aunt! I wear it every day of the week! Let me look different for once! I like people to see me at my best, to look my best, for your sake. No one else will be in uniform!'

'Well, just make sure you're back before dark, you hear? The four o'clock train, otherwise I'll have the police searching for you and you wouldn't like that!'

'Thank you. I promise, Aunt.'

'Go on then, off with you. Oh! And here's a bit extra. Treat your friends to tea and a scone.' She handed her a half-crown, which more than doubled the weekly pocket money, and she was rewarded by the tight grip of the slender arms around her neck.

There was quite a crowd waiting on the platform, and Doreen noticed a fellow pupil standing with her mother and another lady. Olga Morley was in the year below and usually Doreen hardly acknowledged her, but today she walked up with a beaming smile and gave the star-tled girl an enthusiastic hug. 'Hello, Olga! 'Morning, Mrs Morley. Off to the great metropolis, eh?' She stood and chatted animatedly, hoping that Tom Lonsdale would notice she was part of the group, just in case a chance word might get back to Aunt Elizabeth. 'Yes, I saw young Doreen going off with her pal on Saturday morning.' She thought she was quite clever to anticipate such eventualities.

The train hissed in to the buffers at Whitby station before eleven, the white steam and sooty smoke gathering in a pall under the low roof as Doreen passed the locomotive and made her way out into the station square. The day was overcast but mild for the end of February. The gentle slope outside the building was covered with carts and the long porters' trolleys, as well as a collection of parked vehicles, including a couple of canvas covered trucks whose jigsaw patterns of dark and light green proclaimed their military purpose. She had an hour to wait before her midday rendezvous. Her stomach felt hollow, and she was taut with nerves, but also with excitement. She felt rather glamorous, like a beautiful spy, as she made her way across the square, over towards the pointed roof of Paylor's Marine Stores, and the District Farmers' building next to it.

She glanced very briefly to her left, towards the café where she was to meet with the Big Swede. She decided it would not be wise to hang about there for an hour. Other people from Howbeck had business in the town and might well spot her waiting alone. Nor did she wish to sit inside the café for that length of time, which would look equally suspi-cious. So she continued to walk round towards Boots' Corner and the end of the bridge. She would stroll along St Ann's Staith and Pier

Road, past the long line of fishing boats moored two and three deep, and the fish market, where rubber-booted men and fisher-girls were swabbing down behind the stalls where the last of the catch was still on sale to the public.

As she passed these and drew near the lifeboat shed and the west pier, she remembered the day nearly three years ago when she had travelled in dizzy style in Luke Denby's car, with Alice and Elsbeth, and little Algy, and Davy Brown. She felt so good being out with the squire's son, and so conscious of how smart she looked that day, in her new long stockings and pretty frock. She recalled how irritated she had been with Algy and his twisting and turning beside her, and how afraid she'd been that he would put his grubby sandshoes on her nice clean dress.

A gust of wind swirled her heavier skirt as she neared the old battery and the slope down to the beach, and reminded her of the way that the breeze had got under her dress and whipped it up that day, and her coquettish squeals of outrage as she danced about.

And now the handsome young airman was dead. The second anniversary of his death had passed only last week. It seemed unreal, somehow. She still couldn't encompass the thought of his obliteration. A sudden irreverent vision struck her of Luke and Bob Symmonds meeting in the bright mansions above, nodding awkwardly to each other. 'Hello, there. When did you get in?' Would Bob tug at his spiritual forelock? Would he have that horrible, greasy cap with him still?

Her musings were interrupted by the sight of a tall, bulky figure, made even bulkier by an expensive-looking gentleman's overcoat, with an old-fashioned but stylish short cape from the shoulders, in a conservative check pattern. His soft, narrow-brimmed hat in a similar check was pulled well down on his brow against the stiff breeze. The neatly trimmed but extensive beard completed the effect of well-bred elegance. He was altogether a dashing, flamboyant figure for the seaside surroundings. Doreen would have been struck with admiration for him, had it not been for the fact that his light-blue eyes were staring very directly at her and his ruddy face was wreathed in a smile so far beyond polite, impersonal courtesy that she felt the blood rush in a hot flood to her face.

'What? You don't know me, little friend?'

She was still gaping when his booming laugh rang out, and confirmed his identity for her. He had already taken her hand, like a father walking with his child and was steering her back on to the pier in the blustery wind. 'I see you come off the train, so I follow you. Make sure you are alone, ya?'

'I wouldn't . . . of course I'm alone. You didn't think I'd try to trick you.'

'I got to be careful, liddle Doreen. But you not little any more, eh? You very beautiful young lady now. I still know you when I see you.' He pulled a comic face of regret. 'Not like me! You don't know me no more. I change so much, ya?'

She was blushing again, stammering in her reply. 'No, no. It's just – you look so different. Very impressive.'

He boomed with laughter, and now his right hand released hers and his arm slid round her waist, right there in front of the others walking along the pier, and she was strangely disturbed and flattered at the boldness and adultness of his action. Belatedly, she squirmed free, and, still laughing, he took her arm in his, linking her in a more restrained but mature contact. 'I told you, remember? You a real beauty, Doreen. Bet you got boyfriends fighting over you now, ya?'

The wind was so strong as they approached the slim column of the lighthouse that she snatched her dark beret from her head before it went sailing away over the sea wall, and he held on to the brim of his hat with his free hand. He hurried them round to the lee of the tower, and they stood close together, their backs against the whitewashed base. They were facing the long rocky outcrop of the East Cliff. Behind it on the headland the ruins of the abbey stood up, and the squat shape of St Mary's with its square tower. He bent his head close to her, so she could see the pale blond hairs of his moustache and beard, the redness of his cheeks and nose, the sandy lashes and pale bushy eyebrows. His mouth was very near to her face. 'You tell nobody?'

He was not smiling now; his eyes looked pale and she couldn't read his thoughts. She felt taut and breathless, afraid, but with that hollow excitement inside. She nodded, had to clear her throat to speak. 'Not even Alice or Davy. Nobody.'

He asked about both of them and she told him. The smile was quickly back again. 'That sister of yours! I think she should be your brother, ya? So! She go to Egypt! She fight in the army now.' He laughed, quietly this time, and shook his head. 'Some girl, that one!' The smile vanished again. 'It dangerous for me to be here, Doreen. You got to swear me, you tell no one. *No one* about this, understand?'

He leaned even closer and put his great hands on her upper arms. She glanced about in some alarm, for there were several people striding past the end of the pier and on to the wooden extension which led to the stubby little light-tower at its far end. The urgency dropped from his voice. He released her with a playful little shove and growled a laugh. 'I know you my pal, my buddy, Doreen. You the only one I can trust here. I not bad man, you know that. I sorry for Bob. I send his missus money while he in gaol. I send her more now. But you don't talk to her, ya? You don't let her know nothing. I finish with all that. I get out from here, stop all this.' He dug in the pocket of his coat, pulled out a folded paper. 'You get this to that Davy, ya? He still copper.' Another shake of the head, and another laugh, harsher this time. 'I do that for the young bastard. But I know about him.'

The urgency was back. He turned her to face him, and suddenly she forgot about the passers-by, about her embarrassment as his heavy hands seized her again, rested this time on her slender shoulders, those pale-blue eyes holding all her attention, dominating her. 'He in big trouble, Doreen. Big trouble what he do now. But I help him. I got what he want. You tell him, get the letter to him.'

All at once the excitement had gone. The hollow, squeezing sensation was all fear and uncertainty now. 'But I haven't seen him for ages! I'll have to get his address. And Alice is in Southampton. I'll have to write to her. It'll take time—'

'You a bright kid.' One thick finger prodded the side of his head. 'Use the brain, ya? You telephone to York. The police. Just give message that he call you.' The fingers of the hand resting on her left shoulder dug in tighter and tighter, shook her lightly. 'I mean it, liddle one. Tell no one. Danger for me, danger for him. You must tell him.'

'Why can't *you* do it? You get in touch with him yourself.'

He shook his head. 'No good. He don't trust me, I know. It got to come from you. You do it, for your sister, for de young man, and for me, ya?' He bent and kissed her, there in broad daylight; she felt the scrape of his whiskers against her cheek, and the wet touch of his lips before he withdrew and she nodded helplessly.

CHAPTER TWENTY-TWO

'I shouldn't really,' Reeny Lumley said, as she offered Mary Douglas a cigarette from the newly opened packet of Park Drive before taking one herself. 'I'm smoking like a chimney these days.'

Mary's narrow face screwed up as she leaned forward, lips pursed to accept a light from the flaring match. 'Don't be daft! Does you good! Even the doctors say so!'

And I shouldn't spend so much time sitting gossiping with you. But Reeny did not voice this thought aloud. It pricked her conscience, for she had actively encouraged the growing closeness between the two women since Davy was working away so much. She had hardly seen him over the past month. It worried her how much she missed him, how dependent she had become on his presence, and their friendship. Just as much as he missed her, she was sure, the dear boy. But her reflections only stirred the deep unease she was reluctant to acknowledge. They were far more than mere friends. The way he made her feel, their kisses, the little intimacies of their life together. She was like a young girl when she was alone with him.

It was wrong, she knew, and it upset him as much as it did her. It hurt to see that knowledge sometimes, in that serious look of his, the hesitations, the reluctance she sometimes could not help sensing in his attraction to her. He was such a good and honest fellow. So many others would have been quick to take advantage of the situation, or to try. Not that they would have stood a chance with her! But Davy . . . she shied away from the word 'love', but it was something dangerously close. She was a married woman, and a mother, and she should not feel this need for him, this affinity, and the shaming excitement at being with him, the thrill of his touch, his kiss.

Over and over she told herself they had done, were doing, nothing wrong, hammered it home to herself. What was wrong with a few secret kisses, and cuddles? Good heavens! She was living with him, she washed his clothes, saw him in bed most days, went in and out of his room. And never once had she truly betrayed Dick, done anything she should be truly ashamed of . . . but you *want* to! her wicked, mocking mind murmured, and so does he! Any lad just a bit less decent than he was would not have been so patient, would have overstepped the mark ages ago. You wish . . . she hated herself for the insidious thought which was almost like anger within her that he had never forced the issue, never crossed the shadowy boundary in which they were trapped by their decency. A little of what you fancy . . . and you fancy it with him, Mrs Lumley, *Mother* Lumley!

It couldn't go on, and probably it wouldn't. He was away for days on end. Any minute now she expected him to say he was moving out, would have to, because of his work. He spent more time up on Tyneside nowadays, he might well transfer there. That would solve everything, wouldn't it? And she felt sick whenever she thought of not seeing him again. But would it be any worse than this? They weren't lovers, they didn't go to bed with each other – just wanted to, longed for it – it must be the same for him, the way he kissed her, trembled like she did when they embraced. It was like the days of courting, all over again.

She now felt her own helplessness as she began to talk to Mary about him, despite that little pip of reservation, warning against exposing herself too much. Mary Douglas was a gossip. And there was something else, Reeny couldn't explain it to herself, something about the way the little, intense figure encouraged such intimacy, was avid for it. It made Reeny uncomfortable, without understanding why.

'I'm worried about poor Davy. I don't know whether it's his work. He's doing something he can't even talk about now, some special assignment. I never ask him of course. There's so much that's hush-hush these days. Even Dick's not supposed to let on where he's going to, even to me. Mind you, it could be that lass again, her turning up out of the blue like that on the doorstep. Never even let him know she was coming home! Silly girl! It knocked him for six, I can tell you! Thunderstruck, he was! But then that's what she intended.' She leaned forward and flicked the ash with a quick, nervous movement into the ashtray on the table between them. 'It's not right, Mary. I thought he'd got over her after she left here. She's such a funny lass. If she doesn't want him, why does she keep writing to him? And turning up like that, after all this time?'

Mary was staring at her, with the cigarette dangling from the corner of her mouth, and her diminutive face all screwed up, giving her a comical expression. There was a minute pause. She removed the cigarette and, poking out the tip of her tongue, scraped off a speck of tobacco with a nicotine-stained nail. The black eyes gazed at Reeny with an oddly speculative expression, as though she were uncertain of what to say, or was choosing her words carefully. 'He must know by now he doesn't stand a cat in hell's chance with her. No lad does!'

'Eh? What do you mean? He's a lovely lad. And he thought the world of her. He wanted to marry her. He was heartbroken when she left York.'

'Then he's a bigger fool than I thought!' There was that same level gaze, which Reeny found oddly disturbing. 'Surely he must have twigged by now? I'm surprised you haven't. She doesn't want him – or any other feller. She doesn't like men. Doesn't want them. Not in that way.'

The import of her words finally dawned, and Reeny's face showed her startlement. 'You mean . . . she's. . . ?'

Mary gave a hard little laugh, letting Reeny's incomplete sentence hang in the air. 'Come on! Think of it! Have you ever known a lass not wear make-up? How many times did you see her with a bit of powder and paint on? And that curly top of hers! She hardly ever bothered to put a brush through it. And her clothes – she was lucky if she had one frock to her name! And why should she? How many times did you see her in owt but slacks or them trousers?'

'Oh my God! Poor Davy! But he would never know, poor lad. He would never dream . . .' Suddenly she was staring at the figure opposite, her face mirroring her dawning suspicions. 'You knew? How? Did she . . . are you just guessing?'

Mary Douglas stubbed the butt out with aggressive force. She looked up at Reeny, and all at once that monkeylike face took on its more usual air of knowing mischief, and she gave a lewd wink. 'I know, kidder. She told me, about that lass she lived with up in the Dales. And showed me, too, if you must know.'

The tide of red rushed into Reeny's face. 'Really! I'm amazed. I don't want to hear anything more! It's—'

'Then you shouldn't have bloody well asked, should you, missus?'
Mary rose, and Reeny, in spite of her agitation, was struck yet again by
the lack of stature, for the table came to Mary's waist even when she
drew herself upright. Her voice was surprisingly matter-of-fact. 'I didn't
think I'd ever do anything like that meself. But listen! You've got your
man in bed beside you – well, *most* nights, any road. Mine has been
gone three year and more. And I'm not ashamed to admit I miss him –
like that. I never thought for a minute that me and Alice . . . well, just
goes to show, eh?' Her expression was a mixture of bold defiance and
a certain vulnerability, as tears shone in her eyes. 'She brought me a lot
of comfort. And me for her, likewise. All right?'

The colour still stood in vivid spots on Reeny's cheeks. 'It has nothing to do with me,' she answered stiffly. 'It's just – not natural, is it? I
mean . . . I don't understand how you can . . . with another woman.'

Mary gave a bitter laugh, turned and plucked her shabby coat from
the hook on the back of the kitchen door. 'I must admit, I never had a
clue, neither!' She turned, with one last defiant stare and smile. 'Believe
me, though, you can! But don't worry, Reeny, luv. You're still a bonny
lass, but you're far too big. You're safe with me. I'm not the size of six
penn'orth of copper!'

It proved more difficult than Doreen thought to get in touch with Davy
Brown. She was afraid to make a trunk call from home, for Mrs
Eltham, who ran the Howbeck exchange, or her husband, who helped
her out sometimes in the evenings, would be curious enough to mention
a trunk call to York Police to others, especially as Doreen was quite sure
the operator would have no qualms about listening in to such an
intriguing connection, if, indeed, she would even put her through without seeking Miss Ramsay's permission first. Gus Rielke had impressed
upon her the urgency of the situation and her own anxiety grew as
Sunday and then Monday slipped by without any solution to her
dilemma. She had hoped somehow to sneak off and make the telephone call from one of the public booths at the general post office in
Whitby, but there were so many regulations and restrictions associated
with wartime use of long distance calls that she quickly gave up the
idea. She solved it by an inspired thought after a chance meeting with
Evelyn, the prettier of the two land girls who had been posted to the

Howe Manor estate, and who had been friendly with both Alice and Elsbeth.

'It was smashing seeing your Alice again. Will she get up this way again soon, do you think?'

Of course! Mr Barr, the agent for the Denbys, might well know how to get in touch with Davy. She dashed off after tea on Tuesday, making some excuse to Aunt Elizabeth that she had to check with one of her schoolmates about some prep assignment, and caught Mr Barr before he left the office. 'I promised my sister I'd send on something to him. But I've lost the address she gave me. She'll kill me if she finds out I haven't sent it. You couldn't help me out, could you? Please?' She gave her most winning and winsome smile, and the agent was a willing victim of its power.

What a splendid girl she's turning out to be! he thought. A real credit to her benefactor! His mind dwelt briefly on sows' ears and silk purses. 'I'm sure I've got a note of his address in the records. Hang on.' He took some time to search through a buff coloured file. 'Yes, here we are. I'm not certain of his work address, but I have a private one. His lodgings. Even if he's moved on they should be able to forward things to him.' He quickly wrote it down. 'There we are. Don't lose it again! Give my regards to Alice. I was sorry I missed her when she was up here. Tell her to call in when she gets up this way again.'

Up in her room Doreen wrote an explanation to Davy, along with the single sheet of paper Gus had given her, which contained nothing more than a couple of names, with telephone exchanges and numbers beside them.

Please, whatever you do, don't tell anyone about me meeting him. He said you were in danger, and so was he, so please be careful. Just call me, Howbeck 215, to let me know you've got this safely. If Aunt Elizabeth answers, just tell her Alice asked you to get in touch with me, to see how I'm getting on. Do be careful. I know it's something dangerous you're involved in, but I'm sure Gus wants to help.

She was almost certain Davy would still be at this address. Alice would have said if he had moved somewhere else. It was exciting being part of such cloak-and-dagger stuff. She hoped he would be all right, even though she had always felt Davy Brown was a bit too 'goody-

goody' for her liking. And he had been a conchy when all was said and done, whatever he'd done over in Spain, and his work in the police now.

Her mind returned to the day they had all spent in Whitby that summer, and how much more fun Luke Denby had been, always skylarking about. No one could accuse *him* of being a coward. He'd paid the ultimate price, sacrificed his life. He was a real hero, whatever Alice might say about him. She knew why Alice had such a down on him, of course. It was because he had clearly fancied Miss stuck-up-soppy-drawers Elsbeth Hobbs. And even though Al might have thought she'd won her, the snooty bitch had gone off and married some other chap.

Doreen was still thinking about the perversity of her sister's inclinations as she quickly walked along the lane towards the post box set into the wall beside the Oddfellows. She should be shocked, she supposed, but her predominant feeling was one of prurient curiosity. One thing was sure, she reflected as she slipped the envelope into the slot, where its hollow thunk told her it lay in isolated splendour. Davy Brown was definitely barking up the wrong tree if he was still entertaining hopes of wooing Sergeant Glass, and she had time to record a fleeting sympathy for him as she turned with considerable relief and hurried homeward again.

Davy was lying back enjoying the relaxing effect of the warm water on his aching muscles. He had put them to unaccustomed strenuous use from before dawn until almost lunchtime, helping to load sacks and boxes, from a bare, cavelike store between the blackened stone arches of a railway viaduct on the Gateshead side of the King Edward VII bridge, and then riding with them in the back of an enclosed van with the legend F.M. MORRIS, GROCER showing faintly through the grime on its high side. Some of the items on which he and a companion were uncomfortably perched might indeed be groceries. He had not had a chance to explore the contents. But of a certainty they were not part of the MOF-regulated legal distributions of such items. He had done two other similar 'jobs' in his adopted role of call-up dodger, petty thief and general ne'er-do-well. He had hoped and was still hoping they would eventually lead to better things, i.e. a little firmer toehold in the underworld of black-marketeering and stolen merchandise being trafficked in the north-east. So far with little success, as far as his personal criminal career was concerned.

Perhaps he had overplayed his hand as layabout, drinker, sponger and all-round 'wrong-un'. Even the underworld fraternity seemed reluctant to employ him in anything more worthwhile than some occasional pottering, and always in an emergency situation, when it seemed they could not get hold of anyone else to fill in. Yet, as he had told DS Kelly, his Newcastle police contact, he had at least got a toe in the water. He was afraid he might be pulled out, that both North Yorkshire and Tyneside might decide enough time had been expended on the project, with nothing really fruitful gained. They had originally talked about 'two or three weeks' on this undercover trawl, and he had been in place for four now. They were into March already, and York was as short-handed as ever.

Never mind. Friday night, and home again. He rose, with a swirl of the cooling water, and sluiced the remnants of the suds from his body. He shivered. It was still freezing in the bathroom, March or not. He heard Reeny's voice accompanying a rap on the door and he reached involuntarily to cover himself with the towel, even though the door was bolted.

'I've warmed up some stew for you. Hurry up! Dick's popped up to the Institute for a drink. He was wondering if you fancied joining him. He was going to wait, but I said you'd probably be tired, want an early night. You can go up there after your supper, if you want to.'

His mouth twitched in the makings of a smile at the clear reluctance in her voice, then guilt struck again. He had been shamefully relieved in a way to find Reeny's husband home for once, and free of duty until the following afternoon. It served to remind him how he was using the fact of his being away all week up in Newcastle to shelve the acute and growing problems gathering around his personal life. Yet more 'undercover' assignments, he tormented himself. The feelings between him and Reeny simply could not be left as they were. He felt like some grubby Lothario in a bedroom farce – except that the bedroom had never come into it. Not for *real* sex, anyway, only the kissing and the touching, and the steamy unfulfilment of it all. It might be enough for her – and how could he think otherwise about her? But it was still so wrong: this pretend-loving, and the even greater pretence that they were both being decent by their restraint.

Then had come the bombshell of Alice's dramatic reappearance in his life, and the disastrous consequences which it had led to. He still suffered a sense of bewilderment at what he had done – *they* had done, he tried to believe, for surely she could have stopped him? However shocked she might have been, he had not physically attacked her, had not rendered her powerless to resist. Her behaviour afterwards, when they had both recovered from their mutual consternation, had established that. His mind shied away from the mechanics of the act. She had assured him he was the first, and he must believe her. He had even treacherously half-hoped that she might have been impregnated by him, even though that would clearly constitute a disaster for her. A forced union might well prove to be her salvation, as well as his. Maybe in time he could help her to overcome the abnormality of her nature. No chance of that now. She had informed him, in her very first letter from the camp near Southampton: *My little friend has arrived. I've never been so glad of a bellyache before!*

He heard Reeny approaching the door once more. Her voice sounded strained. 'Oh, by the way. Did you see the letter? It came yesterday morning. Very neat writing. Looks like a lass's, to me. Just what do you get up to with them Geordies?'

Her humour sounded a little forced. He had not glanced at the top of his chest of drawers. It couldn't be from Alice. It would have been in the distinctive blue forces' envelope, with her name and address on the back. He quickly pulled on his dressing-gown and hastened to satisfy his curiosity.

Five minutes later, Reeny stared at him, the dismay writ large on her face. He was dressed again, and in a state of excitement bordering on elation. 'Sorry, Reeny! I've got to go out again. To the station. Something's come up. Something important! I don't know when I'll be back! Sorry, love. This can't wait!' He saw the look on her face, and darted forward, planted a clumsy, swift kiss on her parted lips. 'Duty calls!' He left her standing there, gazing at his retreating back, her eyes filling with tears, and her heart plummeting to her slippered feet.

CHAPTER TWENTY-THREE

Davy did not recognize the impressive figure in the merchant service officer's uniform until he was almost on him and already addressing him. 'Hallo there, Davy! The copper's life suits you, ya? You put on the weight. Like me.' Davy was still staring in surprise at the burly individual with the gold buttons and the two interwoven rings on his sleeves when the booming laugh stirred his memory and helped in the identification. The neatly clipped flaxen beard was effective disguise, and added to the charismatic Viking effect. 'No bad feeling, ya?'

Davy felt his hand engulfed by the great paw which reached out to him and shook his arm vigorously. Then they were sitting down at the table in the quiet lounge of the Buck Inn, and Davy fought hard to recover his wits after his signal failure to prevent being ambushed like this. He would need all his acumen to stay on top of this situation. He had chosen this quiet roadhouse and residential hotel seven miles out from York on the Leeds road as a safely neutral spot for this secret rendezvous. Rielke had agreed readily enough, though Davy now realized that the Big Swede was taking no chances. The bluff naval officer had been in the lounge when Davy had entered, and no doubt had had a careful scout around well before the time appointed for their meeting. Davy had arrived almost three-quarters of an hour early, but Rielke had beaten him to it. Not that the foreigner would have found anything to make him overly suspicious. DI Holden had agreed that Davy should run the risk of making this first meeting alone. It did cross Davy's mind that maybe his superior was taking no chance either, and had him under surveillance anyway, without informing him of the fact. But the only other occupants of the lounge at this time of the afternoon was a party of four: two married couples, he would guess, business or possibly farming folk, judging by the girth and complexion of the two males, while their partners, permed and powdered and firmly corseted in their stylish pre-war outfits, were far too authentically matronly to be anything other than what they seemed. Which left the lady tending the bar: long past her prime, despite the painted lips, and as regular a part of the décor as the comfortably upholstered armchairs and sofas. Her beaming grin when Gus Rielke cavalierly summoned her with a wave of his decorated arm to replenish their drinks testified to his enduring 'way with women', and to her need for some long overdue dental care.

'You spoke to liddle Doreen, ya?' Gus said, when the waitress had retreated. 'She gonna be some good-looker in a year or two. She already got the eye.' The trademark of that ringing laugh was as ready as ever. 'How about that sister of hers? Alice? You get anywhere with her yet? She back now, ya? Or has she found some big guardsman to give her what she needs?'

If only you knew! Davy thought, ashamed at the inner fury of his response to the goading tone, then remembering how much he needed to concentrate on the only thing that mattered here. Above all, he must not foul up this amazing opportunity, which had come so unexpectedly. But he did not like this false *bonhomie*, the careful sparring and feinting in the ring before they got stuck in. He decided to speed things up, not to leave the initiative entirely to this imposing, domineering character. 'So! What is it you want? It must be something very important for you to come out of hiding like this. We could put you away right now for a long spell in prison, for what we already have from Howbeck.' The contest had begun, Davy could tell at once, by the change that came over the broad features, the calculation of the narrowed pale blue eyes.

'That was nothing. Liddle bit of dealing.' His lips dismissed it with a hiss of contempt. 'I know what you want. I know all about you, Davy. I know about you in Newcastle, about you meet with the guys up there, in The Ship and The Eagle. ya? Pouf!' He waved a great red hand. 'They nothing, boy! But you look for something big, I know it. Trouble is, you never find it, Davy. Not the real ones, you know. The big boys! They be on to you if you try. And you in danger. I mean it.' He leaned forward and tugged at the cuff of Davy's jacket. 'They soon find you a cop and they do you. I mean it. Proper! You finish in the Tyne – or dumped out at sea. They do it before, I know. I know these boys. The ones you after.'

He smiled, leaned back, relaxed, and glanced up smiling as the waitress returned with the drinks. He pulled a bundle of banknotes from inside his jacket, with a conscious air that irritated Davy immensely, and peeled off a pound note. 'You keep the change, my dear. You look after us damn well, ya?'

'Ooh, thank you, sir. That's very generous of you.' She beamed her bad-toothed smile and gave an embarrassing little bob of servility. It was a generous tip, probably half a day's wages. Far *too* generous, if you were seeking anonymity, and Davy felt a flash of contempt for the rollicking façade, then had to caution himself. The Norwegian was not the affable, above-board fellow he portrayed. He had after all eluded them three years ago, and was now involved with a new and greater set of criminals – or so he had implied.

Davy repeated his question. 'What do you want? You in some sort of trouble with these big boys yourself? What are you after for helping us?' Davy saw something of the danger Rielke himself posed in the transformation of the bearded features, and again the flash of ice in the pale gaze.

'For the start, I save your life!' he snapped harshly, scowling at Davy. 'You making fucking trouble for yourself, I tell you! You got no chance – without me. What I give you.'

Davy waited, scarcely breathing, for Gus to continue. He did, after a dramatic pause, and it was all that Davy had hoped for. He reached into the inside pocket of his reefer jacket, and pulled out a thick sheaf of folded papers. 'I have all you want. I have the names, places, all the contacts. Where it all comes in, where it all goes to, the whole work. Newcastle, down to London, every place. It's big, Davy. Maybe bigger than you think, ya?'

Davy strove hard to contain and to hide his excitement. 'Like I said. Why me? Why now? What is it that you want from us? Unless you've suddenly had a fit of conscience. Maybe you've seen the light, eh? Want to be a good man, suddenly.'

Gus smiled, but not with his eyes. 'Could be, ya. I sure want to get out of here. You know I'm a good chap at heart, a simple guy. I want to get out, make new start. Not here. You boys never give up, you chase me all the time. This war soon be over. You land in France any day now.

Three, four months, the war finish. Everyone know it. I want to get out – now. Now is best time. I go to States. America! That the place. I been there, Davy, plenty of times. After the war, the Yanks gonna be top dog, bigger than you. I get there now. You help me. I need papers. Proper, everything 'bove board, ya? Passport from Britain, seaman's cards. I settle there, no trouble.' He held up his wide hands, in a pledge. 'You never see me, hear me, no more. I swear.'

He leaned forward, put the folded papers on the desk in front of Davy. 'This show you I tell truth. You need more, but this is start. You see I know – there is more to come. If you do for me what I ask. It's good?'

Davy's heart was racing. 'It's not something I can promise,' he found himself compelled to say. 'I'm not a big wheel – not important,' he explained.

Rielke nodded. He was quite calm, had clearly a expected such an answer. 'I know.' He tapped the papers on the table. 'You show your boss. You check up what I give you here. You see it's true. Then you come back, papers for me for America. That's all I want. No money, no nothing. Just let me go, new life. No more crook. Simple.'

He leaned forward once more, and a hand rested on Davy's shoulder, in a gesture that looked like one of great affection. 'You try to send me to prison in Howbeck. I get away, but it make trouble for me. I go back to sea, nearly get my balls blown off in Atlantic, for a year, more.' He laughed more quietly, the blond head shook. 'But still I like you and that Alice. She helluva girl. You know, any time this past month I could put you in Tyne, your head smashed. Like poor Bob Symmonds. I don't do it. I can't. This your big chance, Davy. I trust you. Tell your boss. Next time we meet I give everything. And you give me my papers. But be soon, ya?' He swigged the remains of the whisky in one gulp, his head tilted backwards. 'You go now. I stay. You don't try follow me, ya? I know coppers.' He grinned, a thick finger tapped the side of his fleshy nose. 'I smell them. Even you! You be quick, Davy. If not, you stay out of Newcastle. See you soon.'

He stood beaming down at Davy, who finished his drink in equal haste, the Scotch burning in his throat. The powerful arm fell on Davy's in a valedictory gesture, as they moved towards the bar counter and the doorway. 'You take care now,' he said loudly, with the signature of the booming laugh. 'I stay and talk to this pretty lady.' The stained and crooked teeth were revealed in another simpering grimace. 'Maybe I stay till you finish the work, ya? What's your name again?'

'Vera, sir.' She gave a start, then a freezing look of dignified rebuke at Davy's sudden bark of amusement.

'Take no note, Vera. He crazy man!'

'Just like old times, eh?' Davy delivered his parting shot as he headed through the open doorway.

Davy and his superiors both in York and on Tyneside took note of Gus Rielke's urgency. 'You'd better stick around your usual haunts for a while,' DI Daniels insisted. 'We don't want any of our locals getting suspicious, wondering where you've gone, like. Just till things are sorted with your Scandiwegian mate. Just be careful. And I'll get DS Kelly to fix a bit more back-up. We definitely don't want to lose you at this stage, eh?'

But things were moving within the week. Davy arranged another meeting with Gus, this time outside the Newcastle Co-operative Stores building, in Newgate Street. The impressive recently built flagship store was busy, and assured reasonable anonymity, as they made their way through the doorway at the base of the lofty clock tower. 'You have to come with me,' Davy told him, his voice betraying his nervousness. 'Someone needs to check what you're giving us. I don't know enough. You'll get your papers if he agrees. They're all ready.'

This time, the burly figure was equally nervous. 'I got to trust you,' he said tightly. It was not a question, and Davy sighed with deep relief as he met the cold-eyed gaze. He nodded, and received an acknowledgement in return.

At last it was time to bid farewell to his colleagues up on the Tyne. He was not sorry. Since this whole business with Rielke had started, Davy had found himself living more and more on his nerves in his assumed role and expecting, each time he met up with his newfound ne'er-do-well acquaintances in the shabby pubs by the river, some violently explosive denouement. He prayed that Sergeant Kelly was keeping his word that some cover was in place for such emergencies, and condemned his own suspicions that the tightly stretched resources might not run to it, and that the assurances had been given for comfort but lacked substance.

But after the meeting at the CWS building Davy was finally pulled out, and the last meeting with Gus took place yet again at the Buck Inn, on Davy's home territory. Even his rigorous sense of morality could not compete against his elation and sense of achievement, so that he actually found himself warming towards the bearded betrayer, despite the fact that this arch-villain was walking scot free from a long history of criminal deeds, and doubtless off to a new, even more unsavoury career in the United States. A fine way to repay our transatlantic cousins!

And the connections were strong, as Davy found when the scale of the illegal network and operations were fully revealed. There were a number of Americans, both civilian and military, involved in the chain of corruption, which included smuggling and theft on a grand scale of goods, mainly cigarettes, tobacco, and ladies' artificial silk-stockings brought over on merchant ships or stolen from the vast amount of stores intended for service personnel serving in Britain.

'You've done a damned fine job, lad,' DI Holden told him proudly. 'This is all down to you, and I'll make damned sure you get full credit for it. For a start, you can get off and pack your bags. You're coming with me down to London. Scotland Yard itself, Davy! There's some big names caught in our net, so we've to be down there to be in on the grand finale. You deserve to be there, if anybody does!'

Reeny's face was a graphic map of her mixed emotions when Davy hastily broke the news as he prepared to pack for the journey south. She knew it was something big, even though he could not disclose what it was all about. He had been on tenterhooks for the past two weeks, since he had opened that mystery letter on the Friday night and gone racing out like the end of the world was nigh. She was ashamed of her feeling of relief to learn that it was all to do with work, and nothing to do with that Alice Glass. She always added the prefix 'that' in front of the name now, she couldn't help it, ever since *that* Mary Douglas had made the shocking disclosure to her in the kitchen. And it had been such a terrible shock, there were no other words to describe it, in fact she could hardly find any words at all for such goings-on. There weren't any, no decent ones at any rate! How could there be, for such indecency? She was almost glad that Davy was away, so caught up in his work just then, for she was sure that if she was seeing him every day, if they were as tenderly involved as they had become, she would not have been able to hide her feeling about it. Yet how could she ever find the courage to talk about such a thing, even with him? And now here he was, as wild as any kid going off on a holiday, ready to go racing off again, down to London, of all places, and there was no doubt how she felt about that, as she swallowed the choking lump and blinked back the tears.

She put her arms round his neck, gazed up at him soulfully, and wished furiously that she was not in her curlers and turban, and her pinny and wrinkled stockings and floppy slippers. But then when was she ever in anything else? 'Davy.' She swallowed hard again. 'You're not . . . going to go away, are you? I mean leaving . . . for good?'

He saw the vulnerable beauty, felt the depth of her care, and her sadness, and it added to the weight of guilt with which he was already saddled. 'No, love.' His voice was warm with assurance, even though part of him sternly rebuked himself for the tenderness he felt. 'I'm not. I'll be back in a few days. We'll talk.' He drew her close, closed his mouth over hers, felt that open yielding, the push of her body against his, and the unsteady urgency of his response.

In spite of the excitement of the following three days, of meeting so many important figures in such elevated surroundings, at the very hub of law enforcement, the legendary 'Whitehall 1212', he still found time, in the few moments of private reflection, mainly as he lay exhausted in the small bedroom of his hotel on the famous Strand, to dwell on the instability of his private life. It seemed to him even more complex and devious than his recent professional situation.

Reeny, Alice. The two fought like rivals for centre stage in his troubled thoughts. Except, he reprimanded himself, his landlady had no right to be there at all. It did not help matters to acknowledge that she was at least partly responsible for the predicament they faced. But he could no longer prevaricate, allow their present unhealthy alliance to continue. In a way it would be more honest if he simply went ahead, took the closeness of their relationship to its logical conclusion. Even as he condemned himself for such a thought, he felt his body's keen reaction to it. And that brought him back to Alice, and to his degenerate act on the kitchen floor of Dubry Street.

An appropriate locale for such debased behaviour, no doubt. How could he have let himself do such a thing? His torment was made worse by his acceptance of the fact that Alice had endured it, rather than fighting him off as she could well have done. It was all too painfully clear that she had found nothing pleasurable in it. How could she, someone of her . . . persuasion? He could hardly bear to name it. It was all so wrong, and he wanted so desperately to save her from such a path. If only she would accept the truth, see that there was something so terribly abnormal and deviant . . . accept him, and his love, his spiritual love, for her, he could in time, he was sure, bring her back to the right way. He would be so patient, and loving . . .

All at once it struck him, with the force of revelation. God – Fate for those who could not accept His intervention in human lives – had brought him down here. Perhaps the one who would prove to be instrumental in saving Alice was the partner in her aberrance. Elsbeth Hobbs was clearly aware of the enormity of their deviance. She had turned her back on the relationship once, had fled from it, into the arms of marriage and motherhood. Maybe he could make her see that for the sake of her husband, and her baby, as well as herself, and most of all, for Alice's sake, she must find again the strength to end the unholy alliance for once and for all.

CHAPTER TWENTY-FOUR

Elsbeth's twenty-second birthday had been something of a disaster, even worse than the previous year, when she had been undeniably rounded with Elaine and she had been stuck without Arty up at her home in Margrove, with relatives staring speculatively at her loose flowing gown and new chubbiness. They were almost counting on their fingers as their minds whirred in rapid calculation as to when the 'happy event' might take place and the interval between it and the wedding. 'Married life certainly seems to be agreeing with you!' they said, and watched her turning crimson. 'Nuff said! their looks implied.

This year, Arty had been present – and no one else, apart from the baby, who remained supremely indifferent to the occasion. Aye, that was the rub! Elsbeth had hoped all along that somehow Alice would wangle the time off, even if it was just the night of 7 March. When she failed to do so, Elsbeth could not prevent the mood of disappointment, and then bleakness, from creeping over her, in spite of all her best efforts to counteract it. Arty had made sure he was free – and she had even held that against the poor man, in her desperation. He had wanted to take her out, up west, but, as she had told him, perfectly reasonably at first, there was no one who could come in to look after Elaine for them. How could there be? She knew no one, never went out, except to the shops and the park. Their immediate neighbour, directly above on the upper floor of the old house, was a bachelor who wouldn't know which end of a baby to feed and which end to change. Besides, neither Elsbeth nor her husband had exchanged more than 'good morning' and 'good afternoon' with him in all the months they had spent there.

'Well, we'll have something special – a slap-up meal, a decent bottle of wine, I know a chap who can still get hold of some good stuff, for a

price!' Arty was trying hard, and that was part of the trouble, his determination to 'make the best of a bad job', like all those nauseatingly
cheerful cockneys in the Blitz four years ago. She knew, she could feel
the mood coming on, knew there was nothing she could do against it.
Her face felt as though it were set in cement when she smiled in acceptance of the bunch of flowers Arty flourished like a standard-bearer,
when he returned home on the big day.

'Now you leave things to me. I'll take care of Elaine, give her her
grub. You go up and have a nice long soak, and to hell with the five-
inch watermark! Put on your posh frock and when I've settled her nibs
down we'll dine by candlelight. I managed to get a rare bottle of decent
vino, so we can get sloshed in style. Then . . . who knows?' he concluded
bravely, waggling his eyebrows like Groucho, and Elsbeth struggled to
hide her instinctive clenching of revulsion.

It was doomed, and one of the biggest nails in the coffin was poor
Arty's expensive wine. It loosened Elsbeth's tongue, and her restraint.
She could feel it happening, feel her resistance cracking, and her helplessness to prevent the final crumbling of defence. 'Why couldn't she
have got at least tonight off?' They were sitting in flickering candlelight
after she had picked at the meal she had laboured over so dutifully most
of the day. 'Or I could have gone down there to meet her, if she could-
n't get away.' The approach of tears was evident in her tone. Arty's
woebegone expression smote at her, and made things even worse. 'I'm
off to bed.'

'No!' His cry of protest stopped both of them in their tracks. 'We
have to talk.' He gazed at her miserably. 'We can't go on . . . I have to
say something.'

She felt the last fragments of reserve slip away. It was almost a relief;
it helped her to calm herself a little. 'About what, Arty?' she flung out
challengingly. 'What is there to talk about?'

'About you – and Alice Glass.'

'I'm surprised you don't say Sergeant Glass! I'm sure you feel it
would be much more proper.'

'*Proper*'s the last word I'd use as far as she's concerned.'

'What do you mean? What are you trying to say?'

'You and her!' He sprang to his feet, his thin face working with
emotion, his body jerking. 'I'm not bloody stupid, Elsbeth! For God's
sake! You don't even try to hide it! You never did, even from the first.

191

That night I came back, and . . .' he couldn't bring himself to continue.

'And what? Saw us in bed, sleeping together?'

For an instant, he felt an anger and a hatred of her that made him fear he might even strike her. How dare she try to make him feel guilty, as though he was the sordid one, with sick thoughts and pictures in his head? He swallowed hard, actually felt a physical nausea, a disgust at her forcing him to detail such unnaturalness, challenging him to it. 'You know perfectly well what I mean.' His voice sank almost to a whisper. He sounded weary beyond measure. 'You make no attempt to hide it. You haven't since she showed up on our doorstep. You're obsessed with her. And as for her! She positively gloats over you, the perverted bitch!'

'Perverted *bitches*, Arty! What's that old joke? Takes two to tango. She was my first love, before you . . . before *anybody*!' A sudden image of dead Luke Denby flashed into her mind, and she had a crazy urge to tell Arty about him, too, to confess in one glorious, unholy attestation the secrets of her life. 'I gave it up. Ran away from her, from what we had.' The tears came, rolled down her cheeks, as her breast heaved and she fought to continue speaking. 'When she came back here, turned up like that, I just knew, straight away, that I still loved her. And she loves me. I can't let her go again.'

The rage had drained entirely from Arty's appalled face. Even his voice was softer. 'You're my wife. Elaine's our child. You can't carry on with this . . . this . . .' he shook his head hopelessly. There were no words for it, nothing to encompass the shamefulness.

'I can't stop it.' The passion, and the pain, had gone from her voice, too. 'It never did stop, even – when we married, when I had the baby. I tried so hard to deny it. But it's here.' She put her hand on her breast. 'It's not something I can change, put aside. Sorry.' She was totally sincere in her grief for the stricken figure before her, for all of them caught up in this hopeless tangle, for which there were no words.

Arty felt unmanned completely by it. There wasn't even the outdated concept of pistols-at-dawn to fall back on. Displaced in Elsbeth's affections by another man would have been painful enough . . . but this? It was grotesque, a farce, to which screaming, savage laughter seemed the only response. It was unmentionable. Even a court of law could not provide the answer, not when 'the other man' was a woman.

Arty gave up. He sat on alone, drinking whisky, until the early hours. He thought about retiring to the discomfort of the camp-bed and the boxroom, then crept quietly into his own cold side of the bed, with the curved back of his wife two feet and an unfathomable gulf across from him.

They didn't stop speaking, even though next morning they had nothing to say, beyond the stiff formulae of politeness. He was glad to escape to the war, and began that morning his strenuous effort to make sure he could be released from GHQ duties at the War Office and be included in one of the active units preparing to take part in the biggest combined operation of all time, already known in the top secret files as D-Day. He said nothing of this to Elsbeth. They said nothing about anything that mattered in the days immediately following Elsbeth's birthday.

Until, less than a week later, when Arty came home from duty, he could see a change in her manner, a revived animation in her look and speech. 'Have you heard the news? Yesterday, Mr Butler, the Minister of Education, announced that married women could carry on teaching.' She saw the bewilderment with which he greeted her words and hurried on. 'Don't you see? It means I could get back into teaching. They must still be very short, with so many men away.'

'But how. . . ? I mean you've got – there's Elaine.'

She drew in a deep breath. 'I know. I've been thinking. After the other night . . . things aren't right between us. I can't carry on stuck here all day. And you're away so much. You said yourself it'll get worse the nearer we get to the invasion. I could find someone to look after her, just for a few hours. Or . . .' She could feel her face growing hot, the tension as her voice grew higher. 'I thought maybe I could move back home. Mum would be over the moon to look after Elaine.'

'You mean you want to leave me?'

Even though that was exactly what she was suggesting, his bald statement of it shocked her. 'Just for a time . . . till we can sort things out. You'll be so busy until things start up.'

He knew he should tell her right away that if things worked out he would indeed be away. Perhaps for ever, he thought melodramatically, and was embarrassed by its theatricality. 'I can't physically stop you. But I can't approve of the idea. I just can't understand you at all any more. You're a different person since she came back. Having our baby, being married – I would have thought there could be nothing greater or more satisfying than that. It's the most important job in the world. But then,' he added bitterly, 'like I said, I don't seem to know you at all, do I? Not any more!'

The following day was a Sunday. When the front-door bell rang, Elsbeth's heart raced madly, and she ran down the narrow passage to the front door, fumbling with the lock. They never got casual callers! Al must have got some precious time off. She dragged open the door, her face flushed and alive, the name ready on her lips, and she stared in surprise, then with a sudden great consternation. 'Davy! What . . . has anything happened?'

'No, no!' He responded to the urgency of her query. 'No. I'm sorry. I should have got in touch, but I had to come down to London, to do with work. I just thought I'd look you up.'

He smiled guiltily, recalling the effort he had made via the manifold connections of his elevated colleagues at Scotland Yard, to ascertain the private address of Lieutenant A. Clark, Royal Signals. 'I've got a few hours off, and just thought I'd say hello.'

'Have you seen Alice then?' The directness of her question startled him, and served as a powerful reminder of his purpose in making this visit.

'Er – yes. Just after she got back to England. End of January. And she wrote, after she was posted to Southampton somewhere.' He did not disabuse her of her assumption that Alice must have passed on the Bermondsey address.

Elsbeth seemed to recollect herself, and she blushed. 'Oh, come in, won't you? I'm afraid Arty – my husband – isn't home. He hardly ever is, things are so busy now.' She fussed about, putting on the kettle, introducing him to a snuffly and crotchety Elaine, and he made the appropriate noises of admiration. 'You look very well,' he offered gallantly, when she had settled the baby down in her pram, and he was sitting on the lumpy little sofa balancing his cup and saucer. In truth, he thought she looked somewhat strained and nervous. Her face and figure had filled out, she looked every inch the young matron, but the pride and contentment he should have seen were conspicuously absent – and he was certain he knew why. He felt his resolve and courage seeping away with every awkward minute of polite exchange. He could see she was equally uncomfortable by the falseness of her bright cheeriness. She had never been an outgoing girl, even in Howbeck days, and her efforts to chat away grated on him now. Desperately, he plunged in, cut

194

across her shrill trivialities.

'Elsbeth! I'm sorry – I didn't just call in. This isn't just a social visit. I didn't come because of Alice – or rather, I did – but not the way you think. She's got no idea I'm here. I have to talk to you. This isn't easy, but I have to speak out.' It was obvious she knew exactly what he referred to. She stared at him, her face flushing, her eyes wide, terrified almost. 'I've got to ask you to put a stop to it. To stop seeing Alice.'

The colour was deep now, staining her face and neck above the green jumper. The blue eyes darted away from him, to the pram and the sleeping infant, around the drab little walls. 'You've no right . . . I'd like you to go, please,' she murmured softly.

'It's wrong, Elsbeth! You know it is!' he said urgently, making a conscious effort to keep his voice low. 'I'm not saying it's your fault. I know she was the one who came and sought you out. I know you were the one who left – last time.' He gestured towards the pram. 'You're married. You have a lovely daughter, a loving husband. Even Alice admits – she told me about Arty – how good he is. You can't let this . . . this thing with Alice spoil all that.'

'She said – she came back. And it was all still there between us, all that love. We can't just stop—'

'It's wrong!' His voice sounded loud in the small room, despite his efforts to control himself. 'You know it's wrong! Both of you know it! It's against nature! Against moral law! If you were men you could be sent to prison for it.' For an instant his voice shook, as his mind was filled with the sudden vision of his own ordeal in gaol, the abominations he had been forced to endure. 'You've got to try – to break from each other.'

'We love each other! Is it wrong to love someone so deeply? We just want to be together. We *need* each other.'

Her eyes held his now, shining with tears, appealing. He cleared his throat. 'But it isn't just that, is it? It's physical, too. That can never be right. You know that, as well as I do. And so does Alice. No matter what you say, you both know it's wrong to have a relationship like that.' He stood up, raised his hands to convey his own inability to explain. 'I don't know why some people suffer that way . . . it happens, to men . . . and to some women, too. Maybe it's some kind of illness . . . something that isn't their fault.' His hands moved again, reaching out towards her. 'But you have to fight it, not give way to it. We all have thoughts, urges . . .

but we can't give in to them. I'm not sure what you believe in. You used to go to church in Howbeck, I remember. I don't want to preach, goodness knows I have enough problems looking after myself. But I'm asking you to be honest with yourself. What you and Alice do – is that right, in God's eyes?'

Her gaze fell from his. Her hands were clenched in her lap, and he saw her shoulders heave in an almost silent sob. '*I* love Alice, too,' he went on strongly. 'I know she doesn't love me – not in the way you should if you marry someone. As you married Arty,' he said, slipping in the words like a small, sharp dagger, knowing how much they would wound. 'But I'd still go ahead, even knowing that. I'd hope and pray that that love would come, eventually. It might, by God's grace. But we'll never have the chance to find out. Unless she fights against her inclinations now.' The blonde, pretty, untidy head stayed down now and he could hear her weeping quietly.

He took a step towards her, and put his right hand on her drooping shoulder, pressed hard, feeling the delicate fragility of her bone beneath the flesh. 'And you, Elsbeth. You have to fight it, too. Otherwise it will destroy all you have here. A loving husband, your baby. I'm right, aren't I?'

He shook her very gently. Her whole stance and quiet weeping seemed to indicate that his words had struck home, that she was acknowledging the weighty truth of them. He was astounded when he felt the violent upthrust of that shoulder, the twist away as she swiped his hand from her with startling force. 'Get out! I want you to get out of here at once! You've no right – don't you dare come near me again, you hear?'

She sprang up, her face wild, smeared and blotched with her tears, and he fell back, turned at once and hurried away, pursued by the tortured sound of her abandoned sobbing.

She said nothing of Davy Brown's visit to Arty. He was well aware of the deep brooding quality of crisis in their marriage. It was like being trapped in the middle of a minefield, every contact carried the threat of a violent explosion. Nor did she write of Davy's call at the flat to Alice. Let him tell her, if he dared to face her wrath. But he probably wouldn't dare to say all those things he had poured on her to Alice. Her beloved girl would figuratively tear him limb from limb, and in all likelihood have a go literally if he should be foolish enough to stray within grabbing distance. She found it hard, however, to pen her usual eloquent lines of love, when she made time the following week to sit with her writing pad. Her plans for the decampment back to Margrove and a return to teaching were held up, too, pushed from the foreground of her mind, and she felt the familiar surge of impotent rage against 'Preacher' Brown and his destructive tirade. Above all she needed the all-embracing comfort of her lover's body wrapped about hers, and the melding of hearts that kept everything outside them at bay. Neither her own rambling outpourings of love, nor Alice's often hasty but tender replies, could make up for their separation. Yet the world and the war were determined to keep them apart, for the days passed and Alice was caught in the ever more frenetic preparations for the great assault. Only a week of March was left, and still she had not been able to snatch time for even a night's visit to London. Elsbeth, stunned under the attack of her husband and by Davy Brown's condemnation, remained dormant and sometimes apathetic as the beginning of spring came. She was waiting for the awakening kiss of life from her darling. Nothing else could stir her from this limbo.

The sound of Arty's key in the latch did nothing to rouse her from her lethargy. The meal was in the oven, the room was reasonably tidy – it didn't take long. Elaine had had her evening bath and been fed. Sometimes Elsbeth wondered bitterly whether these days Arty took his time about returning home on those evenings he was free to do so, lingering in the mess or some officers' bar for a drink or two with his fellow warriors? After all, 'the little woman' had turned into something of a dragon. What incentive was there for him to hurry to the familial hearth?

But something was definitely wrong tonight. She stiffened at first, in instinctive reluctance at his swift advance, his arms reaching out, the strength of his grip as he held her to him. Then she saw his face, the stricken look, his eyes – he had been crying, she was sure. 'What is it? What's happened?' Oh God! Her mind raced in panic. Alice? Something has happened to her. 'Tell me what's wrong?' she cried harshly, leaning back against his restraining arms, staring into his tragic face.

'It's your brother. Bill.' His face was ashen. 'There's been a plane crash. He's – gone.'

Gone? Gone where, you stupid man? It screamed in her mind, she didn't say it, just stared in horror as, finally, he managed to say the words. 'He's dead.'

CHAPTER TWENTY-FIVE

Good wireless communication had proved vital to the success of General Orde Wingate's Chindit operations, and he valued highly the contribution made by one of his field communications officers, the newly promoted Captain Bill Hobbs. Bill had been proud to be plucked from the safety of the 14th Army HQ in the border hills, for the dangers and excitement of Operation Thursday, with its flights behind the Japanese lines, and the days and nights living like tribesmen in the jungle, subsisting mainly on rice and local fruits, hacking out the makeshift clearings to get the light planes in and out. The clashes with the enemy were usually short and extremely brutal. 'Keep your head down, young feller,' the general warned him when action loomed. 'No heroics, right-oh? We can't afford to lose you.' They had even tried using gliders in order to minimize the chances of the drops and pick-ups being detected, but the results had been less than satisfactory. The real breakthrough came about when Wingate negotiated the use of a new American plane, the L1, which could set down and lift off 'on a nickel', as the Yanks boasted. And, amazingly, these light aircraft could carry as many as four passengers if required to do so. One pilot held the record of ferrying out seventy-two wounded, making eighteen trips in a single day.

'Wireless and wings, the secret of our success.' The remark was bandied about in various messes and attributed to Wingate himself. It was a suitably ironic twist of fate that the charismatic figure should meet his sudden death in an air crash in the hills of Assam, on his way to yet another hastily convened conference after his re-emergence from the Burmese jungle. He had insisted on taking his young signals officer with him. It was meant as a reward, to mark the start of their 'fattening up' process, ready for the next 'lean' spell behind the enemy lines.

Arty was deeply worried about his wife's reaction to Bill's death. His own response had been extreme enough. He had wept unashamedly in private, then had come dangerously near to some serious insubordination, when he heard a fellow officer, but with the rank of major, say when the sensational news of Orde Wingate's death circulated in the department, 'Well, I hate to say it but it might just be for the best, old boy. I'm not convinced that all the effort that's been put into the Chindits has been worth it. Casualties have been bloody high, and for what? The Japs are still as far forward as ever. Still knocking on the door.'

'For God's sake!' Arty was paper-white, his frame shaking visibly. He found he could not go on, could not frame the words boiling inside his head. Instead he glared, then spun on his heel and fled, while the major stared after him in amazement and growing affront.

'What the hell's wrong with him?' he queried.

'I think he had a good chum who was one of the general's party,' someone informed him.

'Like a bloody school-kid!' the major muttered, but with just the faintest twinge of embarrassment.

Arty believed their sense of loss and deep love for Bill should bring Elsbeth and himself together. The tragedy should heal the breach that had divided them, however bad it might be. And that first night, when he had brought the terrible news to her, he began to think it had. She was dazed. He knew the feeling all too well. He could not believe that his chum, far across the world or not, had ceased to be, had disappeared from the earth. That smiling, sensitive face, the tumbling fair hair, so similar in its colour to Elsbeth's, the lean frame, were all far too real in his mind, he could see Bill so clearly, hear his voice, his laugh. Husband and wife were united in their grief, so close they didn't need words to share it.

So they said virtually nothing. He prepared the bottle for Elaine's last feed, while Elsbeth woke and changed her, and they sat together, shoulder to shoulder on the sofa, while the sleepy little face sucked half-heartedly and fell into a deep slumber again with the bottle still half full. In bed, they lay side by side, still silent, but Elsbeth gripped his hand tightly all the while, until eventually she turned away, let her hand caress his face briefly. 'Let's try to sleep.'

He was half-awake, lying in the dark, when he felt the tremble of the mattress, and realized she was weeping, trying to muffle the great sobs that were shaking her. He gathered her to him, fitting himself round the curve of her back, and he began to weep, too, and he moaned softly. She turned with sudden violence into him, clung fiercely. 'Oh God! I'm sorry! Hold me, darling, just hold me.'

He did, and they lay a long time, their limbs resting together, their wet faces nuzzling, their mouths gently kissing. He was shocked to find himself physically roused, and deeply ashamed, but she was aware of it. To his amazement, and humble gratitude, she reached for him, opened her body, offered it to him. 'Love me,' she whispered, and turned with him, manoeuvred him into her, lay and rutted in time with him, grunting until the brief frenzy of it was over, then lay back, hot and sweating, but keeping their bodies entangled. 'I never meant to hurt you,' she whispered, beginning to cry once more, and he shushed her, kissing the tears, and she fell quickly asleep in his arms.

'I have to go up home,' she said next morning, as soon as they awoke. 'I have to be with Mummy and Daddy, and with Rob.'

He was wretched that he could not travel with her, but events were moving too swiftly at work for him to request compassionate leave. In any case, Elsbeth did not seem unduly upset by the fact that he could not accompany her. She seemed abstracted, somehow distanced from the everyday world around her, which included him, in spite of the physical intimacy they had shared during the night. He managed to take time off to see her and Elaine into the first-class compartment of the northern express at King's Cross. He had spoken briefly to his father-in-law earlier on the telephone. Either he or her brother Rob would meet the train at Durham, so that she would not need to change trains to get to Margrove. 'I'll ring tonight,' Arty promised, as the guard's whistle shrilled and doors slammed. Their kiss was decorous. Her closed lips felt cold. She nodded, smiled bravely. Her blue eyes looked tired, but they were dry. Arty had to blink away the moisture from his own.

Still so much to be said that lay, still unspoken, between them. He watched the carriages move away from the vault of the station, the double disks of the blank rear of the guard's van diminishing, hazing in the hanging wraiths of smoke. He tried to find comfort yet again in the intimacy they had shared in the darkness. Of course, in the starkness of this tragedy which had overtaken them, their own personal problems must be laid aside, but perhaps good might emerge after all, when the rawness of their grief had eased. Maybe he could hope that the shock of Bill's loss might jolt Elsbeth from the unbalance her life had slipped into with the arrival of Alice Glass. She had been trapped, or at least had *felt* so, in the flat, stuck day after day with Elaine, and with no friends to turn to. He banished his ignoble thoughts about her feeling anything other than sheer delight at the gift of their baby, this offshoot of their love, or her refusal to go out and seek new friends, of which he felt sure there must be plenty among the new mothers wheeling their prams about the streets and parks on the south side of the Thames.

It was he who had been selfish, expecting her to adapt to an entirely new kind of life, thrust upon her by the birth of their daughter. She had never been a naturally confident, outgoing young woman. Her shyness, that reserve, her sensitive nature, were what had first attracted him so strongly, when he had met her in her home, three Christmases ago. He could never forget the warmth with which her family had welcomed him, a complete stranger to all except Bill, into their midst. It was in those surroundings he had first known her, and fallen in love with her almost at once. He had been deceived when he met her later, in London, into thinking she had acquired a certain worldly knowledge, a toughness because of her brief experience of dealing with that world in the Wrens. But he should never have expected her to adapt to marriage and motherhood all on her own, far from all the ties that meant so much to her, in their shabby flat. He tried to excuse himself by reflecting that he had been forced to get by alone virtually since childhood, with his mother dead, his father a remote and generally absent figure, and no siblings to turn to. He had been gravely at fault to expect such independence from his wife. Being back home with her loved ones, even in the face of this terrible happening, might help her to get back on an even keel, to break free of this spell the Glass creature seemed to have cast on her. He hoped so, with all his heart.

The letter had arrived and had lain in the small pile on her pillow nearly twenty-four hours before Alice got back to the camp. Stiff with aching weariness she eagerly tore it open. She read the first few lines in a daze, before glancing up at the address. *Margrove*. Her tiredness was displaced by a sudden emptiness, as though her insides had somehow been eviscerated to leave a hollowness that was both leaden and icy. Not again! an inner voice cried, and echoed as she forced herself on, to read of Bill Hobbs's death and Beth's decampment to the north-east. There was no outright cry of *mea culpa*, the groans of sackcloth and ashes and swirling dust in the air and swiping flails. But the guilt was there, all the weight of self-recrimination and vengeance-is-mine that there had been over Luke Denby's death. Alice could feel it, in every word that didn't say so, between every line.

As you'll appreciate, I need some time just to absorb what's happened, to take it all in and get things in perspective. You can imagine how devastated Mum and Dad are, to say nothing of Rob. He adored his big brother, as I did. I'll be up here quite some time, I should think Mum has been hit so badly (Dad, too, though he doesn't show so much). I'm sure having little Elaine around will help. In any case, I've just heard that Arty is being posted to some unit down at the south coast somewhere – in preparation for the big push which is coming soon. He'll be part of it and no doubt part of him will be glad that he'll be seeing active service after so long. I hope that doesn't sound selfish or callous – I do love him and I'll be sick with anxiety for him, especially now. I just meant that men get so het up and guilty about such things. It's a pity they don't give women a chance to run the country. They'd soon end all this bloody bloody waste.

Sorry. All I do is cry at the moment, but it's no wonder. Please take good care of yourself. I'd appreciate it if you'd just leave me for a while, till you hear from me again. Don't be hurt – I've got so much on my mind and enough to deal with up here.

Love,

Elsbeth X

Back to *Elsbeth* and only one X. A begrudging one at that, Alice thought, and immediately felt ashamed at her own selfishness. She realized she was crying, she could feel her tears on her cheek. But she could not deny, along with her grief, that boiling frustration and anger were welling up inside. Damn Beth for that bloody twisted, silly notion of hers of God, the bearded old avenger, with his personal crusade against her and Alice, smiting down her loved ones to 'serve her right' for daring to do what everyone says is forbidden. Watch out, Arty! she thought venomously. You'll be next in line, if we so much as put down more than one X on our letters.

She lay back on top of the creaking bed, the sheet of paper still held loosely in her fingers, the other arm folded, blacking out the muted daylight from her wet eyes. If only we *did* rule the world! she thought savagely. All sorts of things would be different. That was one thing Beth had got right. The world wouldn't be divided into two camps charging about on land, sea and air trying to kill each other. And maybe people like her and Beth wouldn't have to hide away in corners and be made to feel twisted and wrong for their need to love each other with their bodies as well as their hearts. For her darling wanted it as much as she herself did, however much she tore that lovely yellow hair of hers and tormented herself with thoughts of sin and damnation and the Almighty hurling his flaming thunderbolts at anyone who got near them.

Half an hour later, when the tears had dried on her face and she forced herself to sit up and let the world in again, she began to feel something of Beth's bleak fatalism when she opened the second letter which had been awaiting her, whose handwriting she had recognized, too, but had put aside in the wake of the content of her lover's letter. Divine or devilish, Alice could not help the feeling of some great, grinding plan when she read what Davy had written:

I've been debating for quite a while now whether I ought to tell you what happened a couple of weeks ago, during my trip to London. I didn't let you know at the time because I knew how upset – and angry – it would make you, but I guess that by now you've probably heard about it from Elsbeth herself. I know just how angry you'll be feeling. It's no good my pleading that I did it because I care about you so much but that doesn't mean it isn't true. That's not really meant as an excuse, because to be honest I don't feel I need one, whatever Elsbeth might say about it. When I was in London on the business of Gus Rielke etc. I decided on the spur of the moment to call in at Bermondsey – I found out their address from the army.

It didn't go very well, as you will have gathered. Looking back on it, I can see that I should not have interfered, at least not in that way, just turning up out of the blue, in spite of the fact that it was done with the best of intentions towards you and her. You already know how I feel about you, so I can only hope that however furious you are at me you will understand when you calm

down that I acted out of my deep concern and care for you. I can only hope
that Elsbeth may come to see that I meant only good to her, too. Please tell her
how genuinely sorry I am for upsetting her so much, even though I still believe
I am right in what I said.

The final paragraph was another plea for her not to put an end to
their friendship, their 'best matemanship' as he called it. She could
almost hear him begging to let it bring a smile to her lips, however
small. But it didn't.

She groaned aloud instead. She wouldn't call it God – she wouldn't
acknowledge a vindictive deity who would take it out on her and Beth
so cruelly, when what they had was so good and tender and true. Yes!
she thought defiantly, even what we do to and for each other with our
bodies, and all the fiery, unthinking bliss that brings. But *something* –
malevolent fate, call it what you will – was implacably against them.
'Star-crossed lovers'; that was another of Beth's phrases which had
stuck when, long ago when they were happy under their stable roof in
Howbeck, she had read all that Shakespeare stuff she was doing with
those posh pupils of hers.

So be it. It wouldn't stop her loving Beth with heart and soul, as long
as she had breath left in her. Nor, she believed utterly, would it stop her
darling feeling the same, however much she might struggle to convince
herself it was no longer so.

CHAPTER TWENTY-SIX

Alice couldn't trust herself to reply to Davy. She was grateful that she did not have to meet him face to face, for she did not know how she would have contained her outrage at what he had done, at how he had betrayed her. On her scale of reckoning his copulation with her on the kitchen floor of 25, Dubry Street paled into insignificance beside his unwarranted visit to Bermondsey. In a sense, even though their congress had shocked her, it seemed that it was Davy who suffered more in its aftermath. There was even an element of justification when she looked back on it, a feeling that somehow she had paid some sort of debt for his continuing loyalty and desire for her. And underneath all lay that irreverent, bawdy dismissal in her mind – what a lot of fuss over nowt!

But his seeking out Beth! That was different! She could imagine just how appalled her darling would have been, how her toes would curl and her sensitivity wither, at his very mention of the one thing, the one secret thing, Beth had always been so fearful of anyone discovering during the time they had lived together. And to hear it flung at her, to be openly castigated for it by someone who, as far as she was concerned, had never been more than friend, or, more truthfully, an acquaintance. Poor Beth must have been mortified!

And yet, even more ironically, Beth had been prepared, so uncharacteristically, almost to flaunt it in front of her husband, so that even Alice had been taken aback by her brazenness in virtually banishing Arty from her bed in favour of Alice. But still, what did any of it matter any more? Following on from that supreme piece of interference from Davy had come the news of Bill Hobbs's death, to bring everything crashing down to ruin once more. Alice wanted nothing more than to be there at her side, to comfort her and wrap her in their love, but none of it was any use any more.

She remembered her desperate and frantic efforts to cling on to Beth after the disaster of Luke Denby's death, and how bitter the failure to do so had been. However much pain she felt, she must not make the same mistake again. Somehow she must wait, and suffer, and hope that in time they would find each other again.

Meanwhile, there were other distractions. She began to attach added significance to the fact that Davy was the only man to 'know' her in the Biblical sense, for he seemed to be ever more intricately entwined in her affairs, and with her kith and kin. By the time she had learnt of the part Doreen had played in what was proving to be a major triumph of law and order over a wide net of black marketeering and theft on a grand scale, most of the complex operations stretching from Tyneside to the Thames and beyond were completed. Doreen was a heroine, even if largely unsung except for the discreet plaudits of the authorities.

Alice's acknowledgement and praise was rather more stinted.

You could have got yourself killed, you bloody idiot! she wrote. *Fancy going all on your own to meet that swine, without telling a single soul! No doubt you think you've been mighty clever, but I should keep very quiet about the part you played in it all. You never know what might happen if the wrong people get to know it all started from you – and as always the bloke who should really be carrying the can for all of this is safely off God knows where again, just like last time. I shall have words to say to Davy about getting you involved in it all.*

And she had, too, delivered roundly in her last letter. But there would be no more, she decided now, even though it hurt her to break the link. This perfidy of his in seeking out Beth to deliver his soul-thumping condemnation of their wickedness was a betrayal too far. She couldn't drag together her anger and her disgust in words that would do them justice. She wasn't as clever with gob or pen as he was. But her silence would be eloquent. It would hurt him as much as she had been hurt by his action.

And lastly, unavoidably, there was the major distraction of the war. Alice had never been more *grateful* for its demands, with the new spring, and the growing days in the vast war camp which the south of England had become. Her loneliness was there, always, and its hurt, but she carried it like a veteran, part of her kit in the almost ceaseless activity she was caught up in; the feverish activity to keep the stream of vehicles flowing, the convoy trips up towards the capital, across to the east to Portsmouth and Brighton, and west along the coast to Poole, or inland through the New Forest and out to the vast encampments on Salisbury Plain.

She told herself with some justification that she was too tired to face the problems of the long journey up to the north-east in the rare entitlement to a forty-eight hour pass. Instead she ventured no further than Southampton and the NAAFI canteen, the noisy dance. She even got up on the floor for one dance with a Polish sailor, and let him crush her to his dark blue chest and plant his wet, slobbering puppy kisses around her mouth in the dim light of a corner near the toilets, until his hands got a little too intimately busy with her own attire and she ended the *entente* with a short, vicious, clenched fist jab to his ribs and he doubled up in rasping agony, flinging after her departing form a curse which probably did not contain more than one vowel, despite its length.

She was ashamed of her failure to visit her family, but she knew that the thought of the possibility of being less than two miles away from Beth would prove too agonizingly tempting. She did not want to put herself through the ordeal of telling her darling to 'bugger off' again. Alice's mam had written and sent her a cutting from the *Margrove Daily Mail,* carrying a piece about Captain William Hobbs and his gallantry in the Burmese jungle, which had earned him a posthumous mention in dispatches.

It had been hard enough not putting pen to paper or making a trunk call through to Beth's home. And somehow Alice just knew that Beth would stay up there with her parents, hiding herself away from her once more shattered world. Alice even had time to feel sorry for Arty in all this. But then he, too, had a powerful diversion from his private woes. He was part of the armada waiting to set sail from England. Alice felt a keen and bitter envy all at once of him and all his male counterparts waiting at this moment for the great adventure. She found herself wishing that she were a man, with the chance to march or ride or sail or fly off to battle. Instead, here she was, scurrying about the choked-up lanes, serving their needs, of food, of supplies, even of bombs and bullets, only to be left behind when the force sailed, waving them off, and waiting like any wife or sweetheart for news of the grand affair.

April gave way to May. On the Eastern Front Russia was advancing and impatient for the West's second front to begin at last. Polish troops finally succeeded after the months of fierce resistance to secure and hold the rubble of the monastery at Cassino. But at home the news in the *Southampton Echo* was of the first of a revolutionary type of new house, which could be fitted together like building blocks or Meccano, to replace the thousands of buildings up and down the land which had been destroyed by the bombing. Prefabricated houses, they were called.

The tension among the thousands of troops waiting to go, and among those like Alice who served them, was becoming almost unbearable. 'Any day now' was the phrase bandied like a password as the end of May came. Harbours were full of landing craft, some of them mere dummies, and inland fields were filled with rows of the frighteningly basic glider transports, again many of them empty shells. It was an amazingly well-kept secret, when that 'any day' was to be, and, even better kept, where the armada was to land. The 'glorious' first of June came. Still, those endless lines of troops and vehicles cluttered the roads and fields and country lanes. 'Today or tomorrow', came the confident predictions, as the weekend approached.

On the Sunday, 4 June, the fine weather broke, there was a blustery westerly wind whipping the trees around the camps on the common. Late in the afternoon, Alice was called in to the Central Traffic Office. 'Urgent, Sergeant Glass. Three ten-tonners. Got to get to Lee-on-Solent tonight. Packed with gear for the RE base, next to the RAF fighter 'drome. You'll have an armed escort, get there soon as you can. Be careful, there's a hell of a lot of activity going on round there. This awful weather doesn't help. Don't forget you're next door to the GHQ. Might bump into old Monty himself, or Ike. Here are the papers. Away you go. Try and get back by 0-eight-hundred tomorrow if you can. Unless some brass hat grabs you and gives you other orders.'

It was dusk before the small group of vehicles could get away, and by the time they had crossed the river at Northam, then made their way through the wet, narrow roads close by the military hospital at Netley, they were driving with the slitted headlights, worried as always by the difficulties of negotiating the byways hugging the coast, choked as they were by service vehicles of all kinds, and their bivouacked troops. An additional hazard was the number of checkpoints looming at them with ever increasing frequency and abruptness, adding greatly to the strain of what were already difficult conditions.

'Something's up,' Alice told the girl who was her co-driver, after yet another halt and careful check of the crates in the back of the trucks. 'I reckon this could be it, you know. I've never known it this bad, even round here.' The tired girl's face in the dim torchlight reflected her nervous tension. 'Come on, bunch over. I'll take the wheel. It's murder being leader, but it's no good letting our gallant escort go in front. It's a wonder they've managed to keep up with us so far. They're even less clued-up than we are!'

'Thanks, Staff-Sergeant! I'll try to keep my eyes peeled.' She was nineteen, a lean and lanky Rotherham girl, with uneven teeth and a poor complexion. She was also still dog-tired after a late Saturday night recreation in Southampton involving a randy AC2 stationed at one of the fighter aerodromes on the edge of the town and too many rough ciders. In spite of her best intentions, her baggy eyes were blinking, then her head nodded, and, as they skirted Titchfield and Alice searched anxiously for a lane which should swing to the right and allow them to head back to the coast and the village of Stubbington, the Rotherham lass was snorting softly through her blubbering lips.

Alice cursed, but didn't wake her. Not yet, she thought distractedly, and glanced down at the section of the map she steadied on her left knee. It was a brief but fatal error, and when she glanced up she made another, but this one was not her fault. The black shape reared up directly in front of her. She thought at first it was a building – the side of a black wall directly in her path and too close to miss, but then she just had time to record its stretched shape and flying wing, and realized it was a canvas shelter or piece of camouflage, and she saw beyond it the squat turret of an armoured vehicle, the long muzzle thrusting, wreathed in its netting. She swung the wheel violently to her left, standing and wrenching the large unwieldy circle as far round as she could. The truck lurched as Alice's booted foot jabbed at the brake pedal and slid off. The right-hand wing of the lorry's front tore through the canvas and net and leaves of the camouflage screen and smacked into the armour plating of the carrier in a heavy but glancing blow. The wheels were already off the narrow path, which was no more than a farm track skirting the edge of a field, it was later discovered, and the truck ploughed through an insubstantial hedgerow, to fall ten feet down the sheer embankment on the other side.

To Alice the rending and jolting seemed to go on and on, and the dark world stood on end. She felt a tremendous tearing pain, and the clear snap of the limb as her left foot was caught in the mess of displaced metal below the steering column, then there was a final terrifying bang as the door next to her leapt into her and smote her a savage blow which drove the breath from her body. The Rotherham girl was sprawling all over her, screaming piercingly, and all at once Alice's head was amazingly clear. In spite of the terror and the noise and the pain, she knew exactly where she was and what had happened.

The truck had landed on its right side. She could see the faint square of the night sky directly above her, through the passenger door. The girl's body and limbs were flailing, her screams echoing as she fought wildly, utterly lost. 'Get out! Climb out!' The effort of shouting sent stabs of new pain throughout her chest but Alice persisted, dug her fingers into the girl's hair, rived at it wildly. 'Get out!' she screamed again. 'Before the whole lot goes up!'

She could smell the thick stench of the fuel, could feel it soaking into her legs. Unless it was blood, she thought. She struck at the struggling figure a last time, felt all the strength ebb from her and let herself sink back, against the door and its buckled plates, the myriad fragments of glass. She tried to kick at the curved figure, who at last was scrabbling to haul herself through the other shattered window above them. Alice couldn't move her legs at all, feeling only the knifing pain of the nerves as she endeavoured to do so.

She saw the black shape, heard the deep sob, then it was gone from the square and she could see the dimness of the night sky again, and she felt a weary thankfulness. Some of the boxes behind her she knew contained fuses and the flares for Very pistols. She was crying quietly but the stench of the flowing fuel was overpowering, and the torment of pain was too much. She knew she was going to faint and she closed her eyes. Nothing matters any more, was her last disappearing thought as a fuse exploded and the flares lit and met the petrol and sent a great gout of flame and roar up into the darkness.

The crash and its single fatality was small beer compared with the sensational announcement of the greatest ever amphibian operation of all time, which took place just over twenty-four hours after Alice's death. Fred and Maggie Glass were informed by telegram, followed a few days later by a letter from someone from Staff Headquarters, who signed herself as Senior Controller. It was full of praise, extolling Staff-Sergeant Glass's many virtues, including *her selfless courage and supreme sacrifice*. It was an official commendation which was framed and kept as a treasured archive by the grieving family. Exactly a week after D-Day, three flying bombs, pilotless rockets, landed on Bethnal Green, killing six people and injuring nine. Two days later, 244 V1s, as they became known, were launched at London. Of these, one hundred failed to make the English coast, seventy-two exploded in and around London. Another two days, and on Sunday, 18 June, the anniversary of the great victory of Waterloo, one of the flying bombs struck the Guards' Chapel, in Wellington Barracks, where morning service was taking place. Two hundred guardsmen were killed, and roughly the same number of civilians.

The 'spirit of the Blitz' was long gone. Most of Britain was exhausted, worn out with making do and mending, short rations. Just when it appeared the end was in sight and the long awaited invasion of France had come, this new rain of terror from daylight skies dealt confidence and frayed nerves a severe blow. There was a superstitious dread of these robot weapons. Next to impossible to shoot them down, people said, unless our fighter lads were prepared to sacrifice themselves like those Jap kamikaze pilots who dived on to our ships.

The heroism of a north-country lass serving king and country in her own humble but vital role was suddenly seen as a valuable propaganda boost for a badly shaken populace, and what had made no more than a laudatory couple of paragraphs in a local rag was raised to national notice. What was planned to be a private, quiet interment became a much grander affair. The coffin, discreetly weighted with sand, was flag-draped and wreathed, a military guard of honour was organized and drilled, and two buglers gave moving renditions of Last Post and Reveille.

The account of Alice's funeral took up the whole of the front page of the *Margrove Daily Mail*, and was reported in several regional and national papers. The parish church of St Hilda, the most imposing of the town's Anglican places of worship, was crowded, the worshipful mayor and his lady, weighted with their chains of office, were prominent in the front row, alongside Fred and Maggie, Ethel, and Doreen.

To his bitter disappointment, nine-year-old Algy was considered too young to attend, though his grief was as deep as any save Maggie's. Alice's brother George was also absent, but that was because he was already across the Channel, involved in the increasingly difficult resistance encountered by the British forces just a few miles inland, around Caen. He got an honourable mention, under the picture of the pathetically smiling Glass parents in their solemn new outfits.

There were others in the congregation who mourned deeply. Davy Brown was one, and Elsbeth Clark another, who exchanged nods and tremulous smiles, and, in Elsbeth's case, a deepening blush. Tea and insipid sandwiches, thinly spread, had been organized in the church hall adjoining the black, square-towered edifice, surrounded by the equally blackened gravestones, and, at the outer edge, the raw hole and mound of earth into which Alice's remains were ceremonially lowered.

Elsbeth had time to notice a thin figure in an ATS uniform that did not disguise an air of youthful untidiness. She was clearly nothing to do with the official party, and hung well back, evidently not keen to be noticed or remarked upon. She was alone, but then Elsbeth became aware of the girl's diffident but constant stare in her direction after the service. Someone who had known Alice, Elsbeth guessed, beginning to feel just a shade uncomfortable. The girl was definitely sidling towards her, as though she wanted to speak. Then she smiled. The thin, gamine face had a certain ingenuous attraction. She was clearly nervous, plucking up the courage to make an approach.

'You Beth?'

Elsbeth's heart suddenly raced. She nodded.

'Can I have a word? Just for a minute?'

Again Elsbeth nodded, felt the colour mounting. 'Let's go outside.'

It was easier out in the warm June sunshine. They moved slowly along the wide tarmac between the graves and the rather unkempt grass. Some of the oldest stones were so worn that the writing could not be deciphered, and they leaned at pronounced and varying angles.

'I knew Alice!' the girl declared jerkily, her nervousness making her uneducated southern speech sound more pronounced. 'I was with her out in Egypt. Don't suppose she mentioned me? Lynne Manning.' She shot her hand out, and, startled and embarrassed, Beth reached out her own elegantly gloved hand. She noticed the chewed down shortness of the girl's nails, the hint of griminess and coarseness of the skin. With another abrupt movement the girl pulled off her worn cap, with its wavy peak, and pushed her left hand through a mop of raven-black hair, which contrasted sharply with the exposed ears and shaven nape. Like a boy, Beth thought, distracted. But attractive, in a naïve way: a child dressed up in a soldier's uniform.

'Listen! I don't know how to say it, proper like. Did you see her? After she came back, I mean? Did you get together again?'

The brilliant black eyes held her. She could feel the intensity beaming at her, knew that the look they held spoke the truth that couldn't be put into words. But this waiflike figure was determined to try. 'She thought the world of you, you know! She never – you were the love of her life!'

The shocking truth was flung out, hung between them. For a second, they were both joined, part of that truth, knowing it. The girl's eyes shone with tears. 'I can understand why, an' all.' She gave a nod that was almost fierce. 'She couldn't stop talking about you. Only to me. Not to anybody else. I had to tell you.'

'Yes.' Elsbeth murmured, and nodded.

The girl jammed her cap back on, always with the same jerking movements. 'You take care, eh? Look after that baby of yours. You were a lucky girl. She was one of the best was Sarge!'

She turned, and hurried off, almost at a trot, in an ungainly yet somehow touching way, leaving Beth still and silent, weeping as she stared after her.

PART III

O BRAVE NEW WORLD

CHAPTER TWENTY-SEVEN

Sixty-one summers later, another funeral took place, which Algy Glass also did not attend, though this time he at least saw part of it on the telly. He almost missed it. It came towards the end of the news, and he was settling himself into his accustomed viewing chair, anticipating the pleasure he would derive from the first pull of cold John Smith's from the can he was popping open. He was vaguely aware of the solemn stridency of the bugles and the fluttering of the corners of the flag draped over the coffin, but it was something you saw on a daily basis now on local and national TV, and a bloody disgrace it was, all them good lads being wasted out in Iraq and other places you could hardly pronounce. Bring 'em all back, they should! Bloody Labour government, nowt to choose between them and the other lot nowadays. All the same! But he was still thinking mainly about his beer and that first tangy taste, and about the fish and chips young Jimmy would be bringing in later, when his eye caught the thirty-one-inch screen and he jolted upright. 'Bloody 'ell! It's Miss 'Obbs!'

The scene had changed from the sunny exterior of the church down south somewhere and instead had filled with the head-and-shoulders portrait of a pretty blonde girl, smiling shyly, and looking very feminine in a rather conservative and old fashioned way. Winny, Algy's wife for forty-seven years, stopped in surprise as she came in from the kitchen. 'What you on about now?'

The picture had changed to another shot, of the same pretty girl, but this time her grinning face looked small, lost under the camouflaged dome of a helmet and framed by the chin guard and loose straps. Her slimness was shapeless under the loose-fitting army blouse and body armour. Broad bands of webbing crossed diagonally over her breast and she was cradling a stubby, short muzzled automatic rifle. The contrast between that delicate, youthful, grinning face and the military accoutrements she wore and carried was huge, and, to the elderly, rotund Algy, shocking. 'She's the spit of a teacher I used to know when I was a little kid. Elsbeth Hobbs. In Margrove. She went with us when we were evacuated to Howbeck, in the Dales. She was a big mate of our Alice.'

'You and the bloody war!' Winny grumbled. She was five years her husband's junior, born at the end of 1940, and could remember nothing about the war, not even the victory tea and the celebrations at the end of it all. Sometimes she got fed up with Algy going on about it, and in less charitable moments cherished secret doubts that Algy could remember half of what he claimed to recall, with his tales of the bombing raids on Margrove and the rest. And especially about that eldest sister of his, Alice, killed in some kind of accident down south when she was serving in the army. Big hero, they reckoned. His whole family used to go on about it. Algy still had the framed letter the army wrote after she was killed; he'd made a right fuss getting hold of it after his brother George passed away more than ten year ago. They'd all gone now, except for that snooty sister of his, Doreen, who was still hanging on in some posh nursing home down south. Not that she'd ever had owt to do with the rest of her family for years and years, since she was a kid – back to the blessed war again! – and had been taken in by some rich old biddy. She'd even taken over her name, called herself Glass-Ramsay, which sounded even more ridiculous than just plain old Glass, and Winny had got sick of all the daft jokes folk came up with. 'Bet your husband's a right pain, eh? Ha-ha!' 'You got two Glass eyes now, eh, our Winny? Ha-ha!'

But Algy was all eyes now all right, sitting forward in his chair, staring at the set, shushing her to catch the presenter's words. His hearing wasn't so good these days. It was a wonder the folks in the flat above didn't complain sometimes the way he had the volume right up. 'Second Lieutenant Abigail Fuller was only three weeks short of her twenty-second birthday when she was killed by the roadside bomb which injured three colleagues travelling in the jeep with her near the town of Nasiriyah last Friday. Lieutenant Fuller's mother, Mrs Karen Fuller, said her daughter had been keen on an army career since her schooldays, and one of her happiest moments was when she had been accepted for training as a cadet at Sandhurst Military Academy. However, this latest tragedy has refuelled the debate as to the suitability of having young women of our armed forces serving in front line positions exposed to such danger.'

Bloody ridiculous! Algy thought. But then the whole world was topsy-turvy now. Alice would have been all for it, and he chuckled inwardly at the memory of her feistiness. She'd take on anybody, lad or lass, when she got her dander up. He remembered how she'd leathered Doreen's bare backside for her once when she'd been up to no good at Lister Road School, and the recollection broadened that inner grin, at the idea of such a high-and-mighty figure having her arse tanned like that.

He hardly knew how he felt towards his only surviving sister. There'd hardly been any contact with her, ever since he could remember. When he was little all his loyalty and love had been reserved for Alice. She was his champion, champion of all who found it hard to stick up for themselves, like Elsbeth Hobbs herself. It pained him to think of the mucky, scandalous rumours that had gone about, about Alice and the beautiful Miss Hobbs, right up to the end, even after Alice had come back from Egypt, and Elsbeth was married, with a baby. He had always refused to countenance them, even though, later on, he had privately decided they could well have been true. And so what? There *were* women like that – and blokes, too, and if she and Elsbeth had been carrying on today nobody would have thought that much about it. Same mucky jokes, and sniggers, probably, but it didn't matter a damn nowadays.

When it came to that sort of thing, Alice's short life had been blameless, compared with both his other sisters. Ethel – God rest her, she'd been dead of cancer since 1983, at the age of fifty-six. Ethel had been the real good-looker of the family. She was another one who couldn't wait to get away from Maudsley Street – he remembered her moaning after D-Day that she hoped the war would last long enough for her to sign up or get into one of the armaments factories. The Japanese had signed the surrender just two days before her eighteenth birthday. So instead she'd run off with some spiv who was supposed to be going to set her up as some sort of model. He'd been telling the truth, only it wasn't the kind of modelling any respectable girl could be proud of. Ethel being Ethel, she'd given it a go anyway. She came back after a year, pregnant, and with a few tales she couldn't tell anyone around Margrove.

Things had gone from bad to no better, as they say. The stuffing had been knocked out of Mam at Alice's death, and worry over George, who'd been 'lucky' to be wounded in 1945 at the Rhine, and invalided out. Dad was in a bad way with his drinking and his betting. There was some sort of scandal to do with Doreen and old Miss Ramsay who'd taken her over; something to do with Dad trying to get more money out of her. If he did, none of his family, including Mam, ever saw owt of it, and after that they never saw and hardly heard from Doreen again. She was still at that posh girls' school in Whitby, then away to college some-where – and after that some swanky job down in London.

By that time, Mam had gone, too, but just as far as the cemetery, close to Alice. Her heart gave out. She took ill one Friday, being sick and in agony. Algy was still at Lister Road, in the seniors, and she asked him to call in at the doctor's on his way to school, to ask him to do a house call. When Algy came home at tea-time, she was dead. With her Alice again, he liked to think, and hope. And whatever Alice had got up to in her young life, her mam would not have disapproved, he was sure – not after the hard existence Maggie Glass had known.

Ethel didn't appear to learn much from her early experience of life in the big bad world. She seemed to be into one dodgy relationship after another, with two kids from two different fellers, neither of whom she was married to – and goodness knows how many other temporary attachments besides. They'd all popped their clogs now; only him and Doreen were left. The last time he'd seen her had been at Ethel's funeral, twenty-three years ago. She was married to some toff, had a big posh car, a German make, not that she'd been short of a bob or two herself, for Miss Ramsay had passed on in the early fifties and left Northend Cottage and a fair stack of dosh no doubt all to Doreen. Alice used to make folk laugh with her tale of how Doreen had stepped forward that day in Howbeck village hall, soon as Miss Ramsay had walked in, making those goo-goo eyes and twisting the old maid right round her finger. And now Doreen was old herself, wrinkled like a prune for all her wealth, and all alone at some seaside residential home. No kids, nobody to leave her money to. Maybe she'll leave it all to me, Algy thought wryly. Fat chance! Probably go to some dog or cats' home! Who cared? He'd done all right. Winny, and three grown-up kids who were good enough to their mam and dad, nice little ground-floor flat – rented, he'd never been one to fancy being a house owner, in spite of Thatcher and her flogging off the council houses – in a village on the east Yorkshire coast. They reckoned it was slipping into the sea. Another hundred years and he might be plodging in the street outside. Summat to worry about, eh?

The news item had ended. He'd missed the shot of the elegant, straight, slim figure leaving the church. She was the maternal grand-mother of the dead girl who had startlingly reminded him of the long ago Miss Hobbs. He would perhaps have noticed again a resemblance, but he would not have recognized her, for he had never in his life met Elaine Ruth Ferne, née Clark, Elsbeth's daughter. He did not even know of the existence of the shorter figure of her own daughter, who held on to her arm in the warm afternoon sunlight.

Elaine Ruth Ferne clung tightly to the arm of her daughter, Karen, trying to will some of her own stiff-backed strength into the plumper, softer figure at her side. It should have been Keith there to support Karen. After all, he was Abigail's father, even if he had been divorced from Karen since Abigail was eight. But he was keeping well in the background, no doubt clinging for comfort to his 'new' wife, the woman with the pneumatic chest, who was displaying an imposing and inap-propriate tanned cleavage almost all the way down, even in her func-real garb. Instead, Elaine signalled a wordless appeal for help towards her younger sister, Anne, who stepped forward in quick recognition and seized Karen's other elbow. They held her in a discreet sandwich between them and steered her safely, with dignity intact, into the first mourning car waiting outside the crematorium chapel.

Dignity. That's what mattered, at all times. That's what Elaine's mother, and daddy, would have relied on if either of them had been here. But her father had died eight years ago, and her mother six years after him. He would have been bursting with pride at the dignified pomp of the ceremony today: the salute of the volley, the ringing of the bugles. It was generally agreed that Arty Clark's army career during the war, as well as that of his closest friend, the uncle Elaine and Anne had never known, Bill Hobbs, who had died a hero's death in Burma, had played a great part in influencing Abigail's choice of soldiering as a career.

221

'Not just your great-grandpa, you know! Your great-grandma, Elsbeth. She served in the war, too! In the Wrens.' Elaine's mouth twitched in the ghost of a grim smile at the recall of how such complacent remarks had been slid over, eased away from, though not without bringing a touch of pink to her mother's well-nourished skin. That part of the Clark family history was definitely not for too probing an exploration. *Conduct prejudicial to good order and discipline* did not merit too close an inspection. That was the reason given for Elsbeth's discharge from the Wrens at the end of 1942. Some instinct for . . . what? Self-punishment? – had made her mother keep the relevant papers locked away. When she died, Elaine had gone carefully through them. The reason for the dismissal from the services was not difficult to deduce: it lay in two adjacent documents in typically neat arrangement, the marriage certificate, dated 18 December, 1942, and Elaine's own birth certificate, dated 23 June, 1943. It had never exactly been a secret, just one of those things in the well-ordered, civilized regime of the Clark household which was never referred to.

There were others, locked away, but even more closely guarded in the heart, too. There was a small bundle of letters, written by her mother to *Staff-Sgt. A. Glass, Service No. A5196M*, which had clearly been returned to her from the effects of Alice Glass, following her death. The first had been written in November, 1942, and was informing Alice of Elsbeth's engagement to Arty, her pregnancy, and the plans for a hasty December wedding. The second, even shorter, was dated 25 June, 1943, telling Alice of Elaine's birth two days earlier.

Elaine began to read the third, headed 30 May, 1944. Part of her willed herself to have the strength not to read further, but she could not help herself. It must have been one of the last letters Alice Glass received, before the fatal accident, which Elaine knew had happened only two days before the invasion. It made clear the abiding loving relationship the two had shared for the past four years. It began with *My Darling Al*, and ended with *All my love for always, Your Beth XXX*. It was the last paragraph that tore deepest at Elaine's feelings.

I just can't put up any more arguments against our love, and I can't deny it. I'll always love you, but I have to end it. I'm not using God this time as an excuse, not using anything except my own weariness and sadness that the world isn't as we'd like it to be. I can't explain it, but Bill's death, and Luke Denby's death, are there, shadows always around us. And now something else. I know for certain now that I'm pregnant again. It can only have happened when Arty brought the news about Bill. We were both so low and in need of comfort that night, it was the first time for ages we made love. Now I've missed my second month, and I just know by the way I feel. Like I said, I can't argue any more what's right or wrong, and I do still love you and will, always, but we must end it, my darling. Forgive me. Please find someone else you can love too.

Her mother had been among the last of a rapidly vanishing breed, who put the rules for the common good and outward respectability before the needs and demands of the individual. Just a mite too soon, Mummy! Elaine thought, again wryly. Her own generation, those who reached adulthood and bore children in the sixties, had begun the dance to a different tune. No more suppression, no more denial. Let it all hang out! She remembered all too well the polite, civilized restraint of her parents' household, accepted during her childhood and adolescence because they were simply 'Mummy and Daddy', not people with human, basic instincts, certainly not sexual beings. She'd never seen her father kiss his wife on the lips, never tried to imagine them doing so. Cosy, domestic, these were the words she unthinkingly applied to them, until her own attempts at permanent relationships, and their failures, and the failure of her daughter, Karen. Genetic, that was the buzzword nowadays, and there was probably something in it, too, if not all.

The tall, rangy figure, with the long, flowing unrestraint of black hair, the high, needle-heeled boots and skin-tight, superbly styled jeans (forgive the pun), had been generally, if by some reluctantly, accepted as an entitled member of the chief mourning party. Norma Duffy had even been identified as Abigail's 'partner' in the press, accorded the special acknowledgement of the grieving lover. She had held that post since before Abigail's entry to the army and the academy. Karen, and Elaine and Anne as elders, had fully recognized her right, and now, as they progressed deliberately through the busy, uncaring summer afternoon in the stately black car, Elaine felt a great swell of love and pity for her mother, for that silent sacrificial, hidden endurance through sixty long years which had followed the loss of her 'always' loved Al.

Another grave was being tended 4,000 miles away, in hot Ugandan sunshine, in a beautifully kept green cemetery, bright with canna lilies

223

and shady with neat cypresses. The gardener's bare head was white, his brown face seamed and his hands gnarled. The grave was not new. Its occupant had been laid to rest there six years ago, at the dawn of the millennium. He had lived through most of the previous century and died at the age of eighty-three. The gardener remembered him well. 'Bwana Davidi' had been much loved by many, not just his fellow Baha'is, whose beautiful, domed temple lay at the top of the hill.

Davy Brown had come here in the early Fifties, to join the small band of dedicated pioneers from Europe and elsewhere, who had come to teach their faith, and to help build the symbol of that faith, which so fittingly crowned this hill overlooking Kampala. He had been a policeman, in the days of the protectorate, and had stayed on after Uhuru, so that in the end he had lived the majority of his long life here. The gardener, calmly ready for his own demise soon now, had been one of the earliest to become Davidi's friend. He had laughed at their encouragement for him to take a wife, then told him one evening, as the bats circled their simple compound searching, piping, for fruit, about the girl he had lost during the war, and of another, earlier love, whom he had searched for in the chaos of Europe when the war was over. It had taken him nearly two years to discover that she had died in one of those terrible camps the Germans had set up for the Jews and others who had tried to oppose them.

'Like the camps the British are setting up across the border in Kenya now,' one of the young ones had said, and Menya, the gardener, had chided him. But Bwana Davidi had told Menya not to mind, that it was all right. He was a good man, Davy Brown, but lonely sometimes, Menya had felt.

He finished turning the red earth with the trowel, and grunted, straightening and holding his aching back. He squinted up at the sky, paling now, with the mellow light of evening coming. The bats would be wheeling about soon, he thought. Bwana Davidi had loved this time. Menya grunted, spat companionably on to the earth he had just tended, and looked up a last time. He chuckled. Bwana Davidi would not be lonely now, in those mansions of God. They would meet again soon – and he hoped he would not find two of those beautiful maids of heaven fighting over their lord, for David and his fellows had taught them most strictly that each of us is allowed only one wife to share his bed. Would it be the same in Heaven?